THE END GAME

*Other books by
the same author*

THE REBELLIOUS HOME MAKERS
(nonfiction)

THE CLUB (novel)

THE END PLAY

Indira Mahindra

ALLISON & BUSBY

First published in Great Britain in 1994 by
Allison & Busby
an imprint of Wilson & Day Ltd
5 The Lodge
Richmond Way
London W12 8LW

A catalogue record for this book is available from the British
Library

ISBN 0 74900 173 9

Typeset by TW Typesetting, Plymouth, Devon
Printed and bound in Great Britain by
Mackays of Chatham PLC, Chatham, Kent

DEDICATED
TO
KANCHI KAMAKSHI DEVI

GLOSSARY

Baba: suffix after a boy's name.

Baithak: informal sitting-room.

Beti/Bitia: literally, a daughter. Used affectionately when addressing a girl.

Bhaiya: brother. Here it is an informal way of addressing a stranger.

Bidi: inexpensive cigarette made by rolling dry tobacco leaf and tying it with a string.

Chaat: spicy Indian snack.

'Chul, Shaitan': 'Get lost, you devil.'

Dhussa shawl: big, thick shawl, hand-spun, woven from rough wool.

'Dhut, pagli': 'Nonsense, you foolish one.'

Dular: indicates pampering with love, a pun on the name Dulari which means one who is lovable.

Egg-bhujia and pav-roti: egg-bhujia – spicy scrambled eggs; pav-roti – bread baked in four small sections.

Idlis, wadas, dossas: vegetarian snack typical of southern India.

'Jee, hanh. Mera naam Coffin hee hai': 'Yes, truly, my name is Coffin.'

Ka beta: 'The son of – '

Khadi: hand-spun, hand-woven cotton material introduced by Mahatma Gandhi, worn by those committed to free India from the British Raj.

Kriya ceremony: last rites for the dead, after the thirteenth day of mourning, to free the departed soul from its earthly attachments.

Lipphut: pidgin for lift.

Magh mela: ancient religious fair held in January (Magh in the Hindu calendar) at Prayag (near Allahabad) where the two holy rivers, Ganges and Jamuna, meet. Millions of pilgrims, saints and aspiring holy men converge here to pay homage to the united rivers.

Mangalsutra: a distinctive necklace of special significance for a Maharashtrian married woman.

Pallav: free end of a sari which is draped from the shoulder.

Paneer: cottage cheese.

Phiran and churidar: outfit worn by Kashmiri women. Phiran – loose top garment with embroidered neckline and long sleeves; churidar – a closer-fitting pyjama worn underneath.

Pyjama-kurta: ethnic outfit worn on formal as well as informal occasions depending on fabric and design. The pyjama is like a loose-fitting trouser, topped by a loose knee-length tunic with collarless neckline and full sleeves.

Salan and tahiri: salan – Kashmiri name for meat curry; tahiri – their special preparation from rice and lentils.

Salwar-kameez: salwar – ankle-length trouser of light material, with pleats; kameez – knee-length, or longer, loose shirt-like garment worn over the salwar.

Shahtoosh shawl: expensive, warm Kashmir shawl made from fleece of Tibetan antelope called Chiru. The fabric is so fine that its width can be slipped through a ring.

Talukdars: landlords assessed by the number of villages they owned.

Thali: round metal plate of aluminium, brass, stainless steel or silver, with small bowls in which Indian meal is served.

ONE

It was strange. Odd. Nani-ma didn't stretch her arms out to embrace me. Instead she asked why Mother had not come too? Why did I take the risk of travelling alone by train? How was it that Karan had failed in his brotherly duty of escorting me? I moved away from her bed, from her slender form sitting wrapped securely in a shahtoosh shawl, and chose to sit on a chair so that she would have to turn sideways to see me.

'Nani-ma you're smart, but you've failed to move on to the eighties of this century,' I said with a laugh. 'In your days you could step out of the front door only with a male escort, even if he was just a boy. It's not so now. I want you to know that I can take good care of myself on a train. As you see, I'm here, safe and sound with you.'

'So I can see,' Grandmother commented, folding her spectacles carefully into their box, pausing, then snapping it shut. She asked again, 'Why has Bimla not come with you?'

'I wanted to come and see you by myself. There was no need for Ma to come,' I replied as near to the truth as possible.

I could sense that Nani-ma was upset over my unscheduled visit in November. For over two decades Ma, Karan, and I have spent every Christmas holiday with her in Allahabad. Father has never come. Ma expertly overcame our childish sulks, then our teen protests and novel pretexts, to make us accompany her for an annual review of our physical and mental progress by her mother. To make us pliant she devised, for many years, to dovetail a sight-seeing excursion to our holiday month, but we still considered it boring, to be endured for mother's sake. By the time we

1

reached adulthood we became weary of Ma's see-India tours. We mutinied and failed, because Ma neutralised it by agreeing that it was time she stopped manoeuvring us.

Left to ourselves Karan and I came to the conclusion we couldn't let Ma go alone to Allahabad. It could be that we had, by then, become habit-bound to spending December with Nani-ma. And, similarly I presume, she expected to see us in that month, and in that month only. Still, I feel this was not a good enough reason for her to forget to greet me with a hug and her usual words of blessing.

My visit was not a whimsical one. Ma had sent me on a special mission. 'What about sending Karan?' I had suggested. 'It's easier for him to skip classes in college than for me to take leave from the office I've joined less than a year ago.'

'No, I want you to go,' Ma had replied promptly as if she had already considered the alternative. 'I need to harness your gift of the gab.' I knew better than to take this as an unadulterated compliment. It had an oblique recognition of my exasperating expertise in arguing with her. If this was what she needed, I had to agree I was better qualified than my younger brother for her assignment. But here I was, with a bad start. An ill omen. My evasive reply had seemingly irritated the huddled figure on the bed. Nani-ma did not turn to see me, or ask more questions. Most probably she had already concluded that there was a purpose to my extraordinary visit, and that she would have to wait for me to reveal it.

I was too exhausted by the long train journey from Bombay to launch into it right away. I needed to be in total command of myself before tackling an adversary like Nani-ma. I anticipated she would pelt me with a string of probing questions and sub-questions before giving the decision Ma wanted. I had to prepare myself mentally for a long session with her.

For that I first needed to have many sessions with myself to evaluate impartially my role in the family crisis in Bombay. I had had no time or opportunity to think with a clear head. Too much had happened too fast in a short time. I needed to ventilate my cluttered mind and arrange everything in neat piles once again. By nature I'm a tidy person – systematic and orderly. From my playpen days Ma has been saying that I collected most of my genetic strands from Nani-ma. Undoubtedly, my fastidious tidiness has come from that source. I have a suspicion Ma is not too happy that this preference took place in her womb.

Nani-ma's voice startled me. 'You must be tired after your journey. Dulari has kept food in the hot case for you. Eat something and go to sleep. It's late.' So it was. Past ten was much too late for her. She retired by nine every night.

As if this were the cue they were waiting for, Dulari and Mamoo entered one after another. I was surprised that Mamoo had resorted to eavesdropping. We all knew it was a way of life for Dulari. She considered it part of her job to keep her eyes and ears open in order to narrate interesting scenes and dialogues to her mistress. She had been with Nani-ma for as long as I could remember. 'Bitia,' she made the predictable enquiry, 'where would you like to eat your dinner?'

I told her I was sorry I couldn't eat her dinner. The wedding party on the train in the compartments next to mine had kept forcing food on me. I knew Dulari always stocked a packet of Nescafé for our visit. I asked her to give me just a cup of coffee.

'Take a glass of milk with coffee powder in it,' Mamoo recommended. I passed it with a smile, and involuntarily walked over to Nani-ma to claim my hug from her.

This time she said the words I wanted to hear, 'Rest well, beti. May God bless you with happiness and good health.' I went back to the chair to pick up my handbag before leaving the room.

TWO

By the time I connected the thumping sound to Bhoot's tail, I had stumbled on him. I should have remembered that Mamoo's black Labrador was never far away from him. Forbidden from fouling Nani-ma's suite of rooms with his canine odour, he had been waiting in the dark passage outside her door. His gleaming eyes were staring at me. I patted his head and apologised profusely.

'Bhoot, I told you to stay in my room till I returned,' Mamoo unnecessarily scolded him. Without pausing he asked me, 'Gunga, is Bimla not well? Have you come to give us some bad news?'

Taken aback by his presumption I couldn't move for a while. I managed to say in a firm voice, 'No, Mamoo. Ma's health is fine. She's not sick.'

'That's good. Come, let's go.' I heard him release his breath. I was glad he had decided not to ask any more questions.

'Where am I to stay? The guest-room?' I asked.

'I think Dulari has put your suitcase in your mother's old room,' he replied as he followed Bhoot's lead.

There was nothing that suggested Ma's ownership of the room. No mementoes of her childhood, like I have my favourite dolls, stuffed toys, and souvenirs from our trip to England and Europe. I still get a kick out of shaking the small plastic dome enclosing Piccadilly Circus to watch the snow falling like whispers on Eros. There were no frames on the wall displaying her medical degrees and the honours I know she had won. No personal photos anywhere, of herself, the family, or even of the father she was so close to. Not

4

even a fractured stethoscope forgotten in a drawer of her desk. And yet there was no denying it. This was her room. Somehow it exuded her presence stored somewhere by it.

Mamoo left saying he would come back. Dulari made a welcome entry with a steaming mug of coffee. I took it with both hands. I was beginning to feel chilly with just a cardigan over my cotton salwar outfit. From Bombay's muggy climate to this dry cold was quite a switch for me. As I had the first sip of Nescafé, Dulari's expected question came. 'Is Bimla Bitia coming here afterwards?'

I had to admire her diplomatic skill in rephrasing the question I had already answered twice before. I carefully crafted a reply and led her to a detour by enquiring after her family members in the village.

I spared a quarter of my attention to Dulari's family news and made proper responses as she helped me unpack and settle down. I was busy trying to figure out why both Nanima and Mamoo should've been surprised to know that I had come by myself. Perhaps Mamoo missed hearing that I was coming alone by the Howrah Express. I remembered shouting at the top of my voice because the phone connection had been so faint. Luckily he did hear I was arriving on the thirteenth night, and was at the station to receive me.

I remember his confusion and concern on finding that Ma and Karan were not with me. I had not taken it seriously then as I had become preoccupied, like a child, in watching a four-piece band enter the platform leading a convivial group of dancing men and bejewelled women carrying garlands to welcome a bridal party – the party which had dissolved fifteen hours of my life with its pervasive and intrusive presence in the corridor train. It was on seeing this festive group behind the band that I had understood why the women on the train had fussed so much over getting dressed before the train reached Allahabad, while their men had rushed up and down, shouting instructions above the sound of the train, to organise detraining with the party's mountainous luggage.

It was then when I had started packing frantically to be ahead of their disorganised manoeuvre which would very likely block my exit from the train on reaching Allahabad. The engine was on full throttle, running like a child towards its mother. I should've anticipated this when the attendant, coursing down the corridor, announced proudly again and again that we were going to arrive fifteen minutes ahead of scheduled time at Allahabad Junction. It had animated everyone around me, but I had foolishly stayed riveted to the window as the train crossed the river bridge, my belongings scattered on the seat of my coupé. I was fascinated by the shimmering strip of the Ganges between the opaque curtains of the night. It seemed as if she were crooning a lullaby while rocking the half moon on the lap of her gentle waves, sheltered under her dark sari pallav.

To be named after this holy river had been a handicap and a sore trial for me during my school days. Compulsively naughty, I was reminded again and again that I should try to live up to the holy name so hopefully given to me by my parents. All I could do was to change its spelling to Gunga. It made no difference to anyone, but it helped me to wipe off the deposit of failure and guilt, have my own identity, and stay as I wanted to.

Yet, every time I come to Allahabad the meandering river manages to tug at a cord, and pull me towards her. I had to wrench myself away when I heard the train breathing out to stop at Prayag. This was to let pilgrims disembark at the confluence of Ganga, Jamuna, and their third sister, Saraswati. Legend has it that later Saraswati left Sangam, the place of their union. Devotees, however, assert that she is still there in an invisible form – down below, under the surface of the obvious mixing of the clear blue water of Jamuna with the muddy one of the Ganges. What Mamoo told Karan and me, at an impressionable age, was more meaningful. He said that it was appropriate for the goddess of learning to leave Sangam since people had shifted their priority from scholarship to merchandising. After that we cultivated a habit of giving undivided attention to our teachers in school.

I had just managed to stuff the pile of magazines Shiv had bought at the Bombay Station into my suitcase, when the

Howrah Express hiccuped to a stop. There was panic and commotion in the ubiquitous marriage party over the counting of the dowry luggage. It appeared that no one had paid attention to this detail at Nasik as the men, entertained liberally at the farewell banquet, had boarded the drowsy train at midnight in high spirits. I was lying in the lower bunk bed, sleepily turning the pages of a magazine. Sounds of laughter and merriment in the corridor had made me curious. Slipping into my kaftan I had unlocked the security devices and opened my door.

An exhausted, rumpled wedding party was streaming into the reserved compartments next to mine. Expecting dramatic action on the platform, I had screened my eyes to peer through the reflecting glass of the window. It was amusing to see the bride's family self-consciously enacting their sorrowful parting in the glaring lights used by the professional video camera team. A gang of coolies was shouting and shoving countless boxes, trunks, and baskets of fruits and sweets into every available space in the reserved cabins. The veiled bride, encased in a sparkling red sari, was brought aboard as the last item, seconds before the train pulled out. Expecting their exodus to be equally confused and obstructive, I had rushed out of my coupé with a hastily packed suitcase to get off the train ahead of them at Allahabad.

As always Mamoo was there on the platform, wearing a woollen Nehru jacket over his pyjama-kurta with a folded shawl draped on his left shoulder, just in case the mid-November night air should suddenly turn cooler than expected. He hugged me and asked, 'Shall I go in and help Bimla with the luggage? Where's Karan?'

'I've come alone, Mamoo,' I replied.

'It's a long journey.' He must have been distressed, which I failed to notice. The band in their tinselly, ill-fitting uniforms had burst into a Hindi film tune and claimed my attention. I heard Mamoo say on a higher decibel, 'It's not safe to travel alone on an overnight journey.'

That was exactly how Shiv had reacted when I informed him that I had taken a week's leave from *Reflections* to go to Allahabad on my mother's assignment. He offered to send somebody from his office to accompany me. I told him it was ridiculous of him to fuss when my parents hadn't. 'I have an abiding concern for my vested interest,' he said with a playful smile.

It provoked me to exclaim, 'If I choose to come to your bed it doesn't make me your precious possession. I can stop tomorrow if I want to.' His smile vanished. He offered to do my train reservation. I gave in to make up for my rudeness. I realised he had tricked me when I found that he had reserved both the berths of a first-class coupé for me. 'For your safety and my peace of mind,' he laughed and proceeded to mow down my resistance with his amorous pleas. Thereafter, he used all the available time till the guard flashed the green flag, to drill me repeatedly in all the security measures he wanted me to observe throughout the night. Little did he know that his indulgence was to be the source of a novel experience for me.

'Mamoo,' I mumbled, making an effort to give him my full attention. The groom had landed on the platform, and the veiled bride, supported by two giggling girls, was stumbling down the steps. 'I wasn't alone in my coupé last night,' I said. I saw Mamoo gaping at me, panic in his eyes. I instantly elaborated, 'You see that bride there, Mamoo? She spent the night with me.'

It took him a few seconds to decide that this could be possible. 'Where's your luggage?' he asked. He was least interested in marriage scenes he had seen time and again.

Fistfuls of coins, after being superstitiously circled over the heads of the bride and groom, were being flung towards beggars – to assuage their envy of the opulent, happy moment they had converged to watch from as far as the band could be heard.

'Only this suitcase in my hand, Mamoo. Nothing else,' I replied absent-mindedly as I watched the beggars scuffle and scramble, in the dim light of the platform, to find the coins on the ground. It certainly did serve the purpose of diverting their attention. I was wondering if I would ever again have a freak chance to meet the bride. In the same city I wouldn't know where to look for her. I had failed to ask her name, or her address.

Mamoo took the suitcase from my hand and led me out of the railway station, a little too hurriedly as I now recall.

THREE

'You go to bed now, beti,' Dulari said as if tucking me in were part of her duty. 'Don't wait for your Mamoo. I don't think he's coming back.'

She was right, ten-thirty was late for Allahabad. I was tuned to Bombay hours. My generation has earned the disapproval of parents by setting out for our weekend dinner parties after ten, and winding up in the wee hours of the morning. Daylight is used for restorative sleep. That upside-down living was certainly out of context here. 'You're right, Dulari. Mamoo must be very tired,' I said picking up my nightdress and toilet bag.

'Oh no, beti, he must be talking on the telephone. These days he regularly rings up someone after your Nani-ma has gone to bed.' Dulari didn't hide her irritation.

'Haven't you reported it to Nani-ma?'

'Chee, I don't tell tales.' The generous proportions of her body seemed to swell. She tugged at her shawl to cover herself. I was sure she'd been lingering in my room waiting for Mamoo's return. This was her disappointment surfacing.

Long ago it was Karan who had discerned her romantic interest in Mamoo. We had called it Dulari's dular. Later, with better understanding of the world around us, we labelled it DIS – Dulari's Infinite Seduction. It was doomed to be futile. My confirmed belief was that Mamoo breathed on a non-sexual, pure level. Cynical Karan didn't agree with me. He claimed that Dulari's pure adoration could soften Mamoo one day and make him fall.

However, we both were snobbish enough to agree that she was hardly the object of temptation for Mamoo. We used to

10

scream with laughter imagining them as romantic hero and heroine – the dark, coarse-featured, fat Dulari standing alongside the fair, refined, well-bred Mamoo. As I looked at her now I noticed that the years had thinned her hair, made gaps in her smile, and spread her frame. I felt certain that she still nurtured her secret yearning for the unattainable.

'Why don't you also go to sleep, Dulari? I don't need anything more tonight,' I said as I left the room.

In the bathroom I was reminded of my geographical transposition. The toilet seat made me jump up at its chilly reception. Sheer necessity made me sit down once more. I couldn't indulge in lingering over my ablutions and was back in the bedroom in no time at all. Inexplicably, Dulari was still there sitting cross-legged on the carpet.

'Your city is too cold for me, Dulari.' I felt reluctant to slip between the icy sheets waiting for the heat of my body. 'Why haven't you gone to bed, Dulari? Aren't you feeling cold sitting there with just a shawl?'

She found that funny. She laughed, her body shaking like jelly, before she explained, 'For us this is not cold at all. We're used to it. It is next month the winds from Himalayan snow will freeze the blood. You get to bed, beti. I'll sit here with you for a while. I want to know how Karan Baba is. Also your father and all the others of your Sahi family in Bombay. I'm a fool. I talked on and on about myself and my family. Tell me about everyone in your Sahi-Sadan in Bombay.' She resettled her legs comfortably in readiness for a long account. Her smile indicated she expected to be entertained. I wondered if she was asking out of a return courtesy for my enquiry after her family, or if it was another way of hearing about Ma. How could any account of the Sahi family not have a reference to Ma?

I was in no mood to indulge her. My teeth had started chattering. I had to compel my body to slip inside the ice-pack. Between the oohs and aahs generated by the encounter, I somehow managed to say to Dulari that I would answer all her questions next morning. She took my hint and heaved to her feet with loud groans.

But instead of leaving she came to my bed and bent low

to take an anxious peep at me. 'Are you all right, beti? Malaria fever starts just like this. Shall I come and sleep on the carpet here? You shouldn't be alone in case . . .'

I should have found it funny, but just then the ignored fatigue had begun to creep up my legs, demanding recognition. Mercifully, I heard a cough, and Mamoo entered the room with Bhoot three paces behind him.

'Is she sleeping?' he asked Dulari in a whisper. She moved aside saying, 'No, no. She's just got into bed.' To explain her bedside stand she volunteered, 'Bitia said something I couldn't hear.'

He came near the bed holding out a hot-water bottle. 'Sorry, I meant to come much earlier but I got a telephone call. Here, this will warm your bed.' Dulari made sure I caught her significant glance before returning to the carpet. I could guess she was patting herself for resisting the temptation of retiring to bed.

I stuttered my thanks and appreciation to Mamoo for his thoughtfulness, and felt gratified to see Dulari look embarrassed for not having thought of a hot-water bottle for me.

The telephone conversation had definitely relaxed Mamoo. He wasn't upset any more about my travelling alone. He was more concerned about my catching a cold. After giving me tips on how to acclimatise myself to the change, he asked hesitantly, 'Are you very tired? Would you like to tell me how the bride happened to spend the night with you? I should think her berth must've been booked with those of the women in the marriage party. I know you wanted to tell me at the station but . . . but my mind was on getting you home soon.'

'I know, Mamoo.' I could talk clearly, but now my body was demanding sleep. I took a deep breath and decided that the least I could do was to relate my previous night's experience for all the trouble he had taken to pick me up from the station.

Dulari had already settled herself comfortably on the carpet, delighted with the idea of a story. And that too of a bride. Much to Nani-ma's irritation, she still ran compulsively out of the bungalow to the road to see marriage processions pass by whenever she heard a band blaring out a medley of pop tunes. She was enchanted by wedding scenes on celluloid. Ma had stopped us from teasing her by explaining that Dulari, being a child widow, was deprived of excitement and romance in her own life. She needed to fill the vacuum somehow. I knew I had to go into details for this keen listener even if I ran the risk of boring the polite Mamoo.

I propped my pillow on the bolster to raise myself a bit for my audience, and yet stay ensconced inside the warmed quilt. I gave a brief résumé of the arrival of the wedding party at Nasik before coming to the requested story. 'There were so many of them in this party, Mamoo, I'm sure they didn't have enough reserved berths . . .'

'Quite possible,' he commented, 'they must've bribed the guard.'

'They were such a nuisance. It was impossible to sleep, with their loud talk and constant movement in the corridor. I had to weave my way through them to go to the loo. When I returned I found that the women in the marriage party had discovered I had two berths to myself.'

'How was that? Did you bribe too?' he asked with a chuckle.

My tongue slipped. 'No, Mamoo. Shiv booked the coupé without asking me.'

'Who's Shiv?' It was impossible to dodge this. I dealt him a part truth. 'Shiv's my friend.'

'It's a man's name, isn't it?'

'Yes, Shiv Menon is a man.' I struck a light-hearted note. 'Mamoo, you know I work for this magazine, *Reflections*. I sent some issues here for you and Nani-ma. Remember?'

'Yes, yes, I do. I know you are working. Why, I don't understand.'

I ignored his disapproval. 'Women as well as men work for this magazine. Men can be just friends too, you know. At least in Bombay.' Dulari covered her mouth with her shawl.

I quickly reverted to my story. 'You know what happened, Mamoo? Three women from the party came to me. They

13

very sweetly asked if I would allow the bride to use the upper berth in my coupé. Just for the night. The poor tired girl would relax in my company, and be able to sleep, they said. I had no choice. They brought the red bundle to me. Dulari, you should have seen her when she uncovered her head after the women left and I had bolted the door. She was loaded with jewellery. It frightened me. I rechecked the door. Made sure all the other safety devices were secure. When I turned back to her she had thrown off her veil. She was laughing away. My nervousness was very amusing, she said. She thanked me for taking her in. She wasn't that tired, she confided, just fed up with pretending to be bashful. Behave like a bride, her mother had told her.'

'Hai, Ram,' Dulari exclaimed. 'What a strange girl. All brides feel so shy, there's no need to tell them that.'

Mamoo made no comment. He was barely interested in the story.

'You know, Mamoo,' I had to get him involved in the story. 'My eyes got glued to the ornament on her forehead. I've never seen the like of it. You know what it was? Not the usual pendant studded with precious stones. It was an oval gold frame. With a coloured picture in it. Of the bridegroom, I made a guess. Noticing my interest, Mamoo, she unhooked it from her hair to look at it. She burst out laughing and said – "So, this is what the mother-in-law put on my forehead after the wedding ceremony. Isn't it like a suitcase label? She must think I should be her son's piece of luggage. Like hell. Don't you think his face is too ugly to deserve the honour to be on my forehead?" And before I could agree with her she threw the frame on the seat.'

'Was she beautiful herself?' Mamoo was now hooked to my story. I couldn't help laughing. 'No, Mamoo, she was no great beauty to grumble about his face. But her boldness was something. She wasn't from a westernised family. She must've been trained to be docile. How could she be so uninhibited? Incredible, don't you think? On her own she told me that she had studied only up to high school. She was determined to study more. Her parents had forced her into marriage. But she wasn't going to give up her plan to go to college.'

14

'How is she going to do that?' Dulari asked. Her face was aglow with romanticism. I guessed she had found the idea of the picture-ornament irresistible. I was careful in my answer, 'Well, she said that she would first observe the in-law set up. Then she would learn how to manipulate her husband to get her their permission to study.'

'That is sensible of her,' Dulari approved.

'Don't you think she was amazingly cool, Mamoo? Do you think she'll succeed in her plan?'

But I knew she would. What I didn't tell them was that she had equipped herself with a store-house of carnal knowledge. I asked her how could she be so sure of taming a husband she hardly knew? She had laughed heartily at me this time. She thought it was peculiar that a westernised independent girl like me, who could travel alone in style, had no idea of how men could be handled. Was I so ignorant of our ancient heritage, our culture? Had I really not read Vatsayana's *Kamasutra*? That was where one could learn the practical ways of enticing a man, any man. That's how she meant to make her husband do whatever she wanted. Then manipulate his family through him. So easy. Her clear, confident words kept gushing from the upper bunk down on me, like a waterfall.

I found it hard to believe that she could really feel that self-assured by just reading about management of sex. It was something she knew nothing about yet. A pure unkissed, untouched virgin. Was her recitation a device to reinforce her intentions developed through a mere reading of *Kamasutra*? She may have needed to hear herself talk of her acquired armour. The situation was ideal for it. The intimacy of darkness in a transient train; an eager listener; the cradle-like sway of the coupé accompanied by the mesmeric cadence of wheels on rails – the perfect setting to bring out a vital secret and give it an airing. Despite my doubts I had to concede that she was smart. She had not placed her blue chips on the dowry her parents had accumulated to buy happiness for her. She had found and brought her own survival kit.

In clear daylight I witnessed her first act of independence.

15

She was washing and dressing in the morning prior to returning to the compartment of her in-laws. I saw her tossing the head ornament into her vanity case.

'Shouldn't you wear it?' I asked with concern. 'They'll expect to see it on your forehead.'

She shrugged her shoulders, suddenly laughed and said, 'I'd like to ask my mother-in-law to put my picture on his forehead.'

'You're not going to say that, are you?' Bold as she was, I felt she was quite capable of it.

'Don't worry, I'm not going to,' she replied, looking straight into my eyes. 'I'll give the stupid jewel back, hang my head shyly, and whisper that it's too heavy. It's tugging at my hair and giving me a headache.'

'What if they don't believe you?'

'Oh, they'll believe me all right. They'll gloat over the fact that I called it heavy.' She looked so mischievous I had to ask her how old she was.

'I'll be eighteen next month.'

Dulari was disappointed with the story. Her verdict was that such a girl would only make trouble for herself, and for all the others. To Mamoo she was another illustration of the changing social pattern. Inevitable, so why worry about it. He stayed on after Dulari left in case I wanted to unload any burden. I had often sought him out in the past to talk about anything that bothered me.

'You know, Mamoo,' I began, 'whatever you may think of this young bride I can't help comparing her to myself, or to Ma. I'm certainly not that gutsy. But Ma married late, at thirty plus. She's a working woman who could stand on her feet anywhere in the world. I've just found out why she married my father. I'm sure you know it too. What I can't understand is her lack of guts all these years. She could neither manage her husband nor deal with his people. You can't put it down to her marrying out of the Kashmiri community. Or merely to the joint family living of the Sahis. Can you? Am I wrong? Why has she been weak-kneed? You must know. Tell me. I have to know, I have to understand. I do ...' I stopped abruptly. Mamoo was staring at me with a blank, uncomprehending expression. I had bungled; obviously he knew less than I did now.

16

'Don't worry about it, Mamoo. I'm tired. And talking nonsense. I should sleep now.'

'Is Bimla in trouble?' he asked in a faltering voice. 'She's all right, isn't she?'

'She's hale and hearty. At last she's doing what she wants to.' I felt pleased with the half truth I was able to serve up in an unhesitating manner.

'Good night, Bhoot.' I put my arm out to stroke his drowsy head camping on my quilt. He stirred and shook himself before joyfully following his master out of the room.

FOUR

As he left Mamoo pushed the light-switch up on the wall near the door. I turned off the bed-light too. The night, glowing gently in the setting moonlight, crept into the room to encircle and caress me to sleep.

I must have slept soundly for many hours before I woke up in a dark room. Disoriented, my mind was fumbling as to where I was – in my own bed or Shiv's – when I heard shoes crunching on the gravel, and a probing torch spraying its light on the shrubs outside the window. The watchman, I assured myself, doing his routine inspection of the grounds of Nani-ma's bungalow, Atal-Retreat, in Allahabad. I still missed a heartbeat remembering how our ayah used to make Karan and me rush into our beds in panic when we heard that crunch. She had presented him as a phantom who was out looking for naughty children. When Mother discovered this device of packing us off to bed, she scolded the ayah in front of us and made her say that it was not true. When this failed to alleviate our fear she took us out on to the verandah at bedtime, whimpering and clinging to her legs, and introduced the watchman to us. She made us open our eyes and see him smile and salute smartly before walking away. His boots crunching the gravel, his stick held in the right hand, his torch in the left – insignias of his profession.

I wished Mother could help me bury another phantom in my mind which conjures up hordes of people dying in a famine. Not somewhere in Africa, but those who died in 1942 in Bengal and the United Provinces – long before I was born. The newspaper pictures of dead cattle and children have haunted me ever since I saw the old reports about two months ago. The rationalisation by Ma, and later by Karan, when they had learnt, before I did, of the Sahi connection to it, didn't work for me. Perhaps nothing ever would.

Another thing haunting my mind was the question I had asked Mamoo. It was appropriate that I should seek an understanding of my mother in her room. It was here she must have tortured herself to give up the man she loved, for the sake of her parents, more precisely her father. I did ask her why she had taken the path of least resistance by giving up rather than asserting her right to happiness? She had replied that it was the price of being an only child. I couldn't believe this to be the whole truth. Either she wasn't telling me everything or she was deliberately avoiding self-analysis. I told her so.

'What does it matter? It was so long ago. Forget it,' she said, and closed up.

But it did matter to me. My pre-adolescent years were a blur of happiness. And the adolescent years passed in knowing myself – a mixture of painful disappointments and promising possibilities. And now I was appraising my roots. It was the same urge that some years ago had made me ask my most reliable source of information, Mamoo, the reason for Nani-ma's hostility towards my mother.

'Why do you think like this?' he asked.

'Because now I'm old enough to detect the undercurrents.' To coax him into revealing his opinion I said, 'I have to know why. I must. For myself. I won't talk about it. Not even to Karan if you say so.'

He gave me the information I needed, but in bits and pieces. He tested my discretion before trusting me completely. He's had no cause for regret. Now he talks freely to me, sometimes on his own initiative.

He confirmed that hostility does exist and for silly, unfair reasons. When Nani-ma was told that she had given birth to a girl she didn't want to see her. She had wanted to present a son to her husband to shape in his image. Make him into a doctor, as famous a surgeon as he was. In time Nani-ma's disappointment might have blown over. But unluckily for Ma, the complicated labour had ruined the chances of Nani-ma conceiving again. She blamed it on the bad luck her daughter had brought to the family.

Her resentment had no chance to recede because Dr Atal adored his daughter, and showered love and attention on her. Worse still, he treated her like a son and, against the norm of the society of the thirties, encouraged her to take up medicine. Nani-ma argued, quarrelled, sulked, stopped talking to her husband – every feminine wile she could think of – to make him bow to the traditional pattern. She wanted him, like the others in the Kashmiri clan of Allahabad, to arrange their daughter's marriage. Dr Atal was not affected by any of her arguments. Ma continued her medical studies against the background rumblings of Nani-ma.

'I think,' Mamoo said with a smile, 'her real intention was to get Bimla out and away from home after marriage.'

There had been another desperate effort by Nani-ma to displace Ma. Of course Mamoo couldn't include it in his account as it concerned him. Not only us, but everyone in our clan circuit addresses him as Mamoo – Mother's brother. It's a title invested with a lot of respect and a bond of affection, a sort of extension of maternal ties. Karan and I discussed this and decided to consider him Ma's circumstantial brother.

The allusion to circumstances was well grounded. Mamoo was barely three years old when Nani-ma had taken him from a poor relation of hers. His stepmother, we were told, could not bear the sight of him and was beating him black and blue. His father, too mild to do anything, was willing to let him go away with Nani-ma, as the frail boy was sure to die under his roof. Nani-ma, it was easy to guess, had hoped her husband would adopt the little boy and fill the gap in his life of an inheritor of his medical practice. It appears Nana avoided an open clash with Nani-ma by delaying a legal adoption. Soon it became clear that the little boy had a mental block against school. He was taught his three Rs by a teacher who came to the home. His academic lack of interest persisted. Nani-ma had to give up her plans of a higher education for him.

I can understand her disappointment in the little boy she

had brought home with such high hopes. What I don't understand is why she stunted his growth. Mamoo never speaks to her beyond what is necessary. With her he's subdued to a servile degree, even fearful of her, which he tries to hide from us. Both Karan and I made this out a long time ago, but I'm proud that we've always given him respect due to a mother's brother. He has no clue we feel sorry that he had no option but to make himself useful as Grandmother's escort.

Even so he has never allowed anyone to forget his origins. If someone slips up and calls him Atal he is quick to declare he is Gyan Handoo and not Gyan Atal. The only time I've heard his soft, amiable tone replaced by an assertive one is when he has to remind someone that although he addresses Bimla as Didda, the elder sister, he was not Dr Mohan Atal's son but only like a son to him. There is no residual bitterness in his feelings or behaviour. He's devoted to my mother, and truly an uncle to us.

Just then, much to my amusement, I heard a cock crowing as if endorsing my thoughts. It came from the direction of the poultry farm Mamoo had started in the vast backyard of Atal-Retreat with the help of a Peace Corps volunteer. In his will Nana had left him some capital to be used for starting his own enterprise. Ever since Mamoo started making money the gifts he gave us mentioned that they were from him, and from him only. He also looked after Nani-ma's dairy enterprise – a string of Jersey cows and Punjab buffaloes – but refused to handle her money when he started the poultry farm. There was a lot of sense in not creating room for doubt in Nani-ma's mind.

I recalled images imprinted on my mind in childhood, left there to be understood later if so needed. The conversations I had overheard (of people who imagined it was safe to talk in my presence as I was too young to understand anything) began to float in, and fill shades of meaning to my observations of the interactions of elders in my world. In this process of acquiring insight I had looked at Nana's old photo albums to grasp visually the quality of life in Atal-Retreat when he was alive, many years before I came into the world.

21

On my prompting Nani-ma had proudly told me in detail how Nana had personally designed and supervised the construction of this bungalow, solid and functional, and named it Atal-Retreat. Karan and I still make fun of this Anglo–Indian name. Atal in Hindi means that which cannot be moved. It implies a heroic quality of standing firmly on a principle, or whatever is worth fighting for. But the word *retreat* hardly ever implies an honourable move. If he had meant it to be a place that provided shelter, and quiet contemplation, then too the name was more ironical than apt. I wonder if Nana ever realised it.

Although Karan and I had laughed over it innumerable times, even teased Ma about it, I did not find it funny any more. I was overwhelmed by a new awareness of being in a home of deep sadness. All those who had lived here had caused each other unhappiness, directly or indirectly. I wondered if any one of them had managed to be contented and peaceful here. Not my mother, I know. After Nana's death she escaped from Atal-Retreat. After a brief acquaintance, she accepted my father's offer of marriage because he was not from Nani-ma's Kashmiri community and lived in Bombay, far away from Allahabad. Papa had his own reasons for choosing her, as she was to discover after Karan and I were born.

Mamoo and Nani-ma have an interdependent need to stay together. I have often wondered why Mamoo had not married. Someday I'll ask him if I get a chance. My main concern right then was to understand the reasons for the choices my mother made in her life. This might prepare me for the likely choice she would make now. I had to know if she was a martyr who found solace in sacrificing, like giving up the man she loved for the sake of her father. Or did she do it because she was too timid to go against his wishes?

Both these reasons do not appeal to me. I strongly believe that life is too precious to make myself bleed for someone else. Martyrs, who thrive on self-sacrifice, are suspect. At best I consider it a mask for a weak, shaky personality. I would like to think that my mother had made her decision from a position of personal strength.

And the real question that had been gnawing for an answer sprang out of its sheath. It had been waiting for a recognition, and an answer, from the time I had inadvertently opened the closet of the Sahi skeletons. By knowing whether my mother is a woman of strength, or one who falls into self-deception, I would be able to anticipate how she would play the cards she was now holding. As a declarer would she concede her contract as unmakeable? Even if she thinks that way, I'd like her to take a chance by playing on for a skilful endplay.

I found myself making a stereotypical wish – a wish that the walls of her room would reveal the person they knew better than anyone else. They would not rationalise like Ma. They would give a straight opinion derived from all that only they had witnessed.

I felt the walls creeping closer, breathing heavily. I thought if I could relax and make myself receptive I would understand what they were trying to say. I turned on my stomach and pulled up my knees. I had seen infants do this when their mothers made them lie on their bellies to get rid of the discomfort of accumulated wind, and stop crying. I lay absolutely still and waited, but the walls said nothing to me. The cock in the poultry farm was crowing again, but more impatiently this time.

I had no warning I was going to cry. I heard myself sob like I used to when I was sent to bed as a punishment.

FIVE

Sobbing didn't fade into exhausted sleep, as it used to. I felt light and relieved. Also hungry, in need of a hot cup of coffee. It made me venture out of my warm cocoon and go to the bathroom.

I had to switch on the light; it was still dark outside. My quartz watch could not be doubted for indicating that it was about six in the morning. This was not my hour to be up and about. I wondered how I could get a cup of coffee. Atal-Retreat was miles apart from Sahi-Sadan in Bombay where I could buzz at any time of the day or night to get service. I had no idea what time Dulari came into the kitchen to start the day's work.

I was too wide awake to feel tempted to go back to bed. Birds were answering their wake-up calls on the branches of the mango tree stretching outside the east window. I decided to take a stroll in the walled compound of Atal-Retreat. I dressed in my jeans, polo-neck sweater, woollen socks and Nike shoes. Picking up my shawl I draped it over my head and stepped out of Ma's room into the open air.

It wasn't as cold as I expected it to be. It was deathly still, no restless wind with icy claws. The darkness had an opaque quality that my eyes could not penetrate. I felt wetness on my cheeks as if tears had returned, but they had no reason to. I heard the stray dogs, far and near, challenging each other. As I stepped off the terrace I felt the soft earth under my feet. I kept inching forward in an obscure setting despite feeling uncomfortable and disoriented.

'Who's there?' The imperial tone petrified me. I looked to my right and saw a hazy torchlight dancing skittishly. It outlined its owner and revealed the heavy mist which had wet my face. I identified myself to the watchman.

'Sorry, sorry, bitia if I frightened you . . .' He became stuck in the groove of a sorry-and-salaam routine.

'Salaam, salaam,' I managed to interject. 'Don't worry, you didn't frighten me,' I lied. His hand steadied, and held the torch down. Its light bounced off the ground to sketch our presence faintly in the swirling mist.

'You're up so early, Gunga bitia. Any trouble?' he asked anxiously.

'No, no trouble. I need a cup of coffee.' My words sounded muffled. I felt as if I were back in the uterine membrane, and another foetus had come a-visiting.

'You go back to your room, bitia,' he dictated. 'I'll tell Dulari to make coffee for you.' His voice resumed its commanding tone, 'First, I'll tell them at the cattle-shed to hurry up and deliver some milk to her.'

'I had come out for a walk.' I matched his tone. 'Maybe I should come to the cattle-shed with you.'

He hesitated for a second then asked for permission to go ahead in order to light the path with his torchlight.

'That's all right, you go ahead and show the way,' I allowed him gladly.

His outline passed me, moving with confident steps. I felt as if I could jump up and float in the enveloping milky fluid to follow him. But my feet stayed on the gravel not too far behind him.

The shed turned out to be much bigger than I remembered, lit up, and humming with activity. It was already cleaned up, floors mopped and glistening. The attendants I had seen moving around sluggishly with milk cans near the kitchen in the courtyard looked unfamiliar. Here they were tuned to high speed, literally on the run doing their tasks. I counted fifteen cows and buffaloes tied to milking posts, their calves joggling their swollen udders.

The watchman called out to the man in charge, 'Can you hurry up with milking? Gunga bitia needs a cup of coffee.' This drew the attention of all the bees to our entry into their domain. I answered their chorus of respectful namaste with an embarrassed folding of my palms.

'In no time we'll send the milk to the kitchen, bitia,' the man the watchman had addressed said in a comforting tone. He summoned two workers and pushed them to a still higher speed of action.

When the city acquired a dairy system Nani-ma had stubbornly refused to switch to bottled, pasteurised milk. Mother got illustrated pamphlets to impress her with the efficiency and hygiene of the machine system but they had no success in converting her. Grandmother maintained that it was a cunning device to extract the goodness of milk before selling it in bottles to an unsuspecting public. Wasn't that the reason why it did not have its familiar aroma? Mother persuaded her to visit the dairy farm, with worse results. Instead of overcoming her prejudice Nani-ma added one that was beyond reasoning. She was repelled by the mechanical milking device. It was heartless, she said, to clamp metal nozzles to the soft nipples of poor suffering cows. It was all wrong to pump them dry so fast. But as far as we could make out they had the same bovine, indifferent expressions as a cow milked by hand.

Mother had to give up. Nani-ma's cattle-shed kept expanding because she would not sell her new crop of cows and buffaloes to the only buyer, the growing city dairy system. In time she found it difficult to sell surplus milk to the 'unsuspecting' public who developed a preference for the odourless, even-textured milk that could keep for a longer time than the fresh one from Nani-ma's. She started making butter, ghee, and paneer. What was not sold she took as gifts to her relatives whom she visited in turn every evening. I remember once when the drivers of the city milk vans had gone on a flash strike. Neighbours came running to her for milk for their children. Karan advised her to sell it at double the usual price. She had laughed merrily, patted him on the back and said that the money made from the distress of others can never bring happiness. She gave milk free for the children and at the usual price for tea.

'Arre, what are you doing here?' Mamoo had entered unobserved by me.

'Namaste, Mamoo,' I greeted him, relishing his surprise.

He had wrapped his thick dhussa shawl over his rumpled kurta-pyjama and rushed over straight from bed for his first inspection of the day.

'Found it difficult to sleep in your mother's room?' he asked with concern as he sat down next to me on the bench. 'Too tired or worried?'

'Bit of both,' I said turning to gaze at the squatting milk-man holding a pail between his knees under the bound hind legs of the spotted black and white Jersey cow. He was gently massaging her udders before pressing to stream the milk out.

'You want to talk about anything? Now or later,' Mamoo asked.

'I have to talk to Nani-ma first, Mamoo. Ma's instructions. I'd like to talk to you first, but . . .'

'You should do as your mother wants you to,' he said. 'I asked in case . . . anyway your Nani-ma has guessed Didda has sent you for some special purpose. Don't wait too long before you talk to her.'

'I won't,' I said readily, and impulsively asked, 'I need some information. Will you answer my questions truthfully, without holding anything back?'

'Haven't I always been truthful with you? Have I ever misled you?' He looked hurt and a bit annoyed.

I hugged him and said, 'I'm sorry for my stupid way of talking. You know I've always turned to you for advice. Forgive me. Forget it too.'

'All right, it's forgotten. What's your question?'

'Tell me about Shafi Ahmed. Did you like him?'

'How did you find out about him?' He was more than surprised. 'Has he been in touch with Didda?'

'No, not directly. Why?'

'She promised her father that they wouldn't write, or try to get in touch with each other after Shafi left for Pakistan.'

'That was a hard punishment. Why?'

'No, no. It wasn't anything like that,' Mamoo defended. 'It was a . . . well, this was the only way to free them from each other so that they could live separate lives.'

'Who made her give him up? Nani-ma or Nana? Or both?'

'Your Nani-ma was the first one to object, but it wouldn't have mattered if your Nana had not also objected. He would normally have come around. He liked Shafi. But he had serious doubts about an inter-communal marriage in those days.' Mamoo rearranged his shawl to improve its insulation. I had dressed too warmly to feel the chill he was responding to. He looked straight at me and continued, 'Everything is different now, not easy for you to understand. It was a bad time. Hindus and Muslims distrusted each other. That's saying it mildly, I should say they hated each other. Enough to kill neighbours. Riots flared up at any time, just anywhere. And no one stopped to listen to Mahatma Gandhi's appeals for peace. No effect. Jinnah was bent on dividing India to get Pakistan for the Muslims. The country was splitting, like joint families do when there is quarrelling among brothers. How could anyone think that a Hindu–Muslim marriage was a good idea? You see what I mean . . .'

'Was Shafi a fanatical Muslim?' I interrupted his dwelling on the situation I had read about extensively for journalistic knowledge in order to analyse the current Khalistan question. It was fresh in my mind. Indira Gandhi had been assassinated by rabid Sikhs about fifteen days before. Less than forty years before this Mahatma Gandhi was shot by a fanatical Hindu. History was repeating itself in swifter cycles due to fanatics turning into terrorists. I asked, 'Did Shafi's family object strongly? Did they want Ma to accept Islam before marrying Shafi?'

'His family may have, I'm not sure. They must've been staunch Muslims, since they were Pathans from the northwest frontier. That is why he was so tall, so good-looking. A stunningly handsome doctor. All the nurses at the Civil Hospital wanted to work for him. Very fine, straight man, like Pathans are known to be.'

This made me speculate on what Karan and I would've been like if Ma had married Shafi. The Aryan women in ancient times used to select a mate with their sights on genetical factors. I imagine it was a sort of social snobbery to produce quality progeny. Their selection weighed not only physical looks, but also the ancestral stockpile of brain and character genes of the male they invited to their bed during 'ritu' – the period of maximum fertility. That was the age of sexual freedom for high-quality production. The women could have an assorted set of children from their chosen men. I don't think that glorious age will ever come back again. Women began to be tied to the marriage post and children born out of wedlock were dubbed bastards. Denied her free choice, Mother should've stayed single and savoured her freedom to the full, like I intend doing. If Mother had to get married she, being a doctor, certainly should've been alert to genetic factors when deciding on tying the marriage knot with a man from the Sahi stock. Luckily, I'm a gainer from mother's Kashmiri inheritance, nothing to complain about. But Karan is all Sahi – dark in complexion, of medium height, and slight in body. These physical attributes have never bothered me – or him, I'm sure. After my recent discovery of Sahi history I do feel disturbed that Karan's internalisation should also have been carved from the chip of that block.

I became aware that Mamoo had continued his explanation of the Hindu–Muslim problem in the forties. I reined in my rambling mind. It was idiotic of me to remodel Karan with Shafi Ahmed's genes. As his children we wouldn't have existed as such. Our identity would've been totally different. One has to accept oneself as one is, I pacified myself, a creation of one's Karma. Since I had not followed Mamoo's discourse I deflected him by asking a question, 'Mamoo, I'm sure you must've encouraged Ma to stand up against her father?'

'I was in no position to influence anyone. You know how it is even now. Didda knew that. She didn't expect anything beyond my concern . . . and affection.'

'Would Shafi have stayed on in India if Ma had married him?'

'Of course. For him nothing else existed in the world but her.' The expression on his face softened as he said this. After a brief pause he asked, 'You haven't told me how you came to know all this past history.'

'From Rekha first. Then Ma, when she came to know that Shafi Ahmed has cancer. He's in Lahore.' I bit my tongue to say no more. Everything had to be told to Nani-ma first.

'Hai Ram,' he cried out. He bent his head and held it in his palms.

I looked around self-consciously. Some heads turned involuntarily and, on finding nothing alarming, promptly returned to work. It was brighter outside the windows. The mist was battling with the annihilating rays of the rising sun. The cow-shed appeared like a frame in a movie scene, softly backlit outside to highlight the bright lights of the interior. I felt I had unwittingly been cued into a heavy emotional scene. I felt like a self-conscious performer as I stroked Mamoo's back. My spoken line was equally poor, 'Mamoo, you must've been very fond of Shafi Ahmed.'

'I am. Don't talk in the past tense,' he said in a choking voice. He must've seen me looking hurt over his unfair scolding because he cleared his throat and said, 'Yes, it was difficult not to like him.' For a while he seemed to grope to find something more to say. I waited till he asked, 'How did Didda come to know about Shafi's illness?'

'From Dr Davidson. You met him and his wife, didn't you? When they came to Allahabad?'

'Yes. They both came over one morning and had a cup of tea. I've known Dr Davidson from the time he came here as a bachelor to work under your Nana. Both your mother and Shafi were his assistants. Did you know that?'

That Mother had worked under Dr Davidson I had known for years. Way back, when I passed the high-school examination with distinction, she had treated Karan and me to a tour of England and Europe. We had met the Davidsons then. They had us over for dinner at their home in Totnes. We learnt all about their good old days in Allahabad, served with Mrs Davidson's version of Indian dishes she had taken the trouble to cook.

As a prologue, when she stated that her poor attempt was for the two young ones who might be missing home food, Ma's brief glare conveyed to us not to let Mrs Davidson know that we had become devotees of the fast-food joints in

London. Karan ate her servings with such relish that even I was fooled. Later when we dissected the evening, Karan told me, much to my satisfaction, that I had managed to fool him also by my interest in the nostalgic stories the three of them were recalling endlessly. What I deliberately didn't clarify to him was that I was indeed fascinated by their conversation. It was like watching a montage of people and places from the past in a home movie.

I remember now that it was on that evening the Davidsons had talked of their dream of a nostalgic trip some day to all the hospitals he had worked for in India, winding up in Pakistan – Karachi and Lahore – just the way he had done his postings during the years of His Majesty's Service. They'd finally managed to make their dream trip in 1984. They came to see Mother first in Bombay, and went with her to Delhi to call on Prime Minister Indira Gandhi, whom they had known as a young woman in Allahabad.

For their first evening in Bombay Ma managed to lasso Papa for dinner at the new restaurant of Karan's choice, Salaam. That reminded me of the bet Karan and I had to settle. It occurred to me that Mamoo was the right person for that. So I asked, this time tactfully, 'Mamoo, please be frank and give me an answer to settle an argument with Karan. He's convinced that Dr Davidson was, and still is, in love with Ma. Not just a fancy but that he must've been serious, proposed to her and all that. Could that be true, Mamoo?'

'Didn't you ask her?'

'No. How could we?'

'It may be true. Who can tell? There were so many buzzing around her.' I waited. He looked as if he were going to tell me something more when he turned his face to the other side and asked, 'How has Bimla taken the news?'

'It's shaken her up. Made her come out of her coma.'

His head turned sharply towards me. 'Coma? What happened?'

'She's not ill, Mamoo.' I made a mental note that I would have to be careful with my language both with him and Nani-ma. 'It was just a figure of speech I was using. I meant

31

to say that it made her face what she had managed to avoid for years.'

It still didn't make sense to him. I had to peel my statement to the core. 'She's admitted to herself that she's still in love with Shafi Ahmed.'

'Of course, she's always been. She knew it all along, I'm sure.'

'You're a romantic, Mamoo! I've always thought of you as a hard-core bachelor.'

He ignored my observation. 'What about Shafi's wife? His children?' he asked with concern.

'Dr Davidson wrote that Shafi never married. I think this upset Ma more than the news of his illness.'

'Who's looking after him?'

'He's in the hospital where he was working. I imagine his family is looking after him,' I replied uneasily. His questions were coming too close to the point where I'd have to say I couldn't tell him anything more before talking to Nani-ma. I quickly countered the drift of our conversation by begging him to tell me about Nana. 'It's a pity I didn't get a chance to meet him. What was he like? Life around here must've been very different in his time. Am I right?'

'Oh, yes, you're absolutely right. I led a carefree life. He made everyone feel like that by keeping the weight of responsibility on his shoulders. Always smiling and joking. Not once did he scold me for anything. Never . . .' Mamoo's eyes had become moist again.

'Most likely you did nothing to deserve scolding,' I said with a laugh. 'I've heard others joking about him, saying he was so westernised he looked like a copy of an Englishman in the three-piece suit he wore to parties. Was that so?'

'Yes, he did dress like his English colleagues. It suited him too. He was very fair. Tall and well built. But, do you know? He was the only one who didn't tease me when I started wearing khadi on joining Mahatma Gandhi's Quit India movement. He gave me money to make more clothes and give up all the old ones in my almirah. From that day to this, I have worn nothing but pyjama-kurta of hand-spun and hand-woven khadi. Even the die-hard Congressmen have given it up for mill cloth these days.'

32

It was true. I had always seen him in nothing but khadi pyjama-kurta and a jacket. The older generation among the Katra and Georgetown relations tease him by calling him 'Jawahar ka beta' for aping the style of Jawaharlal Nehru's clothes. He, I'm sure, loves that. He's never varied his outfits.

Mamoo was talking, I caught his words: '. . . bad luck he didn't live to see both of you. You're unlucky too.' I could guess he meant because we didn't know Nana. He went on, 'He could love and care like no one else could. And yet be strict. You should be very proud to be his granddaughter.'

'That's notional, Mamoo. I would swap it for having known him, like you.' A couple of years ago I was curious about Nana. I had come to know his bio-data by heart, which Mamoo was reciting for me now. Nani-ma had kept Nana's study just as he had left it, down to the *Lancet* magazine open on the page he had been reading when he collapsed. That December I had browsed in the study, seeing his albums, scrapbooks, papers he had written, his letters, his clothes – just about everything that made him come alive for me. At the end of it I found I envied Ma for having him for a father.

Mamoo broke into my reverie with his exclamation, 'Look, Gungoo, look . . . see, see this beam of sunlight. It glided in just as I said I wish your Nana was around to guide you . . .'

A beam of rising sun had strayed in through the window behind us. It revealed the unseen motes floating, like weightless spacemen. It was an everyday phenomenon. I tried to match his excitement but . . .

'You're laughing at me,' he accused.

'No,' I said emphatically. 'Why should I, Mamoo? You're fortunate to see magic in what to me is Nature's familiar pattern. I can't insult you by pretending to agree with you though, can I?'

'A person just can't stop to exist after death. I believe in the atman, spirit as you say, surviving and staying within the reach of people it has loved. To me the spirit world is as real as all this around us.' He made a sweeping gesture including

33

me with the cow-shed. 'How can our emotions make sense if they are as perishable as our bodies? Don't you think so? . . .'

I was relieved when Mamoo was diverted by the milkman who came to show him the brimming pail of milk he was ready to deliver to Dulari in the bungalow. Mamoo's discourse was becoming too profound for me to grasp without a cup of coffee.

SIX

When Mamoo and I entered the courtyard behind the milkman, Nani-ma was sitting wrapped up in her shahtoosh shawl in her usual place on the divan in the verandah. In her outline she looked exactly as she had last night on her bed. It was as if she were a children's picture book cut-out which could be lifted from one page to the next. Mamoo muttered under his breath that she was up earlier than her usual hour; possibly she too hadn't been able to sleep well. He warned me to be careful and darted off to his room on the right side of the courtyard.

Dulari was sweeping the courtyard, shifting her weight on her haunches to move along with the broom as she swung it from one side to the other. The sari covering her head had slipped off showing a wispy plait lying on her massive back like a book-mark in an encyclopaedia. It was more shocking than amusing. From early childhood I remember being fascinated by her thick, long plait which moved like a pendulum when she walked. For a long time now I had not come out early enough to see her uncovered head when she swept the courtyard.

After greeting and hugging Nani-ma I asked as soon as I sat down on the divan, 'When did Dulari lose her long plait?' After saying it I realised that my question was tactless. Nani-ma's pimple of a bun wound up tightly at the back of her head may also have been a thick plait once.

'She hasn't lost it in one day,' she replied with a chuckle. 'It's been going on for years.' She took out a hand from under her shawl and catching my plait tugged it. 'I've noticed how dry your hair is. Don't you oil it at all? You'll lose

35

your beautiful hair if you don't.' I was relieved that she hadn't taken my question personally.

'No chance, Nani-ma. I'm not losing sight of your will. I oil my hair the night before I intend washing it,' I said lying down on the divan, with my head on her lap.

'You're so cold,' she said as she began to stroke my head, my face. She pulled out an end of her shawl to cover my shoulders, coiling my uncombed plait to tuck it out of the way.

I must have been seven when I decided not to allow my hair to be trimmed. That December my hair was still too short to be plaited. Mother's Kashmiri clan – of Atals, Dhars, Wanchoos, Nehrus, Handoos and so on – invariably asked her, 'Why is she looking like a cave girl?' I might as well have been an inanimate object they were scrutinising. Ma repeated her explanation so often that I'm sure she stopped hearing her own words, 'She's growing her hair long. I didn't ask her to, it's her own idea. All her friends have short styles. She wants a plait.'

My acute embarrassment evaporated when Nani-ma told me how happy she was that I was growing my hair. She declared that I would inherit Atal-Retreat from her, if I didn't give in to the temptation of styling my hair into a short bob like my mother's. Every year after that she examined my lengthening plait, and unfailingly repeated that if I ever snipped off my plait I could be sure of a change in her will. She said I had to make up for my mother whom she had never forgiven for chopping off her beautiful plait when she started working in the hospital. Ma, I imagine, must've found it a nuisance to manage her long hair when she could be summoned to duty at any time of the day or night. I have no such problem in my nine-to-five job. Moreover, my old ayah, Saku Bai, oils, shampoos, and grooms my hair. I love its feel along my spine.

I have yet another reason for keeping the heavy braid attached to my head. It almost reaches my knees now. Shiv adores my plait calling it the snake in his Garden of Eden. When I pointed out that Adam had no cause to love the snake, Shiv decided the first man was a fool who couldn't think for himself. Was it not the serpent who had to teach him the knowledge of sex, its delights? What good was a body without that? Hindus, he said, have been the wise ones. They worship Nagraj, the Snake-God. I had to concede the point and let him call my plait Queen Cobra, while I call it my insurance policy for a roof over my head in Allahabad. Not that I'd need it. I just like the fat feeling of being Nani-ma's favoured one.

Dulari, her head primly covered with her sari, brought a large steaming mug of coffee. With great glee she reported to Nani-ma that the milkman had told her I had gone to the cow-shed to get milk for my coffee. 'No wonder she was so cold!' Nani-ma exclaimed. She instructed me in future to wake up Dulari if I wanted anything. Then she roundly scolded Dulari for not remembering my coffee habit, and for not showing common sense in realising that I would be hungry since I had eaten nothing last night. She ordered her to make quickly a two-egg rumble-tumble with onions, tomatoes, ginger and green coriander – all chopped very fine. 'Make parathas to eat with this, like you did for the Davidsons. Go, go immediately and get to work. You can finish sweeping and dusting later on.' I felt sorry for Dulari, but she richly deserved it for trying to raise a laugh at me.

Nani-ma started telling me of the Davidsons' visit. How unnecessarily nervous she was about talking to them. She said she used the English phrases she remembered, and they seemed to have great joy in exercising their Hindi. They hadn't changed, same as they were. Physically, yes they had. Naturally years had passed. They had to look older, greyer, weaker. But they hadn't changed, same jolly pair as they were before. It was good to see them again, although it made her also sad to think of the old days when Doctor Sahib was alive. I was amused that even after his death Nani-ma couldn't call her husband by his name. What a deeply ingrained orthodox conditioning she had received. I thought of the bride I had met on the train. She belonged to the same school of conservative upbringing but, like a snake, she had already begun shedding the old skin. A social order was coming to an end with Nani-ma; there was no reason to mourn it.

Mamoo, bathed and dressed in fresh clothes, came up the courtyard steps, greeted Nani-ma with a respectful namaste, and sat down on the divan at the far end from her. Dulari appeared with hot milk for Nani-ma, and rumble-tumble and parathas for Mamoo also. The aroma of eggs and onions, mixed with that of coffee, made me attack the breakfast with vigour. Nani-ma picked up my plait which had slipped over my bent shoulders and was falling on my overloaded plate, as if it were equally hungry. Instead of throwing it on my back she kept holding the errant braid as she remarked, 'You have a wild streak, like your mother has.' I knew this was a preamble to her favourite topic, my marriage. 'It's high time this rein was given to a sensible man who can control and guide you. You are over your twenty-fourth year, aren't you?' My mouth was too full to be used; I nodded so that she would continue her usual recitation. 'I know your mother and father are not worried about you. But what about your grandmother, and grandfather? Aren't they trying to arrange a suitable match for you?'

My mouth was ready to speak so I decided on teasing her instead of my usual way of dealing with no comment. 'Nani-ma,' I said slowly with relish, 'as you say, I'm a wild horse, rather a mare. I happen to be in a huge, open space. Why should I let anyone catch me and tie me down? Don't you think you would do exactly that if you were in my position?'

'Chul, shaitan,' Nani-ma said, using my plait as a whip on my back. 'You don't know what you want. You're trying to be different. Just like that. Deep inside you must want to get married.' I looked at Mamoo's corner to wink at him and found that he had quietly left with his plate. Nani-ma started bemoaning how everything had changed for the worse. With education and the new rights given by Parliament, women had started thinking of themselves as equals of the menfolk. They were now the new brown mem-sahibs of India. 'It is Jawaharlal who has given everything to the women on a plate. In such a short time too.'

'Nani-ma, you should be proud that your nephew restored women to their old, high position. Jawaharlal Nehru will be remembered for it.' I tried to give her an objective view.

'He misled everyone, even his father who gave up his legal practice for politics. Where has it taken us? We were better off under the British Raj,' she said with a finality that was above contradiction. I had heard this opinion from all those who wore blinkers and didn't want to acknowledge any progress in the country after Independence. Arguing with them had been a waste of time.

I kept quiet. I was tempted to describe what her position as a widow would've been but for the new rights. She certainly would not have been able to promise to leave Atal-Retreat to me. In the absence of a direct male heir all her husband's assets would've been inherited by a next-of-kin male. She and Ma would have lived on his charity, could not even have been able legally to claim maintenance. Women of my generation knew that once again it was a good time in which to live.

I began to amuse myself by imagining how she would react if I told her that my paternal grandparents had given up arranging my marriage, as they had done for my three cousin sisters who were about my age. All of them had waited decorously at home after graduation doing courses in flower arrangement, gourmet cooking, child-care – anything to pass the time till a groom was found for them. I refused to do that. After taking courses in journalism and mass communication I had started working at *Reflections*. Since then my grandparents had stopped asking me to meet the eligible bachelors from the affluent, conservative bracket they belonged to. In their opinion working girls of the modern, liberated brand had love affairs, even abortions, without letting their families know about it. They, I'm certain, had decided that taking the responsibility of an arranged marriage for me was a bad risk. I had vaguely wondered at that time how they had allowed Ma to let me work. Now I can make a good guess that it was Mother who made the breach for me. I looked up at Nani-ma who was still holding out emphatically on her favourite topic. I wanted to tell her that I was not a virgin, if only to stop her gushing waterfall. But I knew I could never do anything to hurt her. She had been coping with her disappointment in her only child. My ego would not allow me to become another disappointment.

Her observations on the unwelcome social changes were interrupted by the arrival of the vegetable man at the back door of the courtyard. Nani-ma's morning drill had started. Like a school timetable she had fixed different days in the week for the meat, fish, vegetable and fruit sellers. A vendor waited at the back door till she beckoned to him to step inside the courtyard. The big, round open basket he carried on his head would be lowered on the top step of the verandah to enable her to see his stock. She examined the goods, bargained, and bought from her lofty seat on the divan without moving an inch.

After this was over she would go to the kitchen and the store on the right of the verandah. While sitting on the cane stool in the kitchen she would unhook the bunch of keys tucked at her waist and give them to Dulari to open the store. She would give detailed instructions about the menus for the meals of the day. Dulari would measure the exact quantities of oil, ghee, rice, lentil, wheat flour – the lot that would be needed for cooking. Lunch was prepared on wood-fire and the dinner in the antique Ic-Mic cooker, MADE IN ENGLAND still inscribed on it. Grandfather had bought it for her on his first visit to London. Two years ago Mother bought her a Hawkins pressure cooker and took the trouble to instruct Dulari in handling it. As soon as we had left Nani-ma had it wrapped up in a piece of an old bedsheet and put away to give it to me when I married. When questioned by Ma, on our next visit, she said she felt the Ic-Mic cooker was safer for an illiterate woman like Dulari. I could see her point, not that I was aiming at saving that pressure cooker for myself.

The truth was that the slow action of the Ic-Mic cooker suited her better. All that Nani-ma needed was to have Dulari free to accompany her during the daily evening visits alternating between Katra wallas and Georgetown wallas, as the two sets of her favourite relatives were referred to by the area they lived in. While the visit was on, the cooker simmered a delicious meal ready to be served piping hot on their return. This also gave Nani-ma an excuse not to overstay when urged, as she had to keep her appointment for dinner with her reliable friend, the cooker.

After the Ic-Mic dinner Nani-ma played Snakes and Ladders, or Ludo, as her mood dictated, with Mamoo. She drank a glass of hot milk before retiring to bed after nine, content with having conducted the day as she wanted to. It was at that time when Dulari, while pressing her mistress's tired legs, would relate, with Hitchcockian suspense and drama, the stories and gossip she had picked up during the day at Atal-Retreat and from the servants at the place of the evening's visit.

Nani-ma told me to wait for her to return after her kitchen chores. Feeling sleepy on a full stomach I put my head down on the round bolster Nani-ma used as a back-rest of the divan. I remembered Mamoo telling me some time ago why he called it the royal seat of Atals.

'This is really a takht,' he had said tapping the wood under the light mattress. Realising I was not familiar with the word he had explained, 'To you this is a divan for everyone to sit on. To me it has another significance. It's a takht, means a throne in Urdu. I've seen your Nani-ma and Dr Atal, your Nana, talking while he shaved in the mornings here. He would be concentrating on his face in the portable mirror. You know the small one in the leather frame in his room, you must've seen it.'

I had, as a curious item. I nodded and he continued, 'It was a gift from the English Commissioner when he retired and left for England. He had seen your Nana using an Indian mirror, set in a metal frame, in the Dak Bungalow when they were touring together. Anyway, as I was saying, every morning your Nana and Nani would be in a huddle talking in whispers. The slanting razor in his hand, and her serious face reporting and discussing the household affairs, was an awesome sight for me. The outcome of these talks affected us all. We used to post the "weather" signals for those absent from the scene. Now, by herself, your grandmother is a different person . . .'

41

'Not the terror of your young days,' I mumbled. For the first time it occurred to me Mamoo had no personal term of address for his benefactress. I suspected Nani-ma wanted to continue her talk with me on this throne. I wasn't going to allow myself to be scared like Mamoo was when he left with his breakfast plate fearing the clanging of swords between us.

I must have dozed off because the next thing I was aware of was Nani-ma whispering to Dulari to fetch a shawl and cover me. I didn't open my eyes. I started breathing deeply like one does when fast asleep. If Nani-ma was planning to initiate an enquiry on my visit, as I suspected she intended to, I knew I had to dodge it as I was hardly ready for a session with her.

SEVEN

I did take Mamoo's advice seriously about speaking to Nani-ma without waiting too long. But it was not till the fifth day of my visit – I left on the morning of the sixth day – that I was able to deliver Ma's message to her.

It was not entirely due to the internal preparation I became involved in. I think Nani-ma guessed that what I had to tell her was something disturbing. She must've decided that if I was in no urgent need to spill, it would be in her interest to keep the lid on it. She didn't enquire after Ma any more. She aimed her curiosity towards Karan, the Davidsons, Sahis, and of course largely at me.

Since Grandmother was not forcing me to a show of the cards I was holding close to my nose, I also let myself drift. On the third day after my arrival, when I realised I had only two days left before my scheduled return to Bombay, I blamed myself for not taking two weeks off from work, as the 'boss-lady' had suggested. Mrs Singhal had even indicated that I had worked so hard on the October cover story of *Reflections*, also it was so well appreciated by the editorial board, that she would not consider it as leave, but a break I richly deserved.

Although I was quite pleased to hear my editor's unexpected praise, I wanted to show that I could restrain myself from leaping at an advantage. It was only a year ago when Mother, being Mrs Singhal's friend, had managed to place me on her magazine. When I was given the cover story to do, the office folks had sniggered behind my back. Undeserved favouritism, they had called it. Having justified Mrs Singhal's trust in me I didn't want to provide my colleagues with a reason for any comments again. I expressed my gratitude to the editor, and told her that I needed no more than a week in Allahabad to finish the assignment entrusted to me by Ma.

Later, self-analysis revealed the real reason was that I had anticipated Allahabad to be painfully boring. How was I to know that the distressful emotions, suppressed into a heap inside me, would find a healing touch, here of all places?

The delay in a session with Nani-ma was partly due also to my alienating her. It happened when I declared, on the first evening of the day after my arrival, that I didn't want to take the evening chukker with her. I had deliberately left this for the last minute when Hiralal, son of Nana's old chauffeur Ramlal, arrived punctually at six o'clock to drive the car for her ritual visit.

Nani-ma had retired Ramlal soon after Nana's death, but let him stay with his family in the servants' quarters at the back. She had got young Hiralal employed as a driver in a government office. This insured that he would be off-duty promptly by five, making it possible for him to do a two-hour duty for her every day. Thus Nani-ma's frugality, and Ramlal's happiness in staying on in the familiar surroundings, had made a fair exchange.

I had been sitting on a withered cane chair on the lawn just outside the courtyard wall savouring the shade of my old favourite, the neem tree. Its serrated leaves were humming in the soft breeze. Last December Karan had sat yoga-style on the grass where my feet were stretched out. After he had done his deep-breathing routine he had opened his eyes and said with child-like wonder, 'Fresh air. Ozone. I have to clean every sac in my lungs with this neem ozone. This is the compensation for leaving the polluted air of Bombay.' He had just joined an environmentalist group.

When we were younger we spent our time under the tamarind tree, neighbour of neem, looking for its fallen sour pods, or throwing stones to break their slim necks on the low branches of the tree. We would fill our pockets to eat them with a touch of salt carried in the palm. From a distance I could detect quite a few green pods lying around the spread of roots of the tamarind tree. They could no longer tempt my taste buds. I preferred to sprawl in the chair, appreciatively distinguishing the scents of a variety of trees around me, and thinking of time passed and gone. It made me feel as old as Grandmother.

My eyes strayed from the book in my hand to watch the birds around me. The restless sparrows chattering in their squeaky voices had first caught my attention. Soon I was tired of their constant hovering and landing in the grass in search of food. I switched to the pigeons promenading fearlessly all around me. They could be Victorian ladies in hooped skirts and parasols taking a stroll on a beach. The twisting necks of the pigeons snobbishly inspected the others strutting on the turf. Catching the sunlight at an angle their grey neck feathers would flash multiple colours for split seconds, like the shot-silk Conjeevaram saris.

Tiring of this social scene my eyes shifted to the action of the crows on the wall. They were flitting, snooping like newshounds in the private domain of the courtyard for a morsel from Dulari's kitchen. I was snatched from my diversion by Nani-ma calling out from the verandah, 'Arre, Gungoo, aren't you going to change? It's past five-thirty.' I was still in the maroon salwar-kameez I had worn after my bath in the morning.

'I'm not coming with you, Nani-ma,' I replied shutting my book and getting up as slowly as I could. My shawl slipped and fell on the grass, giving me an excuse to take a little more time before looking up at her.

Her rounded eyes were staring at me. She had waited for me to straighten up before exclaiming, 'Arre, why? Aren't you well?'

'I'm all right. I just don't feel like meeting them all,' I said truthfully.

'They're expecting to see you. They'll want to know why you didn't come along.'

'Oh, just say I have a headache.'

'May your enemies have a headache, why should you? God forbid,' she said. 'It's wrong to tell a lie.'

As far as I was concerned harmless lies were merely

strategies of everday living. No sin, they prevented injured feelings. But there was no sense in arguing about grey areas of morality with a senior citizen. 'They'll ask questions I can't answer yet, Nani-ma. You know what I mean. I'll see them later before I leave.'

She tried another angle, 'How can I leave you all by yourself here? Dulari will have to . . .'

'No, no, Nani-ma, you don't have to do that,' I cut in quickly. For Dulari it would be a golden opportunity to grill me with her questions. I wanted to be by myself. How could I make Nani-ma understand that revolutionary social changes had taken place since her time? We girls were no longer over-protected. We travelled alone, lived alone, worked to stand on our own feet, asserted our independence to be on a par with men. Besides, I knew it was highly stupid to argue with someone who was already angry. I used a soft tone to say, 'I'm used to being on my own at home. Ma often had to run off to deliver babies – any time of day and night.'

'Yes, but you're not alone like this, in a bungalow. As you've described to me your father's family lives above and below you. Didn't you say that Sahi apartments are on six floors in that big building called Sahi-Sadan? In Bombay you live like plates piled on the kitchen shelf.' Suddenly her face relaxed; she started laughing.

Her smile was apt and funny. I started laughing with her. 'That is exactly how we live, Nani-ma, on that land re-claimed from the sea.'

And I wondered if, when I talked to her, I should reveal why I was disenchanted by the Sahi stack of plates. And that I had every intention to leave Sahi-Sadan and persuade Shiv not to insist on marriage but let me live with him. I had to make a decision on this, and on many other points. I needed to be left alone. I found myself saying impulsively, 'Nani-ma, can I please spend the time you are away in Nana's room?' I hadn't thought of it earlier but it was exactly what I wanted to do.

I don't know what it was but something made her realise that she shouldn't force me any more, and must let me do what I wanted to. She took out the bunch of keys hanging from her waist. Good heavens, I thought, she's going to trust me so much? She picked out the key of Nana's room which made me think, with relief, that she was going to slip it out of the ring to give me the responsibility of just one room. She handed the key on the ring to Mamoo asking him to open the room for me, turned around and left without saying anything to me.

Mamoo not only opened the room but brought an electric heater. 'Where are you planning to sit? I'll fix it there.'

I made a quick decision. 'There, near Nana's wing chair.'

'I should've guessed it,' he said with a smile. 'Don't be alarmed, Atal-Retreat is as safe as Sahi-Sadan.'

I refrained from saying that I felt safer here. Nani-ma had her own ideas of safety. I heard her instructing Mamoo to lock the front door before returning the powerful bunch of keys to her. I was happy to be imprisoned with my thoughts in Nana's room.

EIGHT

I ventured first into the kitchen and boiled water in the electric kettle to make a large mug of Nescafé. I abstained from milk and sugar to escape Dulari's detection and reporting to Nani-ma. I could wash and replace the mug before their punctual return. I waved to the hissing Ic-Mic, 'Keep my secret,' and returned to Nana's room.

Without any hesitation I sat down in his wing chair with its cracking, but still soft leather upholstery, and put my mug on the peg table where, I imagined, he kept his happy-hour whisky glass. The heater had already warmed the room. I put my feet up and folded my legs inside the shawl, like Grandmother did. I sat for a long time leashing my straying thoughts to concentrate them, as I'd heard mediums did, to make Nana's spirit communicate with me. No one was in a better position than him to have a detached comprehension of the turmoil in my life. Mamoo had mentioned in the cow-shed that Nana would've guided me if I so wished. I did want his guidance to estimate my role correctly in the events of the last few months.

Nothing happened. There was no tremor in the atmosphere. No thought entered my head that I couldn't recognise as my own. Mother's empty room had held her unhappiness. Despite Nani-ma's device to hold Nana trapped in this room, he was not there. At least not for me. Perhaps it was not possible to make a contact with him as he didn't know me. But then spirits are supposed to be all-knowing. Obviously, his atman was not restless. It was at peace. With himself and with those he had left behind on this planet. Could I infer then that, unlike me, he approved

48

of my mother's choices after his death, including the one she had just made, and the last one she was required to make now?

I said loudly, 'God helps those who help themselves.' My voice was dripping with sarcasm. I smoothed my ruffled feathers and decided calmly that I had to be my own counsellor. I stretched my legs out on the footstool and took a few sips of the still warm coffee. I found myself on the couch, and also sitting on a chair with a pen and a pad.

I instructed my memory to go back to the end of July 1984. Before that I had no care in the world. Childhood and adolescent years had had their pangs of jealousies and rough passages, which at that time had seemed giant sized. But there was no disturbance in the river-bed of my life. I had managed to let the winds that rippled the surface pass over me.

In fact, I would say, that I had been like a bird, like a koel, who sits on a branch of the shady mango tree – unaware of the dust, the loo of the unbearably hot summer months – and is absorbed in repeating endlessly her lilting set of notes. My tune in life changed, however, with the assignment of the cover story for the October issue of *Reflections*. I remember clearly the day it was given to me.

It was the usual cloudy morning of a monsoon month. And, as usual, I was running against time. I hastily pinned the pleats of the sari and tossed the free end over my left shoulder, shoved the wallet into the tote-bag, and took a running start out of my bedroom. On seeing Karan in the living-room, I braked involuntarily, and walked sedately. He was lolling on the divan, still in his crumpled white pyjama and kurta. 'Aha, here comes the cyclone,' he called out gaily.

'Learn to bend from your waist and greet your elder sister properly,' I advised him.

'I would if your one-year head start had made you wiser,' he retorted.

'You need a cold shower,' I said. 'Seeing you in the morning brings bad luck all through the day.' And I was out of the front door before he could retaliate.

Saku Bai was holding the lift door open for me. 'Come,

come, Gunga bitia. Someone is ringing the bell for the lip-phut.' She adopted English words on her terms. I did what I had been avoiding like an ostrich. I looked at my watch. It was about nine. My mother was the first one to leave at eight for her scheduled operations at Bombay Hospital. The children from the third floor left for school at eight-thirty. All the others at Sahi-Sadan were late starters.

'Saku Bai,' I said with irritation left over from the encounter with Karan, 'there is no one who would . . .' She thrust the paper napkin wrapped around an omelette sandwich into my hand and let the lift go. This was her daily addition to the cup of milky coffee she served me in bed. No excuse, no reasoning had succeeded in diffusing Saku Bai's breakfast strategy of inducing me to eat in the car. Having taken care of me from birth she had a self-acquired right to bully me. It was just as well she didn't know that I evened the score with her by dropping the omelette sandwich on the first out-stretched palm of a beggar at my car window during a red-light halt.

My blue Fiat, a gift from Aunt Chanda on my twenty-first birthday, was kept ready under the porch by Pandu, my father's chauffeur. He saluted as I ran down the marble steps and held the door open for me. 'Drive carefully, don't speed, Gunga bitia,' he said shutting the door. 'It might rain.'

'Hold back the clouds for me, Pandu,' I said as I drove off.

There was no way I could have speeded, much as I wanted to. The threat of a downpour had brought every available taxi into the three lanes of Marine Drive going to-wards the Fort area. On top of that every amber light flipped into red just as I approached. I was muttering my favourite invectives when I noticed two girls in school uniform laugh-ing at me from the rear window of the car ahead. I waved to them and pretended I had been singing. No longer amused, they turned away. 'Silly billies,' I said as I changed the lane when the traffic began to flow.

I resigned myself to being late and using the elements as my excuse. The south-west monsoon was at the height of its glory. A maddened wind was forcing the usually placid waves of Back Bay into massive levitations against the tetrapods stacked along the sea-wall. They were going way up and crashing down on the promenade on the opposite lane of Marine Drive. I wished I could stand against the sea-wall and let the diving waves drench me. I rolled down the glass of my window and compensated my desire by letting the salty spray wet my face.

The eerie golden haze around me gradually became dark and menacing by the time I neared Churchgate Station. The negative traffic signals continued for me. The policeman's hand had let a stream of cars go, but had to stretch his arm out to stop my car, to give the right of way to the train commuters oozing out of the station like toothpaste. I controlled my impatience by watching their multi-coloured raincoats and umbrellas moving like computer graphics.

By the time I reached the office a light rain had started. It was being whipped around by the wind which tugged at my umbrella as I tried to lock the door after parking the car. I felt I might get airborne like Mary Poppins. The umbrella, not being of the adventurous kind, let the wind invert it. I had no choice but to make a dash for the foyer. A black cat was running in with me. Lucky? Unlucky? I wondered. My plait was wet, my sari limp and clinging. I wondered how I could slip unnoticed to the toilet in the office to change into the spare sari and blouse I carried in my tote-bag for such emergencies.

The office was as disorderly as my appearance. 'Has Mrs Singhal arrived?' I asked the peon.

He smiled. 'Editor Sahib hasn't arrived. All are late. Bad traffic, jams all over.'

When I returned after changing I found everyone crowded around the sloping desk of Kanu. 'You stop fooling, yaar. Stop doodling and listen to me.' It was Maya's voice on a high pitch. 'Singhal will be furious. You're wasting your time. I'm telling you.'

'Goodness, Kanu, you're daring,' someone in the crowd said with admiration.

'Quite an idea, though,' someone else approved. It made

me push in to have a look. Kanu was gaily sketching a Sikh trying to keep his balance on a slice of green earth perched on a rolling pin.

'He just won't listen to good advice,' Maya carried on. She was bending over the drawing board sitting on the table next to Kanu's. Her bare feet were propped on his chair, tucked under his thigh. 'Come on, take a fresh sheet and start another one.'

'It qualifies more as a cartoon than an illustration,' slipped out of my mouth.

'Exactly,' Maya cried out. 'That's what I'm trying to tell him all this time.' She craned her neck to meet my eyes. 'Say it again, Gunga. Pound it into his head.'

'Freedom of choice,' I said noting the indications of her obvious jump from his bed to his desk.

'Hey, Gunga, where are you?' It was fat Renuka, the editor's niece. 'Summons for you from the big cabin.'

'Raise or disgrace?' Kanu asked.

'Who knows?' Renuka replied shrugging her shoulders.

When I returned from the big cabin it was Maya who asked, 'What was it? Raise or disgrace?'

'October cover story.' Now it was my voice which was high pitched.

'Congratulations,' Renuka called out from her desk near the big cabin.

'What's it to be?' someone asked.

'Joint Family Living in Modern India,' I replied. This time my voice was in control.

'Sounds like a school essay.'

'Big spreads are not essays,' I retorted.

'Safe subject for a stand-by cover story.'

'Why her?' a voice cried out for justice.

'Hey, moron, don't you know?' Renuka had the answer. 'She's best qualified here. She's living in a joint family. She should know how three generations live together. Tied up, more by money than love. Question is whether they can continue living like that. Gunga's business family, like some others, works and lives in a joint set-up. Now, who else here can do the investigation better than her? Hanh? Aren't I right, Gunga?'

'I suppose so,' I mumbled. I had never thought of the Sahi life-style as specially significant. Renuka had made it sound as if she had recommended my name to her aunt. It irritated me to be obligated to her. Mrs Singhal knew Ma and the Sahi set-up well enough to think of my handling it. But it was prudent not to challenge Renuka. So, when she suggested I should give a treat to everyone, I told the peon to take the order for coffee and eats from her. She could have the small satisfaction of being my patron.

'Make it an extra-large order, Renuka.' Maya was alluding to Renuka's own consumption.

The Udipi canteen sent steaming idlis, wadas, dossas and coffee. By the time I could get around to eating, the heaped order looked like a threatened species. Renuka's left hand was anointing an idli with green chutney while she was biting on the one in her right hand. 'Good luck, Gunga,' she toasted with her coffee cup. 'Make the most of your first break.'

As it turned out I did need luck most of all. On this re-run of that day in July I remembered that I was infused with over-confidence. I had thought that my determination to work hard and do my best was all that I needed.

NINE

Nana's West End wall clock showed the minute hand skipping towards a quarter past six. Incredibly, one hour had already passed since Nani-ma left. My disbelief swung on the mesmerising pendulum. If it was dutifully wound up every week, as I knew it was, then it kept the right time. My watch was not on my wrist to check it out. I decided to trust the ancient clock. I switched off the heater and the lights and picked up the mug to wash in the kitchen. Nana's room had given me nothing else to take with me. Except, perhaps, to start me off on the track of revising recent events in sequence, and then evaluating and stacking them neatly on the shelves of my mind.

I found Bhoot waiting patiently bundled up outside the door. He got up briskly, waving his head from side to side, his eyes imploring me to talk to him. 'I can't bear to sit inside any more,' I confided. 'The walls are deaf and dumb.' I stroked his neck while he kept stretching it to try to lick my face, an indulgence my love for animals didn't accommodate. I straightened up saying, 'That's enough. How about walking with me in the courtyard? Do you good after lying on the cold floor for so long.' He bounded off towards the steps when I called him back, 'Come to the kitchen first while I wash the mug.' He didn't come inside the kitchen despite my reckless invitation. He knew better. I found a few pieces of old bread, which Dulari was not likely to miss, and offered them to him. He looked at my face incredulously before taking them delicately from my hand.

It was cold in the courtyard. 'Let's walk, Bhoot, to warm up. Quietly. No talking. I have to think.' Covering my head with the shawl I walked round and round briskly to kick up heat in my body. Bhoot walked behind me for a bit. Then, having got the design of the exercise, moved ahead – looking back often to make sure that I hadn't given him the slip.

From the moment my assignment was announced in the office my mind had started working on it. After the coffee-break celebration, when all of us had returned to our desks, I jotted random points on my pad. Next, I tried to think of how I should approach the topic. Like someone had said, it was a dull subject. A glorified school essay, unless I could make the treatment interesting. How? I drew a distressing blank. Looking around at heads bent over desks, I felt I had to get out of that pressure tank. I left hurriedly, saying I was going to the *Times of India* library to look for reading matter on joint families of fifty years ago.

It was while driving in the car that I decided to have a look at Sahi-Sadan as objectively as I could. Renuka had a point when she said my living in a joint family set-up gave me an advantage in writing about it. So, logically I had to start from there in my comprehension of the subject. To be able to judge the system objectively I had to make my perspective a long-distance one.

I parked my car around the corner from home, and walked up the slope to have a look at it as a passer-by would. It was just a simple six-storey building, with no architectural flourish to draw attention to it. Solid, compact, functional. In other words, boring. Next moment it looked very funny, tucked in snugly, as it was, between two high-rise buildings on either side. Like a child held between its parents. I couldn't wait to make Karan see it like this and hear him burst out laughing.

On the upsweep the penthouse garden caught the eye, like a gay straw hat, with its colourful medley of bougainvillea bracts waving joyously in the monsoon breeze. The white, purple, and pink sprays of other vines dripped over the para-pet wall. I could spot my favourite hibiscus bush with its deep-green leaves and the ever-blooming red flowers. It had become special from the time I had listened to a story Ma told us one night of a fairy who became a captive of a flower because she didn't know that it closed at sundown. Very often I still go to this beautiful realm of my grandfather, called Lalaji by everyone, to pluck the closed hibiscus flowers, as I used to when I was a child. I believed I could release the trapped fairy by forcing the petals open.

I wondered if I should start by interviewing Grandfather, Lala Karam Vir Sahi, whose finger was on the pulse of everyone living under his roof. I knew the family's proud story of how Lalaji and his younger brother, Lala Prem Vir Sahi, had risen from landlordship of a few villages near Varnasi to great wealth through their trading enterprises, taking every opportunity which came their way. The two brothers had continued to work and live as one family when they shifted to Bombay after Independence. They wanted to be in the vanguard of the industrial development of an emerging nation.

I concluded, standing on the pavement observing in a detached manner the place of my birth, that the joint family system must have an adhesive quality because the two Sahi branches still lived under Lalaji's patronage although his younger brother was murdered long ago. Lala Prem Vir Sahi's widow, my father's Aunt Chanda, who was till recently a very special person for me, lived on the fifth floor. The fourth floor was divided into two sections for the families of her two sons. The third floor was with my father's brother, Uncle Dinesh. He had only three daughters, my peers, who were married in quick succession. Two of them lived in Delhi and one in Calcutta. The second floor was ours.

My father, Espee as he's called by his initials, is the eldest of Lalaji's family of four – two sons and two daughters. Shanta, the older one, we used to call the mad aunt till we learnt about mental disorders. She was not married. She stayed with Grandmother and Grandfather, on the sixth floor. She had to be confined to the barred room at the back during the time of the full moon. We used to be scared of her screaming obscenities which made us run off rather than listen carefully to unscramble her words.

That was why it's only now that I've come to know that her abuses are aimed at Aunt Chanda. Her uncontrollable anger and her excessive love for her elder brother, my father, were the root cause of her condition. She was not born mad, as we girls had assumed. This was my first discovery of the truths under cover. I still have to decide if ignorance is preferable.

However, my three cousin sisters and I were pretty sharp and aware of what had happened to our father's younger sister, Sita. She was great fun to be with, lively, frank and high-spirited. We four girls had had a great time at her grand wedding. We made more outfits than we found occasions to wear. We changed our sparkling clothes at least three times in one day with heavy jewellery of our mothers' to match. I had a double choice as Aunt Chanda insisted I wear her jewellery too since she didn't have a daughter to enjoy dressing up. I had always been her doll from the time I was born, she declared. Papa had told Karan and I that, although she's our grand-aunt, Chanda was too young to look like one. So, we should address her as Aunt Chanda. But now, like Papa, I've stopped calling her anything. I don't need to, I hardly meet her.

To us four cousins, the marriage of Aunt Sita meant we could dress to kill. We experimented with coquetry with males of any age whose eyes examined us. Fortunately, the women of the family did not frown or pick on us for our boldness. They were too busy flaunting their new stock of dazzling saris and jewellery, and airing their rusty style of flirtation with near and far male relations.

Soon after her fairy-tale wedding Aunt Sita returned to Sahi-Sadan in disarray in the dead of night, in a taxi. That is why all the servants came to know of the scandal. Thanks to Saku Bai I heard of it the first thing in the morning before I left for school. According to her she should never have been given the name of Sita. Like the one in the epic, Ramayana, anyone named Sita is bound to be unhappy. I got nothing more out of the information bureau of the servants' department.

It was Aunt Chanda who told me the diluted truth. She said that, unfortunately, the groom chosen for Sita by Lalaji turned out to be abnormal. We girls knew there was more

57

to that word. We didn't rest till we had ferreted out the real reason. The groom was a sexual deviant. We had long sessions on sex and Aunt Sita's plight in hushed tones. We had to be wary so that our personal maids would not get the scent of what we were talking about, and report to our mothers.

Soon I became isolated because I said I admired Aunt Sita for not waiting till the morning to run away from the fiend she found in her wedding bed. The other three felt she should've behaved with decorum and confided in her mother first. Then Lalaji would've taken care of the situation.

'What if he had told her to go back and bear it?' My voice had become loud to be emphatic. Six hands flapped in the air to lower my volume. I spoke in a low tone but with passion, 'You know what is said traditionally to every bride as she leaves her father's home to go with her in-laws? Don't you remember that darn priest reciting it gleefully? Throw this wheat and rice over your shoulder as a pay-off for the food your parents fed you, he told her. Remember? And the next bit is the bang on the head. Don't leave your husband's home to return here, endure his dictates. You are going to your bridegroom's home in a palanquin, stay there no matter what your fate dictates. You should only leave your husband's home as a corpse, he had said. Remember? Nonsense. Rubbish, I say. I'm so glad Aunt Sita had the guts to run out.' I must've frothed in the mouth like a dragon.

'It all depends on one's fate. You have to accept it,' one of my cousins had said. They're like branded slaves. No wonder I drifted away from them.

I kept my opinions and approval of Aunt Sita's subsequent actions to myself. I felt triumphant when she refused to return even after Lalaji had negotiated a truce with her in-laws. This was exactly what I had predicted to my cousins. Steadily and gradually she manipulated her own destiny.

To begin with she made Lalaji feel guilty enough for what she had suffered to permit her to work for the family business. What had started as an indulgence turned out, in time, to be an asset for Lalaji. During her apprenticeship Aunt Sita discovered her business aptitude and interest. She insisted on doing her MBA. After two years of study, when she returned to the family business, it was obvious that, given equal opportunities to work, her contribution could be on a par with her brothers'. She caused considerable alarm – for my father definitely. I heard him say, without admiration, that she had become a hard-nosed businesswoman. On the other hand Lalaji grudgingly, but proudly, admitted that his daughter had inherited more of his business acumen than his two sons.

Along with her success in business, Aunt Sita's single status was accepted. She was given an apartment of her own by making massive alterations on the ground floor. She devised a separate entrance for herself and made sure that it was so placed that no one from upstairs could spy on her. But Saku Bai and her colleagues had their own grapevine and I was well informed of her visitors. I continued to approve of everything she did.

For the first time, on looking at Sahi-Sadan from a distance, I perceived all of us swarming in this small beehive. But we were far from being clones. We were all so different from each other. How did Lalaji hold his growing tribe with a strong grip? So many pulls in different directions had to be harmonised. The disparities in opinions, varying temperaments, personal inclinations and ambitions which had to be harnessed with strength and justice. I made a mental note that I would have to find out if blood relationships and love in a family were enough to provide the draw-string to close such gaps. Could it really work smoothly to the happiness of all?

The Sahi membership, by comparison to other joint families, was not that large. As far as males were concerned there was Lalaji at the top; on the second rung were my father and uncle; and the third rung held two young people, Aunt Chanda's sons, both graduates of Harvard Business School. One half of the Sahi business was owned by Aunt Chanda and the two Harvard graduates. For the first time I wondered why and how the business symbiosis had worked out between them and those of the old school, Lalaji and his two sons. It would've been logical if the two halves had divided and gone their separate ways. This was the usual pattern in family concerns. It was in this point, I decided, I would find the key to the success of Sahi joint family living.

Lalaji's significant contribution towards this lay in adapting the old pattern of joint living to suit the changing times. Sahi-Sadan was designed to accommodate that revolutionary aspect, we all knew that. Each floor had an independent life of its own. Unlike the old way there was no common kitchen which, it is alleged, created quarrels among the womenfolk to be carried over to the men in the family. In Lalaji's pattern, the nuclear family life on each floor was free from daily frictions. Privacy remained intact. The units were hooked together, Lego style, to form a large power structure for the benefit of each small unit. I was pleased with this visual metaphor of my family's life-style. I wrote it down quickly in case I should forget it.

And yet, some answers were needed still to give a satisfactory understanding. In spite of this beneficial hook-up there was enough area left uncovered for competition, discontent, factions and so on. These expressions are bound to crop up when a group of people live together. How was it smoothed out in this kind of set-up? My research would have to be in this direction also, I made jottings in my notebook standing against the wall of the building opposite my home.

I was about to leave the pavement observation post, when I remembered how Karan had often irritated me by his very obedient behaviour towards Aunt Chanda's two sons, and then criticising them threadbare in private. I could now comprehend the modus operandi he had so shrewdly picked up from his elders. In the office hierarchy of Sahi enterprises he was on the lowest, the fourth rung of power structure. Lalaji on the top; Aunt Chanda, my father and Uncle Dinesh on the second; and then the two sons of Aunt Chanda on the third rung. Karan on the fourth and last rung had to stay on the right side of Lalaji's nephews to get power along with his dues in future when they would be in the driver's seat of Sahi business. This was the same world of manipulations in administrative bureaucracy, or in any business corporation. I suppose Karan had found out for himself that it was each to his smartness to get the most out of the beehive. I know now that he was far ahead of me in worldly wisdom.

I don't know how long I had been on the pavement leaning against the boundary wall of a building, before I became aware of the inquisitive glances directed at me. There was the panwala whose eyes habitually darted around to spot customers as he presided over his gleaming brass tray filled with small containers. His hands kept busy preparing betel leaves according to the demand of a client, usually a pedestrian, who had succumbed to the temptation of pausing to smoke a bidi and chew a pan.

The equally active barber was the other pavement entrepreneur. He was keeping an eye on me in synchronisation with his scissors snipping hair on a head. I heard his customers, squatting around him waiting their turn, commenting under their breath as to what I was up to in a milieu that was clearly not mine. I decided it was time to move.

As I walked back to my Fiat I amused myself by thinking that I was like Marco Polo. The difference between us was that his curiosity had taken him to unseen lands. And my enquiring mind was appraising a familiar setting as if I had never seen it before.

TEN

The monotony of ambulating in the courtyard percolated to me from Bhoot. He had paused many times near the steps suggesting I go up and sit on Nani-ma's divan. When I kept going round and round he continued to follow me, but under protest. Poor beast, he had no thoughts to occupy him. And I was intent on making the most of my solitude. I had to settle the disturbance within me so that I should be clear-headed when I spoke to Nani-ma.

Pretty soon Bhoot's Gandhian satyagraha overcame my resistance. 'Two rounds more and I'll stop,' I promised. I weighed the option of sitting in Nana's room, or my own. Both were rejected in preference for his hint to sit on the divan. We went up the steps together. I arranged myself cross-legged inside the tent of my shawl. I tried to coax Bhoot to come up next to me and share his body warmth, but he refused. He looked happy on the rug.

On the first day of my assignment when I returned from pavement observation to my car I gave in to the temptation to go to Sahi-Sadan for a hot thali lunch. I gave into yet another impulse after the meal. I rang up Shiv Menon to tell him about my new assignment, saying that the piece I had done on him had brought me luck. It was an unnecessary communication which advented momentous consequences. Shiv claims this call made an alteration in the way he had looked at me so far.

I have often relived our first meeting with relish. Mrs Singhal called me to her cabin and gave me a blurb on the new chairman of the prestigious Swiss firm, Zephyr India. I was to find out the rationale behind the appointment of an Indian head instead of the usual Swiss one, as well as present this little-known man to the readers of *Reflections*.

It was not till I had entered Shiv's huge panelled office that I felt nervous cramps in my stomach. Seeing a newly hatched journalist flapping her wings Shiv took over the situation. Soon he knew more about me than I could about him. He took me out for lunch – 'business lunch' he defined it when I hesitated. A series of such lunches thawed me out so much that, in Shiv's opinion, I did a pretty aggressive piece on him.

When the issue of *Reflections* with Shiv on the cover went on sale I saw it in the hand of a magazine vendor while I was on my way to the office in the morning. I had slowed my car to a stop behind a long line of cars at the Churchgate crossing of Marine Drive. A boy ran up with many magazines fanned out in display to sell. I spied Shiv's half face smiling between *Stardust* and *Business World*. I quickly fished out change from my purse and bought his smile. Before the green arrow could make the cars flow, I saw my byline in bold print. My spirits soared. At every stop I bought Shiv from the vendor who brought him to my window.

When I reached the office I was showered with congratulations, and was made to foot the bill of Renuka's order of a coffee-break treat on my behalf. My mouth was busy demolishing an idli when I was summoned to the telephone. The operator of Zephyr India heard me choke when she announced that Mr Menon wanted to talk to me. 'Are you all right, Miss Sahi?' she asked.

I took time to swallow before explaining why I had choked. 'I'm ready now to talk to Mr Menon,' I said foolishly arranging the sari on my shoulder as if I were about to enter his panelled office again.

When I heard his hello it occurred to me that this was the first time I was hearing his voice on the phone. I stammered self-consciously as I accepted his congratulations. 'I've just bought a copy of *Reflections* on the road as I was coming to the office,' he told me. 'It was my chauffeur who first saw a spread of my face on the pavement.'

I burst out laughing. 'You mean you bought it from a

sidewalk vendor? I got mine from those who bring the magazines to the cars. I saw half of your face between *Stardust*
and . . . and *Business World*, I think.'

'I'm today's star. Thank you for sprinkling the silver dust
on me.' Before I could make a witty retort he asked, 'Can
you consider changing gear and having dinner tonight to
celebrate my stardom? Can't mix it with the purposeful
business lunches. It has to be a different flavour. Is it possible?'

It was definitely not possible like the lunches were. I was
reluctant to tell him that dating men was not in the Sahi
book of rules for their girls. They could go out to parties,
shows etc. with their kith and kin – the brothers and cousins,
who did careful screening before introducing any of their
eligible friends to them. Ma had taken the risk of my lunch
dates since they had the screen of working hours. It was
unfair to ask her to swing this for me.

Listening to my silence Shiv asked, 'Is there any problem?
We could dine at home. My Thomas is an excellent cook.
It'd be better than sitting primly in a restaurant. Do you
mind? We'll have a nice relaxed evening. Promise you a
good time.'

Obviously, he had no clue to my level of emancipation. In
any case, preferring his apartment to a public place had a
universal implication which he should've been familiar with.
Was he naive, or was he sizing me up? It made me feel
mischievous.

'Good time?' I said with a heavy undertone.

'Oh yes, just that,' he said hastily and added with a laugh,
'a good time, nothing else. I'm not a rapist.'

'What makes you think I wouldn't be partial to a rape?' I
said with a chuckle.

'Well, it will be as you want,' he said slowly. 'The choice
is yours.'

'That's good,' I said gaily. 'This recalls my mother's first
round of coaching when I reached puberty.' I wanted him
to continue to think I was a liberated, modern specimen of
Indian womanhood. I did go to Shiv's apartment in
Waverley at Colaba for dinner, but not that day. It was to

be soon enough when I broke out of the Sahi corral despite my mother's restraining hand. Thomas produced an excellent *nouvelle cuisine* meal. And Shiv initiated me into the cellar culture of wines with chilled Chablis.

My flight into the past was yanked to the present with a jerk when I heard the telephone ring in the hall. I thought it would be incredible if it was Shiv on the line. It was a call from Bombay, the operator announced. And Shiv's voice was unfamiliarly raised to a high pitch to make his hello audible to me. A very bad connection, but an intoxicating one.

No sooner had we exchanged the news that we were well and missing each other, than the connection snapped. I waited, the bell shrilled and instantly I picked up the receiver. I could hear Shiv trying to charm the operator into giving him a good connection; he had something of great importance to convey to his fiancée. 'You have the wrong number, Mr Menon,' I interjected. 'Your fiancée is not here.'

He exploded into laughter. 'Ma'am,' he said to the operator, 'your connection is correct. The party is under persuasion. Thank you for your help.'

It was the operator's turn to laugh. 'Good luck,' she said and clicked off.

'Gunga,' Shiv resumed, 'to call you girlfriend sounds rotten. Besides, I'm serious about you. When are we getting engaged, and . . . married?'

'What's the important message?' I diverted his flow.

'I love you. Wish you were here.'

'Startling. That sounds new.'

'I'll keep on saying it for a hundred years and it'll still sound fresh and new to you. How's that? Will you, therefore, agree to marry me?'

'What if you forget to say your piece regularly? Wives are taken for granted, they say.'

'Not your kind. I mean . . .' And the connection was broken again. Many a time the connection was made and lost, like senescent memory, till it became annoying. I returned to the divan and let the telephone ring and give up.

Shiv's abortive call left its residue in making me wish I

65

could sip a little cognac. I had deliberately, resolutely, not brought any with me. The one thing Nani-ma, I was told by Mamoo, uncompromisingly hated in her husband she otherwise worshipped, was his ritual of two drinks before dinner. While keeping everything else just so in his study she had removed the drink cabinet. She refused to give away Dr Atal's collection of rare whiskies even to the relatives and others she visited in Georgetown and Katra, although they discreetly begged her to. It would be a sin to distribute such a gift, she had maintained. Mamoo said she didn't trust anyone, so she sat on a stool near the courtyard drain, her nose covered with her sari, and made Dulari empty each bottle of the envied cabinet.

I forced my mind to squash the longing-for cognac and retract to the day I was given the cover-story assignment. I had impulsively dialled Shiv and I was talking to him when I saw Ma walk in. Involuntarily I looked at my watch. It was just after three. Something was wrong, it was way out of her routine to be home. I wound up and said goodbye to Shiv. 'Ma, are you all right?' I called out.

'Of course. Why? Do I look ill to you?' she called back from her room.

She was lying on her bed, with her sandals on. 'Don't be alarmed,' she was responding to the concern in my eyes. 'I was summoned by a minister, house call near by . . .'

'Got a girl into trouble? The usual house consultation,' I couldn't help interrupting her.

'Shoo,' Ma said with a smile. 'Don't ask for the name, journalist. I missed lunch so I've come over for a bite, rest a little, and go back to my preggies scheduled for check-ups. By the way, working girl, what are you doing here?'

Excitedly, I told her of my assignment, and asked her advice about where and how to begin my study of the Sahi family pattern. 'Leave them alone,' she said with a vehemence I find relevant now. 'Study some other families. Research in the library. Why do you have to begin here?'

I wasn't perceptive, or respectful of her advice. I kept on arguing right through the pakoras, grilled chicken sandwiches and masala tea Saku Bai served her. In exasperation

Ma said, 'Why don't you do what I'm telling you without arguing?'

'Because you have to give me a good enough argument for not doing it my way.' I thought I was being very reasonable.

Just then Papa walked in. 'Aha, the working girls are home,' he remarked, but it was a question.

My mother didn't move which was no surprise. I jumped up to hug him and answered, 'We're taking a break, Papa.'

'How are you doing at . . . at . . . what's the name of your magazine?'

Reflections. And my name is Gunga Sahi.'

'Very funny. Why haven't they thrown you out by now?'

'No such luck, Papa. They've hooked me with a prestige assignment . . .' And I explained in detail before asking his advice as to where I should begin the research on the Sahi family pattern. 'With Lalaji, of course,' he suggested without hesitating. Mother didn't contradict him. He went on, 'Take his permission and advice. Interview him like a professional. That'll tickle him. He's an expert on this subject.' I noticed a sickly smile on Mother's face. Even then she didn't say anything, not a drop of the strong dose she had just given me.

Then Papa addressed her with his usual request I had witnessed umpteen times. 'Bimla, can I borrow five thousand from you? I'm short of cash. I have to make some payments at the club.'

She looked irritated. 'Borrow?' she asked with a layer of sarcasm in her voice. She got up from bed and, opening the safe locker in her wardrobe, handed him a wad of stapled hundred-rupee notes.

'I'll settle the lot next month. What's the total now?'

'A lakh and twenty,' she answered without a pause to recall.

'Are you sure?'

'I should be,' she said with a mocking laugh.

'I'll wipe it off soon. Don't worry.'

'It's for you and your Aunt Chanda to worry.' This was a new additive to the old dialogue I had heard repeated many times. After Father left with a wave to me from the door, I asked Ma, 'Why did you say that about Aunt Chanda?'

'Because they lose as partners in bridge at the club.' And she closed the topic as firmly as her locker, and dismissed me by saying she had to leave for the clinic.

I was not informed enough at that time to give importance to her words, or notice her reaction. I thought she was piqued because Papa had been supportive to me. I suppose I was not attentive enough to sense unhappiness and unrest in my mother.

In my recollections, so far, I found no point on which I could prosecute myself for triggering the events which have rent the fabric of Sahi family life. As I go ahead with a sequential examination of everything I participated in, I have to be objective and merciless towards myself to make a judgement worth all the pain I would be enduring for it.

Bhoot stirred and got up with a low bark. I heard the key turn in the front door. This was perfect synchronisation. I was ready to take a pause and welcome Nani-ma's return home.

ELEVEN

I was standing on the sideline of Nani-ma's route to her bedroom, but she ignored me and went by like a programmed robot. Puzzled and a little alarmed, I decided she needed to rush to the toilet – cold weather and a long drive must've created an urgency. I was wrong. I heard her call out to me to come in to her room.

She was sitting on her bed with her legs down as if she were travelling in a bus. She didn't invite me to sit next to her, and without any preamble asked, 'I heard from Hari Atal that Bimla was at the funeral of Indu? Is that true?'

'Yes, Nani-ma. It all . . .'

'Why didn't she ring up to tell me she was going to Delhi? I wanted to go also. She knew that. Deliberately she went without telling me. So I wouldn't insist on going with her and be a burden on her.'

This was an unfair accusation of my mother's motive. At her age how could Nani-ma even think of attending a national funeral. And Prime Minister Indira Gandhi's at that, it was an international affair. And plus, there was the trauma of her assassination, a ghastly one to assimilate for the immediate family, and everyone else for that matter. True, Nani-ma was a family member, an elder connection of the Nehru clan. This was not a family funeral where attendance was noted down. Besides she could've gone to Delhi, if she really wanted to, with the other relations who were going from Allahabad. Her anger was notional, a fresh brew. Now that the mourning was over she could use it as a whip on my mother.

Next thing I knew she had moved me into the firing range.

Her voice had risen in anger to a higher pitch as she flung her accusations at me, 'What were you doing? You're grown up, you could've thought of ringing me up. What's the use of your coming to see me every December if you don't spare a thought for me in Bombay? You're a rubber stamp of your mother. I looked like a fool today who didn't know her daughter had attended such an important family function. I wouldn't have if you'd rung me up from Bombay, or mentioned when you arrived here. Secrets are kept from me by you and your mother. Bimla was always like that. What has come over you?'

The unexpected assault had me at a disadvantage. I wanted to tell her that my mother had a lot more to deal with at the time of the tragic assassination of her much-loved cousin. In fact we were all grappling with the developments I had come to report to her. Luckily, I couldn't get any sound out of my throat. Had I said anything it would've aggravated rather than calmed her tirade. I had imagined I knew all there was to know about her. It made me feel uneasy to see a facet of my grandmother I had never seen before.

She had a second line to her surprise assault, 'Did Sahi-Sadan have an income-tax raid recently?'

'Yes, in the first week of September.' I had to admire her intelligence department.

'Hari Atal told me that Bimla had mentioned it in Delhi to him. He said she had rung up Indu to stop the raid on Sahis. I had no idea about it. Everyone looked at me in sympathy. Secretly pleased because Bimla had not bothered to let me know.'

Getting no response from me Nani-ma began to pack the silence with her words. 'This is what happens to old people. We are put on the shelf. Like you do with your old toys. Taken down if you so wish. Otherwise, forgotten and left there to rot. No one cares.'

A good simile but it certainly didn't apply to her. I laughed, and I could speak, 'Nani-ma, you are no plaything. The truth is, we are your puppets. You keep us on tight strings and we wait for you to make us dance.'

'Dhut, pagli,' she rebuked. I thought I had magically evaporated her anger with my teasing. But her mood was tenacious. She elaborated on how she had seen Indu grow from a little girl to a powerful and wonderful woman. When this awful tragedy took place should she not have been there to be of some consolation to the young people? Wasn't that the role assigned for the older, the umbrella, generation of a family? They must be wondering why she had not bothered to come. And she must've been compared to Bimla, a busy doctor, who dropped everything and rushed to them in their hour of need.

I reminded myself that I shouldn't assume a defender's role for my mother. In essence I had a diplomatic assignment. Meant to be done at the right time, in the right way. This was not the occasion to divulge anything. I still made an attempt to stem Nani-ma's flow and say, 'You know Nani-ma, if you had gone to Delhi you would've sat inside with the women and not seen everything like you did on the television. Don't you agree with me? It was better this way, far better. And Ma represented you, didn't . . .'

'She didn't take my message. She should've rung me up and asked what I wanted her to say. What else do you think I'm grieving about? Henh? They say that you can burn a rope and still it keeps its twists in its ashes. That is your mother's main characteristic. She'll never change.'

She had squashed my line of logic. I tried another one, 'Nani-ma, you could write to Rajiv and Sonia, if you haven't already.'

She looked at me with interest. 'No, I haven't. I suppose I could.'

Relieved, I nailed my suggestion, 'I'll help you if you want me to. This is so much better. They can read your letter again and again for consolation. Show it to those who may ask them why you hadn't come. Better also because at that busy funeral, and in their state of shock, who knows how much their memory could retain as to who came and who didn't.'

Finding success I kept repeating it with slight variations, patting myself for skilfully handling an inflammable situ-

71

ation. I could jump from journalism to the Indian Foreign Service, I told myself.

Dulari came in to ask when she should serve dinner. After washing up we assembled at one end of the big dining table. Mamoo had already placed the heaters and switched them on. The tension of the evening thawed considerably. The steam-cooked meal was not only of top-notch health food standard, but also delicious. Nani-ma was visibly proud when I told her that the salan and tahiri that evening were the best I had ever tasted in Allahabad. Nani-ma switched off my praise with her question, 'Tell me about the income-tax raid. Were you there?'

'I was summoned from the office, Nani-ma, in the middle of my writing the first draft of my cover story. And without being told why,' I began. 'Papa said on the phone, "Come immediately, don't wait a minute." He sounded so nervous, Mamoo, I thought all the way home that someone was seriously ill, or dead after a heart attack. Or maybe Aunt Shanta had this time succeeded in jumping off the roof. All kinds of morbid alternatives.'

I found I had seized Nani-ma's attention, also Mamoo's, Dulari had taken a pause and was leaning against the door. I decided to make my account amusing, rather than tell them how unnerved and disoriented Sahi men were in their castle they had considered impregnable. I had found it highly gratifying as, by then, I had found out about the origin of Lalaji's wealth. Shaken by this first skeleton I couldn't bear to live in Sahi-Sadan. I had moved to the apartment shared by my two school friends, Jeet and Kanta. Ma had let me do that thinking it was a transient phase. She hadn't quite fathomed the depth of my disturbance. I have no intention of making Sahi-Sadan my home.

After swallowing the food in my mouth I switched on a performer's smile to match the style of the account I had decided on. 'On arriving at Sahi-Sadan,' I continued the narration, 'I had thought for a moment that I had turned in the wrong driveway. The usual watchman was not at the gate and strange men were walking all over the grounds. No Sahi driver came running down the steps to take charge of

72

my Fiat. The foyer was over-run with still more strange faces. I was asked to identify myself. This was too much. "What's going on here?" I demanded instead.

' "Madam, tell us who you are," I was asked again. I saw the first familiar face, of our lift operator. But he looked as if someone had cast a spell on him. He answered for me, "She is Miss Gunga Sahi, daughter of Mr Shiv Prasad Sahi, the eldest son of Lalaji."

' "Which floor?" he was asked this time.

' "The second floor."

' "Take her there," he was ordered.

'Nani-ma, you can imagine how offensive and alarming all this was.' I found I was as worked up as I was that day. 'They were leading me around as if I were a dog on a leash. Mamoo, can you understand how helpless I was feeling by then? A tall, burly man was detailed on guard duty over me. The lift operator continued to be scared. He hung his head, staring at the floor, didn't even greet me.'

I continued the story with my entry into our apartment escorted by the burly guard. 'I found Papa talking, more like pleading, with someone in the hall. "Oh, you've come, beti," he greeted me nervously.

' "What's going on, Papa? What's happened here?" I cried out. He told me it was a raid and that he was forbidden to tell me that on the phone. He introduced me to Mr Dixit, who had come from Delhi to organise this massive raid simultaneously on the residences, the offices, and factories of Sahis. I had to be called to unlock my walk-in closet for their search. "What are they searching for, Papa?" I asked in a baby voice knowing full well what they were looking for. I didn't expect Papa to like my joke.

'I stood by him as he said persuasively to Mr Dixit that he did not dispute their right to break the locks, rip the upholstery, take furniture apart, demolish the ornate false ceilings – anything they wished to do and that he had no right to protest. "All I am requesting you, sir, is to wait till my wife comes. She has all the keys of the almirahs. She's going to come as soon as the caesarian operation she's doing is over." He knew, as well as I did, that Ma never carried all the keys.

73

Most of them were with Saku Bai. He wound up by suggesting that, in the meantime, Mr Dixit's team could inspect my room.

'In the living-room I could see what a raid could do. It was in shambles. All the books on the shelves were rifled and thrown on the floor. The gold-embossed leather-bound series no one had read were lying on their spines, staring open-mouthed. Art pieces were turned upside down and abandoned just anywhere. Table drawers were pulled out, rummaged, and left like tongues sticking out for a check by a doctor.

'Nani-ma, I was delighted to see cockroaches running out of their dark corners. That was the only benefit of that raid.'

'You could laugh about it,' Nani-ma said, 'but what if they had come across a lot of cash or foreign exchange. Even some foreign coins, left lying in a purse one used while travelling, has caused trouble. You can't take these raids lightly.'

'No certainly not, Nani-ma,' I conceded. 'But believe me it could be funny if you have nothing to fret about. It was like a scenario from Hindi movies, Mamoo. There was a character with a club foot, and buck teeth protruding way out. He dragged his foot from room to room asking his team mates, "Found anything? Found anything?" He was the comic relief of that drama.'

'Did they find anything?' Mamoo must've been really worried to ask this in Nani-ma's presence.

'No, luckily not. I believe Aunt Shanta created a big rumpus on the sixth floor. The search had to be stopped there because Lalaji asked for permission to let the doctor come and sedate her. By then Ma had come home.'

'That's when she must've rung up Indu to have it stopped,' Nani-ma observed.

'You're dead right,' I said.

'Bimla couldn't have liked doing that?' Mamoo asked.

'No she didn't, but I suppose had to give in to pressure,' I said.

What I didn't describe was Lalaji's descent from the sixth floor. He hardly ever came down unless one of us was ill enough to deserve a brief visit. In a wheedling tone he said to Ma that only she could save the family from disgrace and ruin. I saw that as an opportunity for her to take her revenge by refusing to ring up the Prime Minister, but she gave in tamely. As she was going towards Mr Dixit to ask for permission to ring up Delhi, I kept whispering to her to let the Sahis take the rap they deserved. She glared angrily at me saying it was none of my business.

Later she told me that she had to do it for Karan and me. That I could marry and change my name, but Karan would always be a Sahi. Despite her practical explanation, I do believe she was either too weak to resist, or too tempted to show off her accessibility to her powerful cousin.

'So, that's how Ma had the raid stopped,' I wound up the account. 'Nani-ma, you should've seen Mr Dixit's face when he was called to talk on the phone to the PM's office. He stood at attention saying, "yes, sir", over and over again. After Delhi had disconnected he couldn't move for a long time, as if he had turned into a wax figure at Madame Tussaud's. He stuttered his apologies to Papa while staring at Ma. When he offered to make his team clear up the mess, Papa waved his arm asking him to clear out of Sahi-Sadan instantly. It was a treat to see that buck-toothed character dragging his foot out of the front door looking thoroughly confused.'

The long narrative did dilute Nani-ma's anger. Encouraged, I continued chattering almost non-stop about the exodus of the raiders. It was so unlike me that Mamoo became uneasy. I quickly wound up by asking for Nani-ma's permission to visit Sangam. I hadn't been there for years. By then she had become so mellow that she decided Mamoo should take me there the next day instead of accompanying her for the evening visit.

Mamoo came to my room later and, after much humming and hawing, asked if it was all right with me if he took me to Sangam the day after as he had something scheduled for the next day. It made no difference to me, I said. The hitch in his mind was that I should make some excuse to Nani-ma, not let her know that he had wanted the change. I certainly could do that, I assured him. It left me wondering what made him survive day in and day out with this palpitating fear of Nani-ma.

But the next day I discerned in myself a certain modification of my equation with Grandmother. In my behaviour towards Nani-ma there was a germination of a new element – caution. I dare say, if I had to live as her dependant, I could also develop a psychosis similar to Mamoo's.

I decided I had to hurry up and be ready to initiate my talk to Nani-ma. My body was urging me to be done with my mission and get back to Shiv. His telephone call had defaulted, but it succeeded in releasing my hormonal longing for him.

TWELVE

My grandfather chose his breakfast hour for the interview I requested. His unfailing daily ritual was the morning constitutional walk he took with his friend, Khair Singh, who was picked up by Lalaji punctually at six-thirty from his apartment on Warden Road. They were then driven to Hanging Gardens for their nominated rounds of walking while chatting, and brought back to Sahi-Sadan, sweating and rightfully hungry.

They bathed – Khair Singh's needs were attended to by Lalaji's valet – and sat down on the divan for a leisurely exercise of their palate. Their hour's exertion deserved it, they claimed, otherwise what was the sense of renouncing their sleep to walk round and round like race-horses? Their steady gain in weight was another matter. Was there any appreciable difference in being judged as heavy, paunchy, or fat?

Having adopted an Epicurean philosophy they had no discomfort in making a habit of sharing the multi-choice, sumptuous first meal of the day. After that they parted to work in their spheres. Met again next morning to walk, exchange news, discuss their problems, gossip, and once again eat without restraint for pleasure.

On entering Lalaji's baithak I bent my head respectfully and folded my hands to greet them individually. They blessed me in one voice and invited me to eat with them. When I declined courteously Khair Singh chuckled loudly and said, 'Arre Lalaji, these modern girls are very figure-conscious. They starve to be thin enough to wear fashionable clothes.'

'Sit down,' Grandfather said to me and ordered the head of the relay of servants waiting on them, 'Get a cup of coffee for bitia.'

I sat down and nervously waited for his signal to begin the interview. My journalistic eye caught a new angle of the familiar sight of them on the divan. They made an interesting composition for a symbolic picture of purity. The spotless sheet covering the divan was a fitting background for their white, crisply starched super-fine cotton dhoti and kurta. The narrow border weave of their dhotis had been finely crinkled by the expert fingers of the washerman. Their ample paunches were covered by loose muslin kurtas from Lucknow, white with the finest embroidery done in white thread in a delicate pattern around the neck and the seams. Their white chappals were waiting on the floor on either side of the divan. They were used as long as they stayed immaculately white; slight discoloration and they were discarded for brand-new ones.

The diamond buttons on their kurtas scattered blue flickers of light as the owners moved. They both wore three rings on three fingers – of diamond solitaire, of coral for luck, and of their birth-stone for good health and long life. They wore identical Piaget gold watches.

For the first time I noticed that they had even begun to look like each other. The same droopy eyes, slack jaws, fleshy cheeks, and puffy double chins. Snugly set in their chosen grooves they certainly knew the art of enjoying daily living.

I was flushed out of my visual fantasy by Lalaji's question, 'So, what's this interview you wanted with me?' He placed egg-bhujia cradled in a piece of pav-roti in his mouth and rolled it towards one cheek to ask, 'What's it for?'

I told him briefly of my assignment to write about joint family living in modern India. 'Lalaji,' my voice was faint and hesitant, not like that of an investigative journalist. I cleared my throat and made myself continue, 'You're one of the very few people who have held on to the joint family system. As you know it has been slowly crumbling, in the industrialised, urban areas. The ancient system fitted the agrarian society. The family land was tilled by the related owners who lived under one roof, under the administration of one head. It's now practically non-existent in the affluent level of the society. Especially where the sources of income are independent. How have you managed to hold on to it?' I poured out my prepared opening text in one breath.

'It's making a come-back,' he said managing a mouthful expertly. 'Here in Bombay at least, forced by a lack of living space. The price of apartments has rocketed. Young married couples cannot afford them. The two generations have to live together whether they like it or not.'

'Quite so,' Khair Singh endorsed with a shake of his head. His hands were busy stoking his mouth.

'Lalaji,' I tried to make the interview exclusive with my grandfather, 'that is perhaps a temporary development due to a dire need. The traditional joint family living evolved for the convenience of group-work and financial interdependence which made everyone stick together in one space. Like ants in the ant-hill. I imagine in our case the family business is the strong glue which holds us here, in Sahi-Sadan. Am I right?'

But it was Khair Singh's free mouth which took up my question. 'Family business is all right, but the glue is not there. It's in the wise handling of the younger generation by Lalaji here. You can see what he has done. All the family members live independently on different floors. No common kitchen. There used to be one long dining table in the old days. He's changed all that. Let everyone live and eat as they like. But discipline is . . .'

I was happy to have Lalaji cut in to claim his prerogative, 'It's all right then as it is now. Physical separation is no threat to a family's unity.'

I knew my father and Uncle Dinesh were due to come soon for their day's briefing before leaving ahead of Lalaji for the office. I had to get answers to my prepared questions before they displaced me. 'Can I know how you and Grand-uncle made your first fortune which built up the present family business?'

Lalaji took a slow start and then began to relish relating

the past to me. 'Money we had, plenty of it,' he briefed me proudly. 'After all we had been landlords near Varnasi. More than a hundred villages at one time. Beti, your fore-fathers, as talukdars, lived like kings in their taluks. It's difficult for you to imagine the style in which we were brought up – like little princes. We even had an exclusive college to go to. Colvin Talukdar in Lucknow. We all had suites in the hostel, served by servants we brought from home. Number of servants depended on the size of one's taluk. Some of the bigger ones even brought their horse and syce for the morning trot.' He said this to Khair Singh. Both of them laughed like school boys. Lalaji looked at me and said, 'Those happy days have gone for ever with Independence. It's impossible for your generation to understand our loss.'

Khair Singh took over to relate a story of how the Prince of Alwar had tricked the superintendent of the hostel. He brought a nautch girl dressed as a boy to pass off as his brother to get permission to spend a night with her in his suite. This triggered story after story which they began to recall accompanied by helpless laughter. I was forgotten. My pen drooped on my pad while I watched their bellies bobbing with their giggles. At last the intermission came to an end with Khair Singh belching loudly and saying, 'It's a long time since I've laughed so much.' Another belch. 'I must've eaten more than I should've.' And he fell into a contemplation of what he had eaten.

I jumped into the gap to ask my next question. 'Lalaji, what made you leave your villages and come all the way to Bombay?'

'Well, I wasn't like those who didn't heed the ill winds blowing in the country. I attended some of the rallies of Mahatma Gandhi. Witnessed his non-violence, you know, the processions of satyagrahies which were routed by the mounted police and their lathi charges.'

'You mean, you foresaw that one day his movement would free the country from the British Imperial hold?'

'No, not at all. No one did. Not even Gandhi. I mean to everyone the Independence Movement looked like a fool's daring. You've been made to think of it as a glorious upsurge of the people.' He stretched out his folded legs and leaned back on the giant bolsters at the back of the divan. 'It was my foresight, not India's freedom, which paid off. World War II was on. It was bound to end with inflation. I anticipated that it would be difficult to live the life we were used to from what we got from the peasantry. Some shrewd looking around I did to find out the right opportunity and the right thing to gamble on. It's the bold spirit, mind you, a spirit of adventure, plus luck that pays off. You win and ride out the rough patches. Once you have capital to back you up you're placed high, out of reach of any trouble. Don't believe anything else anybody tells you. All success stories are based on this foundation. Remember, there is nothing like money to give you the power you need to be rated as successful in life.'

This time when Khair Singh took the dialogue over from my grandfather I felt tempted to tape his mouth. With a great flourish of his hand he began, 'Their business, beti, the one that laid the foundation stone, was an ordinary trading venture, nothing risky.' I noticed Lalaji listening to his friend intently, somewhat apprehensively, the reason for which I was to understand soon enough. He spoke of the period just before 1939 when people were guessing if Hitler meant war and just how far it would spread, or how long it would last. The sharp ones began to stockpile the commodities which were likely to be in short supply due to a war. 'Items that used iron were most likely to be affected, like razor blades, paper clips, common pins, sewing needles, nibs for pens. Things that you could pile up without needing a warehouse. During a war guns are needed more than hairpins. So the production during a war was definitely going to be switched to war items. My uncle made a killing in just two items, electric bulbs and hypodermic needles.' He laughed heartily. 'This, beti, your smart elders also did – stockpile and sell at the right time.'

Taking a warning from my watch I asked another question quickly, 'Lalaji, have you been satisfied with your modified version of joint family living? Has it been worth it for you?'

'Aren't you and your cousins in your generation happy to be living together in Sahi-Sadan?' I nodded. I was not only happy to be with my peers but also with my father's generation. My mother being a busy doctor was hardly at home when I returned from school. I could wander off to my aunts to get attention from them. Aunt Chanda, not in age but in position on a rung higher than my father and mother, was my favourite. She taught me sewing, knitting, embroidery – with love and patience. From my kindergarten days I used to run to her on the fourth floor. She had my favourite snacks, a glass of milk, and the current game she had taught me to play – everything ready by her side in her sitting-room. I learnt games, from Snakes and Ladders to chess from her. I have no complaints of a neglected childhood.

Lalaji went on after my nod to tell me that business being the binding force, it helped if all the Sahis lived within easy access of each other. Just then, as if to illustrate his point, my father walked in with a file in his hand. Soon Uncle Dinesh rushed in afraid of a rebuke for being late. Papa knew why I was there but Uncle looked worried. He asked in mime if I had got myself into trouble. My reply was in getting up and saying, 'Lalaji, I still have many questions to ask. Can I see you again, please?'

'Interview your father or your uncle, beti. They can tell you anything you want to know. God bless you.' The interview was over as far as he was concerned. I made my exit with my respectful namaskar to all, including Khair Singh who believed he had been of great help to me.

In the lift going down to leave for my office I flipped over my pad and noticed a gap in my notes. Khair Singh's voluntary information did not specify the item my elders had shrewedly stockpiled and sold during the period of war-time scarcity. When I saw Karan in the foyer ready to leave for college, I called out to him, 'Hey, Mr Know-all, I have a question for you.'

'An intelligent one?' he asked.

I had to ignore his smirk. 'Do you know what Lalaji and his brother traded in to make their fortune during the war?'

'Of course.' And he stopped, deliberately, to make me coax him.

'What was it, you dope, say it.'

'You mean when the World War II was on?' He was taxing my patience.

'Yes, which war could I mean if not that one? I also asked about their first business venture, smart one.'

'Easy, take it easy, I say. You must make your question crystal clear for youngsters.' He paused as if he had to sieve the information from his brain. 'I think it was wheat.'

'Wheat?' I whispered.

'Yes, wheat. What you gobble every living day. A grain. What makes your toast, your chapati. Get it now?'

'They stocked wheat?'

'Yes. What's there to be shocked about? Is it a commodity below your dignity to trade in?'

I registered his taunt but refused to fence. 'You mean they stockpiled wheat and waited till there was a scarcity.'

'What else? That's trading, ignorant woman.'

I said thanks and 'bye to Karan and went to the cabin of our in-house telephone operator to be connected to *Reflections'* office. Mrs Singhal's secretary was in. I told her that I was going straight to the library of the *Times of India* instead of coming to the office first.

Fortunately, at the un-airconditioned library I found a seat near a window. I kept the solitary attendant busy fetching and taking back the folios of the daily editions of the paper from 1939 onwards. I kept turning the yellow, crackling pages carefully to scan the headlines and read whatever caught my fancy. Soon I felt as if I were transported by a Time Machine into a totally unfamiliar world. A different era altogether. The old-style print; the lay-out of news; formally stiff King's English; predominantly British news; the London announcements of the Royal Court appointments; engagements of the Viceroy in New Delhi; of the Governor of Bombay Presidency – all were published in the same column every day. All this introduced me to the world of Lalaji.

The advertisement of goods I had not even heard of, except for a few like Horlicks and Nestlés, were highly amusing. The models for the products were unfailingly English. Tall, blond men wearing Bond Street tailored suits; fair, pencil-slim women with permed short hair smiled persuasively in their off-the-shoulder evening gowns; and most appealing of all were the pink-and-white bonny babies advertising Ostermilk. It was clear that the copy and the format were done in London for the British products for consumers in British India. I was having a glimpse of the world in which my parents had grown up.

My interest in the recent past was satiated by the time I was done with the folios of 1941. I felt stiff in the hard chair. My concentration began to disintegrate, making me aware of the constant traffic of the office people talking loudly as they visited their canteen next door. I stood up, stretched my rigid muscles and sat down again determined to finish my research till 1945 at least.

My resolve began to weaken with the 1943 folio. The fascination with the past was over, the old pages of the newspaper had become familiar enough to be boring. I questioned myself as to what exactly I expected to find in a paper of an era when its news was only meant for a selective readership.

I was about to give up and leave, having convinced myself that I was on the wrong track, when news items, pictures, and small headlines I had been glancing at coalesced. It happened when I came across the screaming headlines on a front page about the Viceroy of India declaring the provinces of Bengal and United Provinces as famine areas. I began to search every page of the 1943 folio. I read the big and the small headlines, and the fine print underneath. The Viceroy's edict against the hoarders who had stockpiled wheat and rice lashed at me like a whip. The editorials ranted against the black marketeers, calling them the 'vultures of society', who had fattened on the profits of hidden grain, released in the market only when scarcity leading to famine had broken out. There was picture after picture of emaciated, starving people in the famine areas; of the cracked land with carcasses of cows and buffaloes abandoned to die by those who were dying themselves; of mothers who clutched their dead babies with no tears to shed. The pictures began to lift off the old newsprint to come at me, mixed with the spicy aroma of food being served in the canteen. I had to leave the table and dash to the toilet.

And once again, here in Atal-Retreat, on reliving that morning in the library, I was forced to leave the warm bed in which I had been tossing with my memories, and run to my mother's bathroom. This time I hung over the basin retching, without gaining relief from it.

I heard soft footfalls and whirled around in fear. It was Bhoot, his tall wagging to brush off a scolding, his eyes asking if I was all right. The retching stopped and sobs began to burst in my throat. I went back to bed motioning Bhoot to stay with me. He placed his head next to my pillow. I put my arm over it welcoming his warmth and body odour.

THIRTEEN

Bhoot's presence and his wordless empathy restored my equanimity. It made me decide that, having started on a survey of the worst sector of my recent past, I should resume my progression of thought from the point when my twenty-four years of innocent, blissful living had come to an end. And that was within twenty-four hours of my starting the cover-story research. I resolved that whatever it may cost me emotionally, exhuming for truth had to continue. It was imperative that order be reinstated in my mind so that I could see my reflection clearly in the mirror of harsh judgements.

On arriving at the office after the exposé at the library, I ensured insularity by sitting down at my desk with a cup of coffee. Signalling that you are engaged in creative production is like drawing a curtain around the bed in the general ward of a hospital. But I failed to find words to pour on the blank sheet of my typewriter.

I was still sitting like an unwound toy when I was given the message that Shiv Menon had called, fourth time since the morning. After the usual opening questions and answers he said, 'You don't sound like yourself. Anything wrong?'

'My work. It's getting me down.'

'Writer's nerves. What you need is to distance yourself from your typewriter. Let me take you out for tea. I haven't had any lunch. Have you?'

The very thought of food constricted my throat. 'I don't want any. I'd rather plod here.' But he managed to dislodge me from my fortress insisting I needed fresh air.

Shiv chose the United Services Club in the cantonment

for tea as it was a good place to talk. Golfers were on the course. There were just two naval officers sitting over their coffee after a late lunch. The vast expanse of Arabian Sea looked agitated. The waves were tossing the reflection of black clouds, puffed with moisture, moving like a woman in full pregnancy. The wind was picking up speed as it swirled inland from the sea.

'Shall we sit outside?' Shiv asked.

'I agree about fresh air but I don't want to be blown off,' I said. 'Besides rain clouds are hovering above us.'

'Right you are,' he agreed readily. 'There's that table near the window. It has a good look-out.'

Shiv ordered a massive tea. Kababs, samosas, cheese pakoras, chocolate pastry, cucumber and chicken sand-wiches, and he was ordering still more when I protested. He said he was hungry. He'd eat the lot. I could nibble. And to the scribbling waiter he said, 'I was forgetting the main thing, the tea. One mint and one plain with lemon. Soon please. Action. I'm likely to faint if you don't hurry up.' The waiter left us without pacing up his kinetic energy.

Watching his leisurely receding back Shiv said, 'By the time he's back with the order you'll be hungry too. You didn't let me order enough.'

'I don't mind waiting for your left-overs.'

'In Kerala it's ladies first. I'll have to wait. Or we could break all rules and eat together,' he offered. I found I could laugh with him.

His conversation hovered over high humidity, monsoon variation of temperature spreading a red carpet for colds and 'flu, the absentee roll in his office, and then he made the landing I was expecting. 'Tell me, what's the problem with your assignment?'

I was prepared to side-track him. 'It's a dry topic. I don't know how to make it interesting.'

'Pull out skeletons and scandals of the joint family living. Sex never fails to catch interest.'

'Too much stink and rattle,' I objected. Little did he know it was a skeleton which was riding on my back. 'What is your experience of joint family living in your part of the country?'

'You're forgetting Kerala has the matriarchal system.' He went on to explain its role in the modern, urban society. 'Whichever system it may be, patriarchal or matriarchal, it demands too much from an individual to conform to the set pattern. Doesn't allow space for natural growth. It machines each cog to fit in a slot.'

'That it does,' I echoed.

To our pleasant surprise the slow coach delivered the eats and tea in quick succession. Shiv, as claimed, ate hungrily after he had made me taste each item first. At the same time he kept talking of how the matriarchal system was dying a natural death in Kerala. Although I knew about all that I let him talk as it left me free to think my thoughts. I became interested in his account when he became personal. He had never talked of his marriage before. He talked of his ex-wife, Chitra. As an only daughter she was the sole heir of her mother's property. After he married her he came to know that he was expected to live on her bounty.

His education in Madras had conditioned him differently. He couldn't accept the role of a drone. She couldn't leave her mother's home, the huge ancestral mansion with its spacious courtyard and pool. 'She just couldn't adapt herself to the life-style required by my career,' he said in a matter-of-fact tone.

'Just for that you let her go, even after two children?' I blurted out and immediately apologised. 'I'm sorry. I've no business to say that. Very silly of me.'

'It's not silly at all. I presume this is an academic discussion. Yes, you're right. It did amount to that. Our marriage hit the rocks on geographical grounds, the mileage between Cochin and Bombay.'

'This ground should've become clear when you were courting her.' I matched his academic tone.

'There was no such period. This is where the system comes in. We were betrothed to marry by our elders. We were young ... I recommend cheese pakoras in this weather. Have one.' I think he had become doubtful of consuming his order single-handed. I took one from the plate he was holding out.

'It started a minute ago,' he said following my eyes turn towards the drizzle building up into a heavy shower outside the window. 'Just as you had anticipated. Expert forecaster.'

We watched the wet golfers running in from every direction. Their jangling bags, loud talk, dropping of muddy nailed shoes in the verandah, calling for towels from the attendants to wipe their wet hair, suddenly transformed the quiet club into a bustling boys' hostel. Impulsively I turned back to Shiv and asked, 'Tell me about the fortunes that were made during the last war.'

He stared at me uncomprehendingly and asked, 'Why? How's it connected with what we were talking about?'

'I suppose war came to my mind watching the military chaps frolicking around.' I said it casually.

He collected his thoughts before explaining, 'Well, it was like in any other war. Production of military supplies of destruction keeps up a constant demand. Fortunes are made there. Catching military tenders, from uniform to guns, I should imagine. Construction work in cantonments, camps. There are a hundred different ways to catch bits and pieces of profits during a period of heightened activity.'

'What about consumer items?'

'Yes, that too. Trading in coffee, tea, blades, sharpeners, knives – hundreds of things like that which are in short supply.'

'You mean traders stockpile before war and sell when the price is high?'

'It could be that way, or the usual way of supplying a demand.'

'How would you feel about a fortune made in this opportunist manner?'

'No different than during peace-time. Trading is an old game of supply and demand. Legitimate.'

'Cigarettes, nylon stockings, chocolates etc. from army supply started the black-market. In Italy, isn't it?'

'Well, in war zones, yes.'

'Black-money is not honourable, right?' I had to pursue the topic I had touched off. I had to know if I wasn't over-reacting to the information I had unearthed.

'It's the way you look at it. It used to be a hush-hush transaction between dubious characters. Time and its need have scrubbed its face. The way I look at it is that it has saved India from a bloody revolution, something like the Russian upheaval.'

I had to make my question more clear than I had intended to. 'Would you be comfortable to use a fortune made in this questionable manner?'

'Hey, you're getting deadly serious about something I don't know enough about. I've been in company service, not in business.'

I had to know his reaction. 'Still, you've done business for your company.'

'Black-money is a transaction between two willing parties. It doesn't force anyone. Unless personal interest is involved no one needs to be a party to it. It's not an exploitation.'

'All right.' I was too worked up to let go. 'What about those who invest in grain stockpiling and then sell in the black market?'

'You still have the choice not to buy from them. Use your ration card.'

I had to be even more specific to get the answer I wanted. 'Some traders stockpiled wheat and rice and created the famine of Bengal and UP to sell for huge profits. Would you classify that as legitimate trading?'

Shiv looked penetratingly at me before turning around to see if anyone was hearing our conversation. He said with concern, 'No, that's not trading. That's downright evil.'

It helped me to hear that out loud from someone else. I continued to be upset, but it also calmed me. I began to pick up the eats without waiting for Shiv to hold out a plate to me. He was happy to see me match his hunger, but he looked uneasy. I decided to get back to Sahi-Sadan and find out how the others in the family had digested this base to their rich status. And finally find out if Ma knew about it. And if she did, how had she managed to live with this knowledge?

FOURTEEN

When I turned my blue Fiat into the driveway I spied Aunt Sita getting out of her car at the porch. I raced in and caught up with her in the foyer. 'Aunt Sita, can I come in? I want to see you for a few minutes.'

I asked her if she knew the source of the capital base of Sahi business. She replied, flopping down on the sofa in her charmingly furnished living-room, 'Of course, I know. I should. I work with my father.' I noticed she said 'with' and not 'for my father'.

Aunt Sita had carefully groomed her personality to impress as a businesswoman in her own right, not to be taken as her father's dummy sitting behind a big table. Her office saris were of subdued colours but always of rich fabrics with smart designs. Her office-wear blouses were of a standard tailored pattern – sleeves up to the elbow, midriff covered, clinging Chinese collar. The sharp contrast of her party blouses was stunning for those who met her for the first time in her office. They were sleeveless, neckline low in front and back, short at the waist for a slim midriff to be saucily exposed. Her hair was styled short in such a way that it looked severe during the business hours, and sexy in the evenings when she stepped out. She was a person worth watching and emulating.

I made a short and precise statement to get her opinion. I connected the famine of 1943 to Lalaji's stockpiling to off-load in a starving market. Aunt Sita said without hesitating that the famine was due to the failure of monsoon, and the drainage of government resources by the British imperialists. Tainted money? Nonsense. Business is business. Everything goes.

91

I didn't expect such a stereotypical answer from her. I was disappointed in her intelligence which had so placidly accepted the blame placed on the British Crown. But then she was a survivor. There was no doubt in my mind that she was honest with me. She had said what she had to believe in.

I met Uncle Dinesh in the lift and asked him about black-money. He laughed heartily. Took out his wallet and showed me two banknotes of five-hundred-rupee denomination. 'Do you see any difference between the two?' he asked.

'No.'

'So there. Where's the difference between the black and the white? They're both in circulation. Right?'

My father was dressing to go to the Willingdon Club with Aunt Chanda for their regular rendezvous of a bridge evening in the card room. When I asked him my question he wound his tie and checked the knot carefully before answering, 'Don't worry your head about such things. That's the trouble with you girls when you take up jobs. I was never in favour of your wasting time in that congested office. You have fun in life. Leave all the worrying to us. Keep your mind on clothes, jewellery, fashions, parties, and so on. Okay?'

Papa said what I had expected him to. Even a weak opinion from him would have surprised me. And yet something must have splintered inside me on hearing from him what I had heard a thousand times before. Sahi girls were expected to be like paper dolls. Put glue on their picture, then sprinkle it with gold and silver dust, and let them sparkle. Aunt Sita had not really succeeded in altering the Sahi male attitude. The reason why this time the familiar words made a fresh impact was because I had come to know the price of their gold and silver sparkle.

On the way to my room I heard Saku Bai loudly declaring, 'Karan baba, today I'm going to tell your mother that I will no longer work for you . . .' I went to the living-room. Karan was watching cricket on the TV ignoring the tray within his reach. Saku Bai was flailing her arms in time with her words warning him to eat the cheese toast while it was hot, and to drink his milk before the cream formed on top, because she would not take it back to the pantry to strain it. When I walked in she welcomed me to her sermon alleging I was no better than my brother. The two of us had meant nothing but trouble for her from the day we were born. When I refused her offer to eat something as I had had high tea earlier, she left the room muttering, audibly enough to make us hear her.

I had thought of dealing my question to Karan but crossed him out because I decided he was too immature to take it seriously, and give me an answer worth the trouble. Seeing his lordly behaviour towards Saku Bai I felt like shaking him up. So I put my question to him in a dramatic form climaxing with, 'So what do you think of the first Sahi fortune built on skulls?'

'Ugh.' He stopped chewing the toast and sat back. 'A ghastly way of saying it.'

'You knew about it, did you?'

'Of course. Didn't I tell you what they traded in during the war?'

'So, how have you managed to digest it?' And I made a mental note that some other time I would ask him why he hadn't told me about it before.

'All that damn business belongs to the past, Didi. Why rake it up now? It's like beating a dead snake.'

'It's a comfortable way of arranging your sensibilities. It's not a dead snake. We are taking our nourishment from it. It's like being attached to an umbilical cord that can't be snipped off.'

Karan leaned forward and inspected his glass of milk. Cream had formed on top. He lifted the thin film with a spoon and dropped it on the plate. 'Why bother with the karma of our elders, Didi?' he said resolutely. 'That goes to their account. What matters to me is the present and my future. Like Papa, Uncle Dinesh and the two cousins are doing straight business, sharp but straight. Like, I'll have a clean slate. I'll have my turn to make a choice as to how I work and make money. That will be my karma.'

'But your starting point is cursed by the dead. I feel we're all cursed. This Sahi-Sadan is cursed. Each brick is a soundless cry. I can't . . .'

93

'Come on now, don't over-dramatise something we can't do anything about.'

'I'm going to. I'm going to leave and live on what I earn.'

'Cool it, Didi.' He got up to sit down next to me and put an arm around my shoulder. I fought the tears building up. It wouldn't be right to cry in front of a jerk of a younger brother. He continued his comfortable logic: 'My first reaction was just as severe. The logic I worked out is not for self-indulgence. I'm right about karma. We bring harm on ourselves with our actions. All this business of curse-verse is for stories. Don't you believe in all that nonsense.'

I couldn't trust my voice to speak. I could hardly recognise this version of my brother.

For a while we were both silent with our thoughts. He cleared his throat and remarked, 'I had found Papa and Aunt Chanda's liaison more difficult to digest. I'm not sure I have even now.'

'What liaison? What are you talking about?' I exclaimed.

'Oh, shit,' he moaned. 'I thought you knew about that too. Damn it, I've shot my mouth.'

When I asked him to tell me he kept on repeating, 'Forget it, forget it. It's nothing. Forget it. Forget . . .'

'If you say that once more I'll scream. Come on, tell me what you meant. Tell me what I don't know. Aunt Chanda is special for me, has always been . . .'

'That's why don't ask.'

'All right then, I'll have to ask Ma. I have to know.'

'Oh, shit, what have I done? Don't ask Ma. I'll tell you. Wait. Don't hustle me.'

Once again he tried evasion. 'It's a tough story, Didi. Why do you want to hear it today? I promise I'll tell you another day.'

I wish I had let go like he wanted me to. Another day would've given me time to cushion myself for this second blow. But I was hardly in a state of mind to entertain second thoughts. I exerted all the pressure I could to make him tell me. I said, 'How can I wait, Karan? Tell me now. Begin, for heaven's sake.'

He told me the sordid tale slowly, in detail. He anticipated everything I would want to know. I didn't seek any explanation afterwards. Karan started with the time Lalaji's younger brother was murdered by the son of a man he had cheated in the grain business. Aunt Chanda was only twenty-seven years old then. She was his third wife, much younger than him. The main purpose of marrying her was to make her bear children for him. The first two had failed to do so and had been sent back to their parental homes with generous endowments. Aunt Chanda gave Lala Prem Vir Sahi two sons, much to his joy. She was pregnant for the third time, hoping for a daughter, when he was brutally murdered in her presence. The shock aborted the conception.

Karan said Aunt Chanda took it very hard. I had known that as the reason why she showered affection, and attention on me. Tragic as this was the problem for Lalaji was that his brother had been his partner, owning half of the Sahi business. He had died without a will. Had he died a year earlier his half of the ownership would have come to Lalaji as a matter of course, as the head of the family. In 1955 the Hindu Code Bill had been passed giving due rights to Hindu women after centuries of deprivation. The Bill made Aunt Chanda an equal partner of Lalaji in the family business. His fear was not that she would be difficult to handle, but that if an adventurer lured the young widow into marriage it could be disastrous for the family. She was very attractive, still is. And widow remarriage was not socially taboo any more to prevent her from being tempted.

To combat the threat Lalaji decided to use his eldest son, my father, who was only twenty-two then. Papa was directed to look after his young bereaved aunt. Give her his company so that she didn't get lonesome. Anyone could've predicted the consequences. Lalaji, as a strategist, must've aimed at sexual gratification for his young business partner to keep her in-bound in Sahi-Sadan. When the internal arrangement of the Sahi family began to lead to gossip Papa married my mother, and we came along to cloak the liaison for Papa and Aunt Chanda. Their daily bridge game at the club was an acceptable escort duty by a family member whose wife was busy with a medical career. So the double role worked out for Papa. The only person with a right to protest was my mother. It was impossible that Ma could've remained unaware of this liaison. I could be non-discerning as I was soaking in Aunt Chanda's love for me. But Ma would have to be a moron not to notice what was happening under her nose. Why did she let it go on? Why?

'How did you come to know about it?' I asked Karan.

'I happened to hear sly remarks of Aunt Chanda's two daughters-in-law. They were watching Papa from their balcony and calling, "O Romeo, ah Romeo" softly. They didn't know I had come in to pick up a file Papa had left there. I froze in my tracks to hear them make fun of him and Aunt Chanda.'

'What was your processed logic, your acid thinking which dissolved this poison?'

'Don't tear me to pieces. Repair jobs are delicate.'

'I'm sorry, bad habit. I'm serious. Tell me, I need an adhesive to put myself together.'

'Well, finally, I concluded what the hell, Ma has taken this shit. She's made her shell. She's working, is financially independent. Also, she pretty well does what she wants to, with herself, with us. This must be her bargaining point. I mean, no interference from anyone. I observed her. She seems to be at peace.'

'On the surface, maybe.'

'Good enough for her, I suppose. It works smoothly. She must have her reasons. She expects me to be ignorant of it and work with Lalaji. Damn it, so I do. The surface works for me too.'

'Just that, is it? Is it good enough to mulch the whole rotten scene?'

'Try and understand Lalaji's desperation, Didi. I mean his strategy was nothing but desperate . . .'

'Yes, desperate, but where were his morals? Was this the only solution?'

'At that time, like, it was important to keep the small, private company intact. I mean, today it's spread out like a banyan tree. Mean, you have a branch break off, no damn difference to the rest. Like, Lalaji today would snap his fingers at . . .'

'Okay, so financially it's a very secure scene today. What about an exemplary moral tone for the family? Hasn't he messed us all up?'

'Come on, Didi, change your lenses,' Karan said with difficulty, his mouth was dealing with a big chunk of toast. 'Like, the great-aunt was not raped, or forced. I mean she was a willing party. The three main people involved have balanced the scene. So why should we worry for nothing? Now, when I know that Papa is spending the night on the fifth floor it's just a matter of location. You see, moral judgements change with angles. Change the lens, change your sight. Simple. Right?'

No, it still wasn't right for me, but I let it go with him. There was no need to unsettle him. I had to settle myself, in my way.

FIFTEEN

I had a sudden urge to get away from Karan. I left him to his toast and milk in the living-room. I heard him switch on the TV to swing back to the interrupted cricket commentary.

So much had happened to me and the day had wound up to just about six-thirty in the evening. I needed Ma to talk to. To tell me that the skeletons which had rolled out were part of a nightmare, that the Bengal famine had nothing to do with Sahi trading, that Papa cared for Aunt Chanda as a family member who needed help – his friendship, which was being misconstrued by her daughters-in-law, by Karan, a consequence of their limited understanding of the world of grown-ups.

But Mother was not there to sort out the extraordinary day for me. Except for leaving at a set time in the morning, barring when she had a case at night, Ma had no other predictable slots in her day. There was no choice but to wait for her to come home.

Involuntarily, my feet decided to turn to go to the fifth floor. I knew Aunt Chanda would not be there, having gone to the club with Papa. I made an excuse to her maid that I was looking for a book I needed. I examined the shelves when she was around waiting for her to lose interest in my silent presence and go off to the back of the apartment for better company.

For a while I sat where Aunt Chanda and I had played games. Looked at all the familiar paintings on the walls, at the decorative pieces and artefacts I knew so well, and let my eyes stray over everything, down to the design of the carpets on the floor.

I went to her bedroom. A sky-blue lace negligée set had been spread on the bed for her. Huge cushions, with convent-embroidered covers, were fluffed up on the chaise-longue. This is where she sat in the mornings, a cup of steaming coffee on the side table entreating her to wake up with its invigorating aroma.

Her dressing-room was clinging to the perfume she had sprayed before leaving. In the long mirror I seemed to see her, fresh and glowing. I calculated she was no less than fifty-six. She could easily pass off as forty-five or less. No wrinkles, no sagging of the facial features. A result of beauty masks I had seen her using. She would try out any cosmetic routine she came across in fashion magazines. I could now detect anxiety and apprehension in the preoccupation I had earlier assumed was natural in any pretty but ageing woman.

In her bathroom I sat down on the edge of the sunken tub. I had often sat here and watched her using elaborate herbal aids while chatting to me. They were stacked on the shelf as I had always seen them. I got up and forced myself to open the mirrored frame of the cabinet above the wash-basin. And there they were, my father's shaving kit and his brand of after-shave lotion and skin tonic. A man of habit. In his bathroom too he kept his toiletry in the closet above the wash-basin. It had never occurred to me that there could be any other curious implication to my parents using separate bedrooms and bathrooms. It appeared as sensible and convenient due to Mother's odd hours of work. I had found the proof I had hoped not to find. I suppose I had come to Aunt Chanda's home to bid farewell to my childhood, a childhood which had persisted to my twenty-fourth year.

I left the fifth floor and walked slowly down the staircase to our second floor.

My ears were keyed to the sound of Mother's low-heeled sandals at the front door as I tried to pass the time by making notes at my table. The only light I could bear to have in the room was from the flexible lamp curled over my typewriter. I sat there a long time trying to distract my mind before admitting I was not on my normal functioning level.

Inside, all my vital organs were on hold. In a state of

anaesthetic shock, I was like a heart patient waiting for life-giving bypass surgery. In the surrounding gloom of the evening, the light over the typewriter acquired operating-theatre wattage. In panic I switch off the light and went to my bed.

I lay on my back breathing deeply, attempting a yogic sleep. I wasn't aware of curling up, my knees almost touching my chin. In the silent darkness, the passage of time was of no consequence any more. Awareness of myself came back with the touch of a hand on my forehead. A touch I had known as a new-born. 'I have no fever, Saku Bai,' I whispered, 'I'm tired, that's all.'

'Why do you have to work, beti?' It was not a question from her, it was more like an instruction. 'Work is for people like me. You were born to sit on soft cushions.' Usually voluble, she said nothing more after that. She sat down to gently stroke and press my body.

After some time she must have felt I had fallen asleep because her hands stopped pressing. She left as quietly as she had come. I said to myself I was lucky to have yet another mother surrogate. But, luck was running out, I thought as I reviewed my situation. I was not a hardy plant any more standing high and proud in the sun. I was becoming a weed underfoot.

On the first morning after our arrival in Allahabad, Karan and I used to run to the kitchen garden of Atal-Retreat to look for the Touch-me-nots hiding under the taller weeds. We would stub them with our toes to see their leaves fold up. Our laughter and triumphant cries would convert the garden into a battle-field.

Now, for the first time I was the weed. I was down under crouching with fear as I watched two immense figures looming above, their threatening feet about to strike. I had to fold myself up to survive their surprise attack somehow.

It was about a quarter to nine when I heard Ma come in. I sprang from the bed and ran out of the dark room to greet her.

'Hello, Ma.' She looked as if she were about to sink with fatigue. I embraced her tightly. 'Looks like a grim delivery kept you on your feet, Ma.' And I decided to wait for some other opportunity to talk to her.

She laughed. 'Not one grim delivery. Quite the opposite. Four easy ones – one after the other.' As I released my embrace to let her go she hugged me back to her and asked, 'What's happened, Gungoo? Something on your mind?' She divined my state without examining my face.

'I want to talk to you, Ma. Some other time perhaps. You're too tired tonight.'

She held me at arm's length to look at me. 'How can I anticipate a time I won't be tired out?' She stroked my face and let me go. 'Give me time to change and have something to eat. I've survived on cups of tea and coffee.'

Saku Bai appeared like a genie.

'Will you have a whisky with me?' Ma asked.

'Yes, why not?' I replied. She had decided I needed it. She ordered the drinks and substantial snacks before turning to go to her suite of rooms. I tailed her.

Ma kept talking about her cases, her hospital, her clinic, to shun the silence which she may have found uneasy. I was content to watch her drop her clothes one by one on the rack. While she was at the basin splashing water on her face I could see that she could be in as good a state of preservation as Aunt Chanda with the obsessive use of cosmetics. In fact my mother did nothing to attract attention to her physical assets. I had seen pictures of her as a graduate – young and alluring. Now it seemed as if she had put all that in deep freeze. She and Aunt Chanda were about the same age. Ma showed her years, Aunt Chanda didn't.

'You remember Dr Davidson, and Mrs Davidson, don't you? They are . . .' she was asking me.

I remembered meeting them in London. She briefed me on their imminent arrival in Bombay to meet her, go with her to Delhi to call on Prime Minister Indira Gandhi before starting on their nostalgic trip to the towns they had lived in, in India and Pakistan. As she talked she slipped into a smart kaftan, brushed her hair, and announced herself eager and ready for the happy hour of chota peg.

Ma's glass was half empty and snacks had reinforced her when she said, 'All right, I'm ready for you.'

The expression in her eyes conveyed her expectation of

hearing about the man in my life. I felt sorry for her as I began in a shaky voice, 'Ma, you do know, don't you, that speculation in wheat by Lalaji and his brother caused the Bengal and UP famine in 1943?'

Her expression changed to alarm and then deep sadness. 'Such a famine couldn't result merely . . .'

'Oh, well, they were one of the many. But the foundation of the Sahi business, spread out as it is today, is from that fortune. Isn't it?'

'Yes. I came to know much later, after you both were born.' She turned her eyes away and said in a low tone, 'That's why I didn't want you to get your matter for the cover story from Sahi-Sadan. I'd hoped you wouldn't get to that. Who told you?' I let go one hope of her denial. I held on to the other one. It was the more important one anyway.

I told her briefly about my research in the library. 'Karan has known about it for a long time. You should've told me.'

'Why? Why do you have to know?' she said vehemently.

'Ma, you can't keep us in an egg-shell for ever. I want to know how you could take that? Didn't you feel like getting away and not being a part of this scene?'

'You mean divorce your father? The price would've been to lose you both, definitely Karan . . . It was a matter of adjustment. I've lived on my own earnings, never taken any money from your father, or from . . .'

'You've given him money, not taken, I should know.'

'It gives me perverse pleasure to have a Sahi in debt to me.' Ma looked mischievous briefly before saying seriously, 'I live my life as I like to, no dictation, no interference. I've been able to bring up both of you as I wanted to. I think I've been a gainer in this bargain.'

'Had you wanted to break off, law would've been on your side. The Hindu Code Bill had come in.' I watched her to see if this would mean anything more in context. It didn't. 'I don't think Papa would've contested . . .'

'In families like this one, children are important. Your father would not have been allowed to let Karan come to me. You? Perhaps. Or they could've been nasty and made me out to be an undeserving mother. False witnesses and that kind of unpleasant court handling. Law is open to interpretation and argument. Besides, its working is long-drawn-out and painful.'

'You and I could've had a good life on our own,' I said wistfully.

'Easy to say so now.' I could see Mother was getting a little impatient with me. 'Had I done that you may have accused me of selfishness, of having deprived you of your father and his family, and of their rich life-style. We all have an idealistic layer. Practical factors have to glaze it to keep it intact underneath. I had two Sahi children to bring up. I couldn't change that reality, could I? Then there was my commitment to the marriage vows I had recited. You have to exert to your outer limit before you can justifiably call it quits from such heavy responsibilities. I wasn't so desperate as not to consider all the aspects of my action. The only sensible thing for me to do was to make myself as insulated as possible from the unsavoury setting I found myself in. Which, as I told you, I did to my satisfaction. I haven't lost sight of my idealistic cravings either. I have given them another direction. In my work, the sphere I can control.'

What she elaborated for me could apply also to the Aunt Chanda liaison. I wanted to hear her rationalisation on that front which must've been a much harder reality to adjust to, for any woman.

'Ma, today was an extraordinary day. A hard one,' I began and paused to prepare her a bit.

She was impatient. 'What was it, Gungoo? What else happened to upset you so much?' I decided it would be considerate to come to the core of my question without meandering, 'Ma, I also came to know about Papa and Aunt Chanda. Don't ask me how.'

She looked as if I had struck her head with a stone. 'Oh, no,' she whispered. She took time to recover. I waited, with a blank mind. She walked over slowly, took my head in her hands and kissed me on the forehead. Wrapping her arms around my neck she pressed my head against her abdomen, as if wishing I were back in her womb. She began to sway back and forth saying, 'My baby, my darling baby, no wonder you were so upset. I'm sorry . . . I'm sorry you came to know of it. I should've been careful . . . I could've . . .'

The hope of Ma pronouncing the liaison a sheer fantasy shattered like a mirror slipping through the fingers. I said in a mechanical voice, 'Stop blaming yourself, Ma. How long do you think you could keep me in the incubator? We had to know sooner or . . .'

She let go her hold and turned my face up to look at me. 'You mean Karan knows it too?'

'Of course he does. Long before me.' I didn't want to tell her that I had come to know through him. She went back to her chair and sat down limply.

'Why did you allow me to go to the fifth floor, Ma? How . . . how could you let me become fond of her?' I demanded the explanation she owed me.

'She's truly fond of you, Gungoo. For her you're the daughter she should've had.'

'I know that, Ma,' I said roughly. 'Even I could guess that long time ago. I'm asking about you. How could you tolerate that?'

'You needed attention. I was working. I couldn't give you the time she could when you returned from school.'

I felt an upsurge of anger I didn't know was inside me. 'So you could let her be your substitute for me? As she was for Papa?' I wanted to wound her – deeply, unsparingly. 'Wasn't your love for me possessive enough? I think you must hate us. If Karan and I were not around, you wouldn't have been forced to accept such a God-awful compromising situation, and therefore . . .'

'No, that's not true,' she cried out.

I couldn't stop myself. Anger burst into a thousand flares, like fireworks in the sky. 'Oh God yes, it has to be true, Ma. The only thing that makes sense. If we were not there you'd have left this set-up and lived with self-respect. We've trapped you here. Because of us you had to become the third side of the triangle to enclose a space. An arrangement which suited the Sahi purpose. Why, Ma? Why? Why? . . .'

'For God's sake stop. Don't go on saying that.' She stretched her arms out to me. I was beyond hearing her.

'What makes me mad is that you took all this shit because of us,' I went on relentlessly. 'If I were you I still would've left with whatever options I could extract. Children can never be taken from a mother. We would've come to you. Who could've stopped us, Ma? Didn't you know we loved you even if you . . .' I couldn't say it.

I paused. When she didn't say anything I said in a controlled voice, 'You married for love, didn't you? You showed guts to go against Nani-ma who hated your choice of a non-Kashmiri, and a dark-complexioned one at that. You left Nani-ma, and all those relatives in Allahabad. Your work in the Civil Hospital where Nana had left you the legacy of respect he had earned.' I was getting breathless. I gave her the choice to say something.

She didn't. She was sitting with her hands supporting her head. I felt my anger flowing away from me. I said slowly, softly, 'I should also mention Mamoo who adores you. All this couldn't have been easy for you, Ma. Why didn't you go back to Allahabad? What happened to your guts? What softened you?'

There was no response from her. I felt alarmed. I touched her and asked, 'Ma, are you all right?'

'I'm too exhausted to lie on the psychiatric couch and answer your questions, Gungoo. Tell me, is there anything else on your mind?' Her voice was weak, exhausted.

I heard myself saying, 'Ma, I want to leave. I can not bear to live in Sahi-Sadan built on a foundation of skulls.' I saw her cringe, like Karan had.

'Why do you want to leave me?'

'Karan is here with you, Ma. His survival kit is sound. I'm not so logical. My brain is controlled by my heart. I can't change the make-up you've given me.'

'You need a break. Go away somewhere. To Allahabad. London, Europe – anywhere.'

'Ma, you're not listening to me. I can't live here. The fifth floor is crushing me. I can't play-act and pretend to be affectionate with Aunt Chanda. I don't want to see Papa doing his double role. I guess you've been a celibate. But I have an imagination that will travel with him to the floor above. No, no Ma, I can't take it. I have to go away from here.'

'Lalaji won't let you, even if I do.'

'I thought about that, Ma. You can say I've shifted to stay with Jeet and Kanta to work on my cover story. I know you've never liked them, even from school days. But they're the kind of friends I can be frank with. They would welcome my addition to their shared apartment and . . .'

'Have you asked them already?'

'No, I have to. All this has happened only today. I know they would be delighted to . . .'

'I knew from your school days that they would turn out to be wild girls, and they have. I don't like your staying with them.'

'There's little choice, Ma. Staying with them gives me a cover you need for the Sahis.'

Ma was not wrong about Jeet and Kanta, I couldn't dispute her opinion. She had never asked me to break off with them. She had been fair in allowing me my choice of friends. The three of us had been inseparable from the sixth standard. As we attained our adult heights we unconsciously walked together in a gradient. Tall Jeet, five feet eight; then me, five feet five; and then Kanta, on my other side, stretching herself up to five feet three. We were nicknamed as the Himalayan Slope by our class girls envious of our unbreakable bond. It had survived time and my disassociation from their social life.

Jeet as Air India hostess, and Kanta as the Banquet Manager of the Golden Palm hotel, had convenient settings for their life-style. 'I'm not likely to turn wild, Ma, by living with them. I could by now have been pretty wild if I wanted to be. I need space to find out what I want to do. I have to get out of here or I'll be screaming like Aunt Shanta. I can now understand what made her skid on the thin line.'

'You are a natural lawyer, aren't you?' Mother said. 'You can argue endlessly.'

'Not without resilience, Ma,' I defended myself.

I wish Ma had defended herself by challenging my claim to understanding. It was much later, not till I knew about Shafi Ahmed, that I realised Ma married Papa to get away from Allahabad.

I had kept in contact with Ma after leaving to stay with Jeet and Kanta, but after the income-tax raid I did not take the initiative to ring her up. When she rang up or dropped by at our apartment in Saket building in Cuffe Parade, I was formal and aloof with her. It could be that my attitude influenced the decision she took which upset the balance Lalaji had maintained for years in Sahi-Sadan. I felt I had played a part in it.

SIXTEEN

I was looking desperately for a square cloth. White and square, no other shape was acceptable. I was obsessed about finding it without knowing why and what for. I had to have it. I was searching and searching everywhere. I was on the move looking for it – here, there, and anywhere, not caring whether it was a bizarre or likely place to find it. Just seeking, desperately, obstinately with a racing heart.

I heard an ear-splitting, tearing sound – pause – and then a repeat of the sound. At the same time I felt as if my front teeth were being pulled out, as if I were in the dentist's chair. But I wasn't. With a groan I woke up. My front teeth were aching but I was in bed and it was dark. I stretched my hand out for the switch. Fumbled. Then remembered I was not in my bed, or Shiv's. That I was in my mother's bed in her room in Allahabad. I knew then where the switch was and I could put on the bed-light. I saw a piece of white, square cloth held tightly in my left fist. My heart began to beat faster, and faster.

I breathed deeply – yoga style – quite a few times till my racing heart had slowed down. My fist released the white cloth I had searched for so desperately in my dream, a bad one obviously. I sat up slowly and looked down hesitantly at the drawsheet of the quilt. What I had feared was there in reality. A gap in the white sheet. My teeth had bitten off a perfect square from the top end. The piece from my left hand fitted that square. I took some time to get over my disbelief, which gave way to terror. There was no doubt I had slipped on the razor's edge and become as mad as Aunt Shanta. Like me she also had not been able to accommodate the shock of her favourite brother's, my father's, liaison with Aunt Chanda.

I looked for Bhoot all around, and under the bed. Finding me asleep he had gone back to Mamoo. My watch said it was ten past five in the morning.

Saku Bai says that early-morning dreams, between four and five, come true. Was this a warning of my coming madness, or had I become mad already? A piece of information tucked in my brain rolled out on the conveyor belt to assure me of my sanity, at present anyway. I had heard that the insane never admitted they were mad. They thought the rest of the world was mad, not they. The day they reversed this opinion, or became sexually aroused by the opposite sex, it was notched down as their first milestone towards recovery. So, since I thought I was mad, I was not. And my longing to be back with Shiv was the ultimate proof of my sanity.

My terror had subsided with this rationale but it lay low, waiting for reassurance from clear daylight. I slipped the white square under my pillow, folded the drawsheet to hide the torn portion, and crawled back inside the quilt. It was a while before I felt warm in my cocoon. I decided to resume my sequential recall to distract my mind from the trauma it had experienced from the bad dream. This time I kept the bed-light on as I relived another slice of my recent past.

Next day after an hour's work at the office I went to see Kanta. After graduation she had done a hotel-management course and started working in the Golden Palm Hotel. As she rose in the hotel hierarchy she was given an apartment in Saket, a condominium in the cluster of new buildings on the land reclaimed from the sea at Cuffe Parade. Jeet shared this apartment with her, and now I wanted to move into the third room used as a TV lounge. That is if they welcomed me with open arms.

In the foyer of the hotel I had to pick my way between the heaped luggage of a tourist party, the colourful gypsies on the wagon of the twentieth-century technology. I found Kanta in her office. She disengaged herself and took me to the coffee shop where we could talk.

When I asked her if I could move in with her and Jeet, she

said, 'You don't need to ask. But why, what's happened? How, or why, is the Sahi-Sadan system setting you loose? Don't mind if I'm surprised and curious.'

I gave her the background, unburdening my feelings of deep disgust of Sahi affluence, and of disappointment in Mother for compromising with her circumstances and becoming gutless. Kanta took a few minutes to absorb the shock of my revelations and then remarked, 'I can't help feeling sorry for your mother. I know you're mad with her. I see her as a tragic figure, not spineless. She has a strong personality.'

'Naturally, you'd think that,' I retorted. 'She pulled you out of a jam.'

'I could've had it done elsewhere, for a fee. I always liked her. You know that. Way back from school days.'

I restrained myself with difficulty from telling her what Ma thought of her and Jeet. 'Where's Jeet?' I asked instead.

'She's here. I've left word for her to join us.'

'What do you mean by she's "here"?'

'She came in by last night's flight. She stayed on here with Martin Coffin. I haven't seen her yet.'

'Martin Coffin? Spelt C-O-F-F-I-N?'

'Yes. I think so.'

'Must be Jeet's joke. Has to be. Is he her latest acquisition?'

'She is his acquisition. Apparently he's fallen hard for her Nefertiti neckline.'

'What is he, an Egyptologist?' We both had a good laugh. 'What's new in your life, Kanta?'

'Nothing exciting. Same old hotel carousel, some getting on the horses, some getting off.'

'Reaching your saturation point?'

'Far from it. Here comes Jeet.'

I looked over my shoulder and saw her entering with the swinging-down-the-aisle walk she had cultivated.

'How long do you both think you can stretch this champagne-bubble period?' I asked Kanta under my breath.

She waved to Jeet and replied with a smile, 'For ever. Thanks to the tiny pill. Till someone worth marrying comes along.'

After introducing Martin Coffin, Jeet exlaimed to me, 'Long time, why no see?'

I said in Hindi that she had been romping around forgetting my existence. Before she could contradict me I asked if her guest's name was really spelt as pronounced.

Kanta said, 'I've told her but she won't believe me. She thinks you're joking and . . .'

Martin said, 'Excuse me,' to Kanta for butting in and addressed me in Hindi, 'Jee, hanh. Mera naam C-O-F-F-I-N hee hai.'

We three were stunned, staring at him in disbelief and discomfort. Jeet was first to recover, 'Oh damn, do you speak Punjabi too?' Turning to us she explained, 'I talk in my sleep in my mother-tongue.'

'If you did I didn't hear you,' Martin said laughing heartily. 'Now I have an incentive to learn Punjabi. I can pick up languages with ease.' Perhaps we still looked uneasy because he added as a footnote, 'Believe me, I'm not an American CIA agent.'

This encouraged us to ask him one question after another till we satiated our curiosity about him. He had first come as a hippie to Goa. 'I know every inch of it,' he said.

'Drugs? Nude living?'

'All of it,' he replied. 'My good karma. I became interested in spiritual search. Varnasi, Rishikesh, Hardwar, the usual circuit. Gurus, ashrams, tried everything.'

'Found what you wanted?'

'Yes, that no one has the long-term answer. But I came to love this country.'

And we led him to give us two vital answers. That he collected artefacts for museuns, and that he was married and divorced. His wife had urged him to change his surname. When he refused she changed hers anyway, he said to make us laugh. 'It's a rare name. It registers fast and is not easily misplaced. It sinks in.' He was pleased with his double meaning.

Looking back I think it was from that moment, if one can fix such a moment, that I began to look at Kanta's and Jeet's life differently.

Ma, as usual, was right in her apprehension about my living with them. My inhibitions began gradually to drop leading me to decide on the revenge I could have for the disenchantment Lalaji had brought into my life. The germ idea was conceived when I watched Martin and Jeet in the Koli Fisherman's Village I had written about for my magazine. It was Kanta's idea that I should take them there as Martin would be interested in seeing it.

I tested the interest factor in Martin, hoping to be let off the trip if he wasn't. I told him a bit from what I had researched. Encircled by high-rise buildings of the metropolis the fishermen lived in an exclusive colony on a strip of land off the Bay on Cuffe Parade. Their fishing boats set out to the Arabian Sea from there, and returned to anchor near their hutments that were perched on prime real estate of the city. What was more significant about the village, I had written in my piece, was the exercise of Koli fishermen's right of occupation as the original inhabitants of Bombay. The municipality of the city had no right to displace them. The fishermen, and their women, were too smart to be tempted by the alternatives offered to them. They knew the value of land in terms of money, and still more as the shore from where their ancestors had set out for fishing.

'This is the rainy season. It would be slushy and filthy,' I said to discourage Jeet, if not Martin. She surprised me with her enthusiasm saying if it didn't rain around five we should go as Martin wouldn't have another chance to see it. She would dress in her rough clothes, so would he.

The whole afternoon, as I worked in the office, I kept watching from the window and praying for heavy rain. But Martin's luck held out. There was not even a drizzle to support my case for cancellation.

While our taxi waited for a green light at an intersection near the village, three Koli fisherwomen carrying gleaming brass water vessels, two on the head and one at the waist, crossed the road on the zebra lines. 'My God, a rural scene in an urban setting,' Martin exclaimed and promptly took a picture. 'I suppose the Municipal Corporation is not giving them the benefit of a water connection.'

'Like in a village, the women have to fetch drinking water; here it's from the opposite buildings, for a fee. They don't want to pay municipal taxes so as to keep their legal standing intact.' I had to play the role of a guide.

When we entered the village Martin grinned and said, 'This looks so phoney, like a film set.' And he kept shooting the scene with his camera.

It was slushy, but the flagstones they had placed at critical places kept us moving. The children clamouring to be photographed followed us and like movie stars posed for Martin. I refused to translate their comments in Marathi to Martin, telling him it should be an incentive for him to learn the Bombay language to get their viewpoint on us. But it didn't need any interpreter to know that the boys were gaily imitating Jeet and my cautious negotiation of their muddy pathways.

I could see that the stench of garbage and dry fish being cooked was overwhelming Jeet, but she dared not cover her nose with her perfumed handkerchief since Martin wasn't reacting at all. He was admiring the fisherwomen for maintaining a sleek, tidy appearance in such a mucky milieu. All of them had oiled, neatly combed hair twisted into an intricate bun at the nape of the neck, with flowers tucked in. Martin's camera was busy focusing on them in their brightly printed saris, with matching brief blouses exposing bare midriffs. Their golden earrings and weighty necklaces topped by the auspicious mangalsutra proudly declared the earnings of their hard-working men.

'They make me feel dowdy in jeans,' Jeet said with a pout. 'No wonder their men are not even looking up from their mending of nets to ogle us, like Martin is ogling the swinging backsides of their women.'

An old woman sitting on her haunches in front of a hut beckoned to Jeet and asked if her sahib would take a picture of her grandson. The child was in a crib made from a pensioned boat held together with nylon ropes. As Jeet took Martin inside the hut she asked me, 'Why does she think he's my man and not yours?'

'I have the unstuck look,' I said detecting a tinge of jealousy in my heart.

113

When Martin was ready to oblige the grandmother she moved into the frame and fixed a smile on her face. Her two front teeth were missing; the rest were discoloured due to the tobacco wad bulging in one cheek.

Martin pointed to the old boat planks, obviously left-overs of the crib boat, nailed to the wall to serve as shelves for pots and pans at the kitchen end of the hut, and said, 'What an ingenious interior.' His camera selected the daughter-in-law preparing tea at the stove as his next subject. This started a playful banter between Jeet and Martin as they went from one photogenic subject to another in the village. I don't think they noticed my drift towards the beach where the fishing boats with fluttering flags were anchored. The boats seemed to be fed up with idling during the monsoon months. They were tossing around in a tantrum demanding that they be freed so they could set out towards the open sea on their own.

Looking over the restless Bay, the towering buildings, the threatening black clouds which were creeping overhead, I decided I would also, like Jeet and Kanta, direct my own life. So far I had had no desire to revolt against the Sahi conservative conditioning in me. I may not have sat around for a marriage to be arranged for me, like my cousins did; thanks to my mother I had taken up a job. But in the final reckoning I had also, like them, adhered to the fear of losing my virginity. Similarly, I had responded to the same legend drilled into me that no respectable family agreed to accept a girl as a daughter-in-law, if she was free and easy in her social conduct. Sort of 'goods once sold . . .' warning. But as Kanta had said, thanks to the pill, we girls could also, like men, shop around for a man worth the gamble of marriage.

I clearly remember it was while standing on that beach, feeling the sea-breeze ruffling my hair, that I identified myself with the agitated boats. I decided I had to break from the grip of Sahis by freeing myself sexually. Only then would I be compelled to keep going on a path of my choice.

I was startled by a scruffy character sidling up to me to ask in a low tone if I was looking for foreign cigarettes, perfumes, cosmetics, VCR, transistor – anything I wanted he could get in ten minutes. I shook my head many times, more with irritation than to make my 'no' firm. I noted that the source of gold on the Koli women was not entirely from the catch in the nets of their men.

I turned back towards the village to find Jeet and Martin. I passed an old fisherman and his wife sitting on a block of wood lying on the beach. It was a huge weathered piece of a wrecked ship that the Kolis may have towed in with their boat. The pair was eating hardboiled eggs and spicy fried black grams spooned up with bits of bread. The two tumblers of piping-hot tea waiting by their side on the block tempted me sorely. It was time to go to Saket where I had sent the small suitcase I had packed and brought with me in the morning. Time for tea and nourishment, I decided.

On reaching Saket I was busy counting the change to give to the taxi when I heard a familiar voice say, 'So, you've given up self-service for this expensive transport.'

I turned around and faced Karan. 'I knew you'd be tempted to come here, but not this quickly.' He did not smile. 'What induced this burst of energy?' I asked.

'The burst of energy came from your prized possession. I had to bring it back to you,' he said dangling the car keys. I looked to his right and spotted my blue Fiat in Visitors' Parking. 'Why, couldn't you find anyone to read the note I left on your pillow?' I asked but failed to insert the old bite of sarcasm in my question. In that note I had gifted the car to him; I couldn't very well return it to Aunt Chanda, much as I wanted to.

'Allowing you to work was a hideous mistake,' he said. His usual teasing tone was missing too. 'I see the point of girls being married off at eighteen.'

'Daughters do return from disastrous marriages. Don't look for an end to your sister there, you punk,' I said laughing.

'Why did you have to leave the incubator?'

'For you. There's room for only one,' I said lightly. 'Come on, Karan, you know why I have to. I can't think and feel differently and continue to live there. Do you see me like that?'

115

'I don't like to see you tramping round in taxis,' he said shyly, with his head bent to hide his eyes from me.

I put my arm around him and said, 'Let's go up to the apartment. I might be able to make a decent cup of tea for you.'

'Not today. Another time.' He turned to leave. When he was beyond arm's length he asked, 'Will you take my old Fiat in exchange?'

How could I? That car was from the Sahi stable, I thought. So are you, retorted my next thought. I called out to my brother's back, 'Okay, fair exchange. Send it over whenever you can. No hurry,' and added with my next breath, '. . . thank you.'

SEVENTEEN

'Arre, bitia. Oye, Gunga bitia. Are you sleeping? I must know, your Mamoo has sent me to find out and tell him. Why are you still in bed? Aren't you well? He wants to know.' It would be Dulari who would wake me up to find out if I was sleeping. To surface from a deliciously deep sleep to answer all her questions would irritate a saint. I mumbled, 'I am sleeping, Dulari. Can't you see?'

'But you're talking.' She sounded genuinely puzzled.

How could I even hope to trump her? 'I want to sleep,' I said and covered my head with the quilt.

'Were you reading late? This light is still on,' she said switching off the bed-light. Instantly I recalled the torn square white piece. I came up from underneath the quilt as if a pair of tweezers had pulled me out. My hands rolled the sheet back and kept it pressed down after my eyes had made sure that the torn part was out of sight. 'What time is it?' I asked the startled Dulari.

She looked at the slant of sunlight on the drawn window curtains and replied. 'It should be well after nine.'

'Nani-ma must've gone for her bath.' My observation was a question.

'She should be coming out to sit in the sun,' Dulari said turning to go. 'Shall I get you a glass of milk – hot milk? It will take away the puffiness under your eyes.'

'Hot coffee, Dulari, but later. Can you ask Mamoo to come here?' I reached out for my dressing gown. She searched my face for an explanation but, mercifully, left without fussing.

I described my dream and showed the white square piece

117

to Mamoo. 'This is what a mad person would do, isn't it, Mamoo?' I should've known he would react negatively to a direct question.

'That's nonsense,' he said instantly and kept on staring at the piece for so long that I became quite nervous. At last he said, 'Mad people are destructive but this was different. This person set out to find something. White, square cloth. Nothing else would do. A very clear, determined mind. A person who ... who will not give up, or ... or alter the demand. And somehow or the other, she gets it.' He kept quiet and became contemplative again. What he had said was complimentary; I was relieved and highly pleased. Then why was he looking so disturbed? After an unbearable lapse of time I ventured, 'Mamoo, what's bothering you?'

He looked up; there was deep sadness in his eyes. 'Gungoo, this kind of determination and obstinacy can only make a woman miserable in life. She's meant to be giving, not demanding. In a man these are heroic qualities, in a woman ...' His voice trailed off.

'Times have changed, Mamoo. Men and women are equal. A woman with these qualities need not be a loser.' I was amused to note that I had adopted this third-person reference to myself.

He smiled. 'All this equality business is like a cyclonic storm. I may live to see the liberated women decide they want to combine rather than compete with men. You'll see, that day will come. Nature has meant the female in all the species to be a mother. You'll understand what I mean one day. There's time. You'll know.' And he added, 'I hope.'

'What should I do, Mamoo?' I asked, risking another philosophical dissertation from him.

'Well, the problem is the torn sheet.' I realised he had misunderstood my question. I let it go. He went into the strategy of replacing my bedsheet with one of his so that Dulari would not know of the incident and carry it eagerly to Nani-ma. 'How would you explain the torn patch when the sheet is found with you?' I asked.

'I'll think of something,' he said nonchalantly. I thought of the favour-for-favour price he would have to pay Dulari.

I got up from my chair and took the torn piece he was still holding. 'Mamoo, I'll tell Nani-ma about it. Let me use my determination during daylight. I might find her reaction interesting.'

He was alarmed. He argued for a while without wearing me down and surrendered by saying, 'Well, I'll watch the result of your obstinacy. I might find it interesting.' I was happy to see him smiling.

The self-confidence I had pumped up for Mamoo began to leak slowly and steadily as I washed and changed into the woollen Kashmiri outfit, of purple phiran and churidar, to please Nani-ma. She was sitting in a cane armchair positioned in the sunny part of the courtyard, her crossed feet in beige socks resting on a footstool. The mutton-man had weighed the meat she had selected and wrapped it in newspaper for Dulari to pick up. Fortunately, his back also was towards me as I stood in the verandah plaiting my hair and mustering my will-power before going down the steps to greet her. He was imparting the news of the neighbourhood to attentive Nani-ma as he folded his hand-balance, collected the scattered weights, and carefully tucked them alongside the chunks of goat's meat in the wicker basket he was going to carry on his head down the road, from house to house. I was in no hurry either. I had to think of a satisfactory opening line to use with Nani-ma.

I was still wondering what to say when Dulari spotted me. I quickly finished the tail-end of my plait and swung it over my shoulder as I went down the steps towards Nani-ma. She hugged me, anxiously enquiring why I had slept so late. Did I have my usual menstrual pains? I handed her the square torn piece of her linen, and the story of my dream tumbled out, diluted, and shorn of the description of the terror I'd overcome.

She folded the piece and held it in her hand like a handkerchief. She didn't look at me, she sat absolutely still, thinking. Sitting on her footstool I was squinting in the sun as I watched her face. I felt my nervousness draining, replaced by a strange reassurance. She looked up, met my eyes, smiled and said, 'All my bedsheets are very old, and worn out. Don't worry.' And she proceeded to call out to Dulari and instructed her to place a chair in the shade for me, by her side. And ordered a cup of coffee, deleting her usual recommendation to me of a hot glass of milk.

'Do you remember the time of your dream?' she asked me.

'About five.' I felt a sudden rise in my heartbeat. 'The early-morning dreams come true, don't they, Nani-ma?'

'Well, you made this one come true,' she replied and laughed loudly, which she rarely did.

'Seriously, Nani-ma,' I implored, 'do you think this is the first indication of madness? Like my Aunt Shanta. The same Sahi genes . . .'

'Come here,' she ordered, opening her arms invitingly. She gathered me to her bosom and held my head pressed down with her hands. 'May your enemies go mad. You don't have Sahi genes, good or bad. You are a cent-percent Kashmiri. Not the Atal strain. You've taken after my side of the family, the Nehrus. Haven't you heard everyone say that you're like me? Nothing will go wrong with you. We Nehrus are tough.'

It was fortunate that Mamoo had already propped me up earlier or I would've burst into tears belying my tough inheritance from Nani-ma's family. It was also because her tender consoling was a novel experience for me. She was to surprise me still more.

I ate the cheese omelette and crisp toast hungrily. I was on my second cup of coffee when Nani-ma began what she had clearly been waiting to say, 'I've been watching you and I've come to the conclusion that something has happened in Bombay to upset you deeply. It may be you and Bimla have quarrelled, and you've come here to discuss it with me. Or just have time to think everything out. I don't know. But I'm sure you are very badly upset. You may not want to talk about it, but . . .' She held the torn piece up and said, '. . . This is the result of whatever problem is on your mind. Not madness, it's just worry.'

I put my cup of coffee down and stared at her. She was right, of course, in a way. That hardly mattered. It was the right of way she was giving to my privacy. This was not the grandmother I had met every December of my twenty-four years. Or the mother who had driven my mother's life off-centre. In the past I had never been scared of the Dictator of Atal-Retreat, as Karan and I used to refer to her privately. But I also had never felt as close to her as I did right then. She, reclining in the sun on her chair, shading her eyes with her palm, and I sitting stiffly in the shade of the courtyard wall. It was then I realised I had run out of time. This was the fourth day of my five-day stay. My mind was clear enough to talk to her right there and then. I sat back in the chair and said, 'You are right, Nani-ma. I have problems to sort out. I have come to talk to you . . .'

'You look completely drained out.' She lifted the palm shading her eyes to stop my flow, like a traffic policeman. 'You had a bad night. Gyan is taking you to Sangam this afternoon. That will be good for you. We can talk tomorrow morning.'

Impetuously, I went to her, held her face close to mine and kissed her.

Mamoo who, I knew, had been observing our session as he went about doing his usual chores, called out from the verandah that there was a call from Bombay. As I turned to go Nani-ma stirred in her chair saying that she was coming also to talk to Bimla. Before I could tell her that it couldn't be Ma's call, Mamoo informed her that it was someone else calling for me from Bombay.

Knowing no one else but Shiv would telephone, my hello was almost a caress. In the hum of the static I heard Shiv shouting his repeated helloes. I had to shout back to let him know that I was alive at this end. To be audible, he said at dictation speed that he was worrying about me, was I all right?

'Don't worry,' I shouted as clearly and slowly as I could. 'I am fine. Everything is going well.' I had to choose every word carefully as my voice was accessible to Nani-ma in the courtyard. I took the risk of Shiv wondering why I was so cold and impersonal. I had to tell him that I was returning, two days later, as scheduled, so he shouldn't bother to call again. Shouting on the telephone was hardly worth it, I reasoned. I could hear him saying that the connection last night was good, he would try calling at night. 'No, don't,' I said emphatically. 'I'll be out.' I yelled good-bye, heard his response, and was relieved to put the receiver down.

As I passed Mamoo he said under his breath, 'That was a grand use of obstinacy. I'll add another compliment to it, you're also a clever strategist. Congratulations.'

'I'm keeping your adjectives in the Fixed Deposit,' I said grinning happily. 'Don't you make a withdrawal.'

As I expected, Nani-ma asked me who had called. I was tempted to spare her the truth but I changed my mind and said, 'It's Shiv Menon. A friend.' I could see her making an effort not to ask any more questions. She postponed them for the session scheduled for next morning.

EIGHTEEN

Parents, grandparents, aunts, uncles – they all look for opportunities to expound on the virtues of telling the truth (always, regardless of consequences) to those they regard as their grave responsibility. From the time the children stand on their feet, and begin to have a reference library in their heads, they are constantly exhorted by a big body bending over, index finger held out like a gun, to tell the truth always and nothing but the truth. That alone, they allege, could assure one of a trouble-free path paved with goodness and happiness in life.

A long time ago in school, before we had the benefit of hormonal wisdom from menstruation, Jeet, Kanta and I had shared our experiments with truth, and concluded that the path elders recommended to us was not trouble-free. After discussing the subject from every conceivable angle we had unanimously decided that elders did not have the capacity to digest truth when they heard it.

The final conclusion we reached was that telling lies that betrayed no one, did no damage to people or situations, was truly an act of charity. We made a pact that unless pure truth was demanded, and only after the demander was given due warning of the risk he was taking, were we to speak nothing but the truth. It was imperative that we should consolidate the habit of being always charitable. And through the many years that we had observed our ideal, the impact of our charitable habit had made our paths comfortable to commute – causing no unnecessary agitation, or any emotional upset to the people we dealt with.

I found, however, that the years of cultivated habit had

peeled off, to reveal the embedded conditioning of the pointing index finger. I regretted mentioning Shiv to Nani-ma
when one simple half truth that a friend from the office had
called would've sufficed. Instead, I had to prepare myself by
inventing credible lies in reply to Nani-ma's additional gril-
ling the next day.

I could well anticipate Nani-ma's questions, and I amused
myself with speculating on the result of answering truthfully.
Shiv's age, and that he's a divorcé with two teenage children
were enough to make her write him off the eligible list for
me. And if I told her that I agreed with her, I had no intention of marrying him . . . *but* that I intended to live with him
she would literally froth in the mouth with anger. And if I
wickedly offered the truth that I already had a sexual relationship with Shiv both Mamoo and Nani-ma, in all likeli-
hood, would have a stroke. So, charitable lies were a
necessity. I had no uneasy conscience about lying. I had to
make sure there was no skidding on my part. My problem
was to try and remember what I had handed out as truth.

Nani-ma had gone back to dozing in the soothingly warm
sunlight of mid-morning. She would open her eyes just a slit
to check on any movement around the courtyard. On the
whole it was quiet, the vendors had come and gone keeping
to her schedule. Dulari had finished her sweeping and dusting and was working noiselessly in the kitchen, fearful of
inviting a lashing from Nani-ma's tongue should a spoon fall
on the floor and wake her up. Mamoo had gone out to attend to a misbehaving television of Mohan Kaul, Nani-ma's
relation in Katra. And I looked as if I were absorbed in
reading Ludlum's tumescent publication, shifting my chair
to stay with the slipping shade of the wall.

I had hardly read two pages after the book-mark when my
mind reverted to the sheer necessity of spinning lies. I considered the consequences of revealing my relationship with
Shiv to Nani-ma. Tell her of the morning when I woke up
to find my face tucked into his armpit, his hand pressing on
my back, like a paperweight, keeping me pressed down on
his bedsheet fragrant with Capucci's Punjab, his perfume.
That sometimes I find my forehead grafted to his chest

heaving with his breathing. Often, lying awake by his side, I become interested in the varying scale of his soft snores. That I anticipate in a few years, if I am still with him, his snoring would become a loud soliloquy which would keep me awake till I would gently make him turn on his side. That, right now, it was sheer happiness to have his sonorous presence in the dark assure me that he was by my side, for that night at least.

If Nani-ma could recover from the shock of hearing all this she would definitely ask me if Shiv, the old divorcé and a father who should know better, had tempted me into this sinful relationship. She wouldn't use the word seduce because there is no word in Hindi quite the same in meaning. And I would enjoy bringing her up-to-date with the social evolution of the emancipated Indian woman. I would tell her with relish, in as much detail as she could endure, of my planned seduction of Shiv Menon.

I heard Bhoot barking wildly as if chasing a stray dog or cattle out of the compound he considered his domain. When I didn't hear the sound of any other feet but his four, I wondered if he had spied a snake. Suddenly his barking stopped, as if switched off. Afraid he may have been bitten by a cobra I was just getting up to check when I saw him enter from the back door of the courtyard. He had a long drink from his bowl in the corner. He turned, gave a speculative stare to the dozing figure in the armchair, found me in the shady far side and without a second thought decided to pad warily over to me. Apparently, Bhoot knew that Nani-ma's naps in the courtyard were not tuned to the sounds outside it. I put the fat book away to give him the hugs and caresses he was seeking. 'Don't be scared of Nani-ma,' I advised him. 'She looks hard, like a coconut. But inside, she is also pulpy and watery.' He seemed to understand what I was saying, but was reluctant to agree with my analogy. He moved his head away from my lap. Twisted into a doughnut and flopped on the floor, resting his snout on the paws to do his own thinking.

Bhoot's behaviour reminded me of Shiv. He would listen, with undivided attention, to whatever I had to say, and receive my opinions seriously. If he didn't see eye to eye with me he wouldn't engage in a discussion right away. He would take his own time to think before giving his comments. During the early part of our relationship, before I became used to his style, my immaturity almost ruined a particularly beautiful launch of a Sunday I had managed to spend in his apartment.

It was the period when my mind, while coming awake in the mornings, had to try to fade in on the locale of my body. Its familiarisation exercise would waver from my old bed at Sahi-Sadan, to the new one at Saket, to the double bed I had occasional access to in Shiv's apartment at Waverley. The final assessment was done by my leg moving like a pendulum, in an ever-widening arc. If it struck a hairy limb I would rejoice that this morning belonged to the red strip of Sundays on the calendar, combined with the luck that Shiv was in Bombay and not visiting his factory in Poona, or away on a tour.

On this particular Sunday I was still in a deep sleep when I felt a hand on me. I was instantly wide awake and my fist reflexively struck out. It was Shiv's hand lifting my nightdress and stealing into my underwear. My head eased back on the pillow, and concentrated on Shiv's progress as he gently separated the hair to seek the clitoris. I kept my eyes shut and my body inert. I referred Shiv's act to the professional section of my brain which captioned it 'Rape in Sleep', promptly demanding I collect matter on the subject for future use. But I found it hard to continue the pretence of being asleep. My pelvis had begun to respond with tremors and jerks, as it felt the build-up of his hardness. The next instant his pace accelerated as he transformed into a man in haste. In one co-ordinated movement he jacked up on his elbow, reached for my breast, and took my lips in his mouth. My remonstrations shattered his pyramiding harmony. I pulled my mouth away and turned my face to the other side imploring, 'Not before we've brushed our teeth.'

'You unfeeling woman,' Shiv cried out as he fell back with a thud on the bed. 'Have you ever seen a hot scene in a movie interrupted by a cut to the bathroom?'

'Unhygienic romance belongs to the phoney world of celluloid.' My wit had made a quick recovery. 'Consider realism. There's the Listerine ad. on the television. The love-light snaps off in the eyes of the willing girl as soon as she gets close to the odorous mouth of the handsome suitor. What about that?'

'That is this.' He rolled to his side, sat up and said, 'I have to project this . . . this long shot of a scene of realism, down to earth so to speak.' He stood up, tilted his back at a dramatic angle to pronounce in a theatrical intonation, 'Sorry, my darling. You'll have to wait. I have to pee.' And he strutted off to the bathroom.

My laughter was still acclaiming his exit line when the telephone rang. I let it ring in case it was for Shiv. Thomas picked it up outside and buzzed to tell me the call was for me.

It was Kanta telling me she had to begin her one day of rest with two lies. My mother had rung up for me and Kanta had to say that I was on my way to Dadar to interview Maharashtrian joint families. Why on a Sunday, she had asked? Because this is the one day when the working couples are at home. Ma had left a message for me, she said. It was to remind me that Dr and Mrs Davidson were arriving on Monday and I was to keep Tuesday free for dinner with them. 'She added the information that your Papa was also coming for the party. What's more she very politely invited Jeet and me also,' Kanta said teasingly.

'That's a sacrifice on her part,' I teased her back.

'I knew you'd say that.' Kanta laughed. 'That's why I had to tell her a second lie, that I had a banquet at the hotel to handle that evening. You'll have to compensate for it when Jeet returns from her flight next time.'

'Done. It's a small price for a big favour.'

'All right then. When do we meet Shiv?'

'Not till I'm sure of my ground. Lay off, you two.'

'Another favour granted you. Remember that. By the way, don't forget the pill . . .'

'I know, I know. I'm not that stupid.'

By the time Shiv emerged from the bathroom I had

worked up my anger with Ma. When I told him of her call and the message he said, 'There's nothing to be upset about.' I told him that she was such a phoney. She would pretend to the Davidsons that she was deliriously happy in her marriage. She may have been weak enough not to have had the courage to divorce but surely she didn't have to lie about it. My mother, I told him, cannot face truth. About herself or anyone else. She is like an ostrich, head in sand all the time. Nani-ma doesn't pretend, she's honest about herself. Giving truthful answers to her questions is another matter. I knew if I did, it would crush her. For instance if I told her the truth about my spending some nights with him it would be unfair to expect her to accept it, much less understand. So, why tell her? I wouldn't, that's all. Simple.

At this point of my outburst Shiv put away his newspapers and listened to me patiently through two cups of tea. I monopolised his attention to clarify the point I had made earlier. How would it be if Ma were to see the cards I held so close to my nose, like a poker player? She was of a generation closer to me than Nani-ma. Plus she was highly educated. A product of the era of Mahatma Gandhi. A close relative of the enlightened Nehrus, Saprus, Kitchloos of Allahabad, which had been the cradle of the mass movement for Independence. She was one of those who had tearfully heard free India's first Prime Minister's midnight speech of a Tryst with Destiny. And most important of all, she was of the first adult generation of women to benefit from equal rights with men. As a Hindu woman she knew what it meant to have the Parliament pass the Hindu Code Bill in 1955. Despite this conditioning, I felt sure Ma would react very much like Nani-ma. She had been so evasive with her own life. She hadn't exactly taken advantage of the social changes of her period. Does she even know that my generation has moved on much further than hers?

I realised I had been talking almost non-stop. That he hadn't made any comments at all. I asked him if he agreed with me, wasn't my anger justified?

'You're right, you're talking in anger,' he said thoughtfully. 'Your thoughts are confused.'

His comment didn't help, I felt irritated. 'That is why I asked for your opinion,' I said icily.

'I need to think. It's a serious accusation.' He paused. Since my eyes were still on him he continued, 'Your mother got you the option to work. She must've put up a fight somewhere. I'm sure she understands how you feel. She's screened your escape. I haven't met her, I don't know anyone in your camp. It's tough for me to give an opinion, don't you think?'

His patronising answer irritated me still more. Sensing that, he put his cup down and got up. He took my full cup of tea from my hand. 'It's cold. Thomas will get us a fresh pot of tea ... Later. Now I want you to come with me.' Taking hold of my elbow he said, 'We have to do something about that anger of yours.' I thought he was planning to force me into the bath-tub to give me water treatment like they did for Aunt Shanta.

'We have unfinished business ...' he murmured as he took me back to bed and held me close, stroking my head and back. His fingers were getting entangled in my open hair. He gathered it gently and spread it on his chest saying, 'Don't you ever cut your hair. I adore it.'

'My Nani-ma will disinherit me if I do,' I said reassuringly.

He took me back in his arms whispering, 'No talking now. We have to do justice to our Colgated breath.'

But he couldn't stop me from thinking. Not of my mother, but of him. This man was well worth seducing, I thought as we made love. I congratulated myself for having taken the initiative to do that. He would never have touched me till he had decided to propose marriage to me. He told me that he was debating on the pros and cons of marrying one so much younger than him. What he really meant was immature, I think.

The plan of seducing Shiv had germinated in my mind on the day Jeet, Martin and I had visited the Fisherman's Village on Cuffe Parade. The gambit was to wait for him to repeat once more the invitation to have dinner in his apartment rather than go out. Unlike the last time I wouldn't

129

wheel it off skilfully, but accept it after a light touch of hesitation. The invitation came earlier than my forecast, perhaps because he expected I wasn't beholden to anyone but myself at Saket.

I stuffed my toothbrush and a change in the capacious tote-bag. When I told Kanta and Jeet, who happened to be on a two-day layover, that I may not be back that night they reacted worse than my mother would have.

'What's come over you?' Kanta demanded. 'Just the other day you were critical of our life-style. Why this change? What's going on with you?'

Jeet pulled in her dropped jaw and said, 'Don't do it. Don't imitate us, yaar. It's not for you. Not your brand of fun. Besides, your family is here in Bombay. My family in Amritsar has no clue about my life-style. Believe me, I wouldn't shit on my own doorstep. Forget it.'

'That's exactly what I want to do. Shit on the Sahi façade. What do you ...' Shiv's chauffeur rang the bell; he had come to pick me up. 'We'll talk tomorrow when I'll be in your league. Promise, I'll have no remorse. No regrets. I know what I'm doing.'

'God, she's cool, yaar,' Jeet said to Kanta flinging her arms in the air. 'It's not for the hots.'

'It's a crusade,' Kanta said softly. 'But your cause, Gungoo, is not good enough for you to kill yourself,' she said in an entreating voice.

'Who knows? Maybe the cause is an excuse. At least I'll find out.' I realised I'd said something significant I hadn't thought of on the conscious level.

'Oh then, have a potful of fun,' Jeet said to me and then turned to Kanta to say, 'Anyway, it's high time she launched herself.'

'Break a champagne ... no, a coconut, to bring me luck,' I said over my shoulder as I stepped out of the door.

NINETEEN

Sitting in an unfamiliar car, driven by an unknown driver, I began to feel as if I were a leaf floating further and further downstream, away from the shelter of the tree of shade, Sahi-Sadan. It made me sadly resigned to the decision I had taken.

At first my fury had tempted me to break the roots of the tree I was attached to, but I realised it belonged to many others too. I had a right to my life only. The others who had chosen to sit under its canopy, like Karan, had a right to do so. So I had dropped off, like a leaf on a tree when it couldn't draw nourishment from it.

From Cuffe Parade to Colaba Post Office was hardly a distance of a five-minutes' drive, at the most seven. Shiv's chauffeur was negotiating it in an unhurried manner, letting every car overtake his Mercedes. I suppose for him it was a dull routine to fetch and return the girls his master dated. I could be one of those high society call-girls on an assignation unknown to their parents, or husbands. And some of them, it was well known, did it for their parents and husbands.

I began to wonder how Shiv was evaluating me. A fun-girl, a rich spoilt playgirl belonging to the new liberated generation? Had I not accepted his invitation to spend an evening with him without the compulsion of a romantic interest? There had been no emotional expressions of any kind between us. There was just an evident enjoyment of each other's company – talks, discussions, arguments – and a lot of laughter. Nothing more. I had progressed from business lunches to this first dinner in his bachelor habitation. Shiv

131

would naturally conclude that I conveniently stayed with my friends every now and then to have access to social freedom.

By the time the car was entering the narrow lane, leading to the luxurious Waverley condominium on the island's harbour shoreline, my hands were sweating with nervousness. I steadied myself by quoting a saying often used by Nani-ma – if you've had to put your head in the mortar why worry about the impact of the pestle? 'Here you go,' I said to myself when the chauffeur hurried around the car to open the door. 'Paste a smile on your face.'

The chauffeur politely asked me to wait in the foyer till he had parked the car so that he could escort me to the apartment. I nodded, the smile pasted firmly on my face. His bodyguard drill on such an assignment amused me. It must be to make sure that the girl doesn't knock on the wrong door and find a welcome. I might as well, I decided, be the call-girl I was assumed to be. In any case, it suited my purpose as it did for Shiv Menon.

The door was opened by Thomas, I presumed. He was in the immaculate white uniform of a valet-bearer. He ushered me into the living-room in his best expressionless, professional manner. He informed me that Shiv Master was getting ready, he would be with me soon. Would I like him to serve a drink, anything I wanted? When I said I'd rather wait for his master, he requested me to make myself comfortable and left with a measured stride.

I busied myself by looking around critically. The room was an impersonal work of an interior decorator on a large budget for a company's chairman. The usual highly polished granite flooring, glass and chrome furniture, expensive Jacquard fabrics, Ahuja carpets and cushions – all totalled up to reflect a modern, western look. A few photo frames lent a feeble personal touch. I walked over to look at a large silver frame of a handsome woman with a smiling girl and boy on either side. It was easy to guess that that was Shiv's family in Cochin. I bent down to peer at her. She looked proud and possessive, very self-assured. In another frame the same children had grown into serious, awkward teenagers.

'Welcome, welcome to my humble . . .'

'. . . abode,' I finished it for Shiv as he called out on entering from the door behind me. 'I've heard this phrase especially from those whose abode . . .'

'. . . is not humble.' This time Shiv finished my sentence. 'The score is even now. I'm sorry I wasn't at the door to greet you. I had expected you to keep the car waiting for a while, so I sent him as soon as he dropped me here from office. Sorry – I should've known you'd be deadly punctual.'

'I hope it's meant as a compliment.'

'But of course . . .'

'I now understand why your chauffeur was driving so leisurely,' I said noticing that his damp hair, freshly scrubbed face, tee-shirt and casual trousers made him look like a collegian – very different from his corporate appearance in the office.

'What will you have to drink? Thomas tells me you elected to wait for me – thank you. What will your drink be?' He asked again as he moved to the bar.

'I'll leave it to your expert choice.'

'I had anticipated you and asked Thomas to chill a bottle of Chablis. Remember you had asked for it when we lunched at Ménage à Trois and they didn't have it?'

'No, I didn't add that bit to my memory bank.' I felt flattered. 'Seems my advantage was in forgetting it. I'd love some tonight.'

Wine began to mellow my nervousness till I forgot I had ever felt it. As always it was effortless to talk to him. He asked me how my assignment was going. I felt tempted to tell him all about my discovery in the *Times* library but I checked my tongue. 'Wine seems to loosen one's tongue, doesn't it? How much have I had?'

'How much are you used to?'

There it was, he did think of me as an adventurer. 'Not used to it at all,' the truth slipped out. 'Once in a while. Am I high?'

'I'll ask Thomas to give us dinner if it's all right with you?'

I was startled by the two-candle silver service Thomas had laid out with champagne waiting in the ice-pail on the chiffonier. Shiv's Jeeves, I thought, at a snap of Master's fingers could produce the perfect atmosphere for a seductive evening. I felt annoyed and at the same time remembered that I had that very purpose in mind for the evening. Instead of dribbling, as I had been doing, I decided all I had to do was to let Shiv score his goal. I could use Shiv's purposeful candle setting to my advantage.

Much later I was to know that Shiv was just as much surprised and embarrassed as I was by the grand design of Thomas. Also, that both the chauffeur and Thomas, his old retainers from the family home in Cochin, were particularly excited that evening because their master had, for the first time after his divorce, shown interest in a woman. I often wonder how I would've behaved had I known this that evening.

'Gunga,' I heard Shiv calling softly. I looked up. 'Thomas is about to cough to catch your attention.'

Thomas wanted to remove my dinner plate. 'I'm sorry,' I apologised moving back in my chair. 'What a delicious meal, so delicately prepared with herbs. You have a French cook, it seems.'

Shiv burst out laughing. 'There's my chef,' he said pointing to Thomas. I saw a smile flickering on Jeeves's face. Shiv gave his bio-data: 'Thomas is from Cochlin, an old acquisition of my father. He came to work for him when he was barely twelve. He's my inheritance. I was afraid he would elect to stay with the children when Chitra and I split up. Why, Thomas,' he addressed him as he came back through the panty door with a tray, 'you don't miss Cochin, do you?'

Thomas took a few seconds to think before saying tactfully, 'No, not Cochin, sir. I miss family, three grandchildren.'

'Of course you do,' Shiv said sympathetically. 'That's why I send you home twice a year at least.'

'Sometimes more, sir.' Thomas smiled this time. 'When you go foreign you send me Cochin.' He added to me, 'Master very generous.'

It made me happy to see Shiv embarrassed. He changed the topic to politics, his business. Right through the dessert the mood of the evening didn't change to a romantic note.

It remained prosaic and dull. He didn't make an attempt to touch my hand on the table as a tentative opening bid. I began to feel that he didn't find me attractive, sexy enough to take to bed. I couldn't figure out what he was getting out of dating me. The candles flickered, going lower and lower as Shiv talked. We drained the decoction coffee. He was holding out the silver dish of petits fours for me to choose from when Thomas came and whispered something in his ears. 'Oh, I'm sorry, I forgot,' Shiv replied non-confidentially, 'tell him to go off-duty. I'll drop Miss Sahi home.'

This was exciting news to me. Shiv had some plan after all. Next moment the projection changed when he asked me, 'What time do you have to get back?' I answered instantly, 'Today I'm not operating under the curfew orders of Sahi-Sadan.'

I began to feel convinced that Shiv meant to take me back like a brother escorting a school-going sister to her boarding school after a privileged outing. What would I tell Jeet and Kanta? That I was unattractive to the male I had selected as my target? Or worse still, that I had behaved like a nun? The thought precipitated a decision to confess boldly my expectations from the visit. Desperate? Undignified? I had no choice.

As soon as Thomas was on the other side of the pantry door I said, looking straight at Shiv across the dripping candles, 'I intend spending the night with you, Shiv. May I?'

I could lip-read a soundless, 'What!', before he looked over his shoulder to check on his Man Friday. I did not shift my eyes from his face. I saw the young collegian revert to the chairman of a company, who wriggled in his power seat before starting to negotiate across the table. 'Are you feeling sick, you want to rest here?' My laugh interrupted him but he continued, 'Has the wine disagreed with you?'

I applied brakes to my laughter which was beginning to sound hysterical, and said, 'No, no I'm not feeling sick. Wine in fact has done me good. I want you to make love to me if . . . if it's not too disagreeable for you.'

It was his turn to laugh, but not hysterically. I was examining my words to find what could've caused such mer-

135

riment when he got up from his chair and came to me. 'Disagreeable? What a funny word to use. Do you realise . . .' Just then Thomas was coming from the kitchen. 'Come, Gunga. Let's get out of here.' He took my arm and led me out of the dining-room formally.

In the well-lit living-room he made me sit next to him on the sofa. I thought it was an encouraging sign till his carefully delivered question squashed it. 'Forgive me if my laughter upset you. It wasn't meant to. I was laughing at myself, for . . . for having been stupid. I'm feeling ashamed that you've had to say what you did. At my age I've no business to be so obtuse as not to notice your reactions. It's obvious I've been giving wrong signals, creating a misunderstanding. Can you forgive me for that?'

'There's nothing to forgive,' I said feeling proud of my clear thoughts which I could articulate without stumbling. 'You haven't been obtuse. You've given no signals, not at all. You're not reading me right.'

He looked distressed. 'Something is wrong with me. I'm usually not this dense. I can't grasp what you're saying.'

I smiled. I felt on top of the situation at that point. If humiliation from a negative answer was coming my way I felt I could take it. 'I'll spell out everything to you, Shiv. Don't blame yourself for anything. I chose you to do me a favour. Something like choosing a surgeon to lance a painful boil. Don't ask me why because I can't tell you, not tonight anyway. I want to end my virginity and I expected you would be the best person for that experience.'

'Oh my God.' He leaned back on the sofa and closed his eyes. I sat quietly, without moving till he opened his eyes and said, 'I'd like know the reason for your urgency . . .' I was about to remind him when he added, 'I know you've taped my lips but can I ask why you chose me? From many contenders, I suppose.'

I had to think that one out. I carefully chose my words. 'This is not a trick to hook you. For that, my technique would be different. I surely wouldn't want you to think that I was a whimsical, wild sort of woman. I mean I can't help it if you had reason to think so.' He was watching me intently. My voice remained steady. 'You were the only one, no contenders . . .'

'Doesn't sound like a compliment.'

'It's not a matter for a compliment. It's a dictation from my need.'

'How do I fit your need?'

'The truth is not always pleasant. Let this question go.'

'I have the big grinders inside me for chewing. I'd like to hear.' And he added after a pause, 'Please, if you don't mind.'

Again I had to select my words carefully. 'For one, you were within reach. I felt attracted to you . . .' I was watching him just as minutely as he was watching my face. His facial muscles visibly expanded on hearing this. It warned me to be still more careful not to hurt him. I think at that point I had the first glimpse of my love for him. I went on to say slowly, 'Your age and your experience with women were a plus point. I knew with you I didn't have to pretend to be in love. Or make any commitments. What I'm trying to say is that there was no danger of a hangover of the one night I needed. That . . . that I could get back to my life without having to erase the blackboard.' I laughed at the word I had unconsciously chosen. I had to explain my laugh, 'My conditioning is so deep. That word, blackboard, is symptomatic of that, don't you think?' He laughed with me and then waited for me to go on. I thought I had said enough.

He prodded me out of silence by asking, 'What made you so sure I'd let you go after one night, or ten nights? Whatever.'

'You're making me say what I don't want to.'

'I want to understand you. It's important to me.'

His unexpected statement puzzled me. Before asking for a clarification I had to satisfy his curiosity first, 'Well, it shouldn't be difficult for you to let me go. In your position I wouldn't be in a hurry to get involved. I would enjoy my freedom. Wine, women and song. I expected I could be easily scratched off your social roster.'

Shiv threw his head on the back of the sofa, stretched out his legs and roared with laughter. I couldn't make out anything funny in what I had said, or in the situation in which I had placed myself. Utterly bewildered, I watched him helplessly, trying hard to control my temper. When his private amusement subsided he got up and poured a generous level of cognac in a snifter for himself. He didn't even ask me if I wanted any. He came back to the sofa and asked, 'What's your plan if I don't bite your bait?'

I felt my face flush. 'Next time I'll offer payment for defloration service.' I sprang up and picked up my capacious tote-bag with my nightdress and tooth brush stuffed in it. 'I want to go back to Saket,' and added a please to it.

He put down his snifter on the coffee table and gently released the bag from my clutching hands and put it back on the sofa. 'That was truly stupid of me. A crude statement. I didn't mean it at all. Do forgive me.' He exended his palms out as if he wanted me to rap them with a ruler.

When I didn't move he came forward and put his hands on my shoulder. 'I can explain my unforgivable behaviour.' He waited for me to look up at him. 'I was amused by the stereotype in which you slotted me. During the interviews I thought you were estimating me as someone very special, unique. And the piece you did on me for your magazine was complimentary. Afterwards, you accepted my lunch invitations, all very flattering, encouraging to an old man . . .'

'You're not an old man,' I objected involuntarily.

'Almost as old as your father.'

'My father is fifty-five. You're ten years younger than him.'

'For you I should be in my twenties.'

'I'm not shopping for marriage,' I grounded his high lob.

Shiv laughed before saying, 'But I am. Shopping only for you. Now you see why I was so amused? Here I was in love with you debating if I was overstepping. And there you were thinking of me as a man-about-town you could spend a night with. I have been hesitating because I was getting no positive signals from you. Naturally, I thought it was unfair to weigh in my teenage children along with myself as your burden.'

I felt exhausted, my knees were threatening to go off-duty.

Fortunately, Shiv decided to take me into his arms and hold me tight against him. He didn't say anything for some time, rested his face on my head and stroked my back gently. He picked up my plait and twisted it around his wrist murmuring softly, 'I think I was smitten by your plait writhing on your back as you moved or talked. Like a cobra. Queen Cobra, to be precise. Mesmerising. Bewitching. Like the women with long tresses in ancient sculptures, and frescoes.'

I was critical of the kind of conversation we were having during our first physical contact. 'You seem to be using my bewitching plait as your handcuffs.' I tried to mix in some humour. It gave him a cue for his major speech.

'You're right! So it looks, doesn't it?' he agreed happily. 'My unconscious desire surfacing. Feeling better?' I nodded. The expression on his face was making me uneasy about his next move. 'Come and sit on the sofa.' He seated me as if I were a fragile doll trusted to his care. He gave me his snifter, instructing me to take a delicate sip and roll it in the mouth. As the first sip trailed warmly down my throat he said, 'It's medicinal. It won't make you high.'

'I'm not sick. I need something to make me feel high,' I said.

'Aha, that's my assignment.' He kneeled, took my left hand and asked, 'My Highness, would you consider me worthy to be your consort?'

'You've got the wrong hand, Knight-Consort. I've resolved not to marry.'

'You're giving me the royal boot. You don't consider me worthy of sharing your life.'

'Nonsense.' I kept the play-acting tone. It was an easy way to convey the truth. 'I've bestowed the greatest favour on you. I'm sharing your bed.'

Shiv got up from his knees and sat down next to me. He said in his natural tone, 'I'm serious. All this virgin bit – why don't you wait? You tell me how to go about it with your parents, grandfather, whoever is to be approached. I'll do my paces and take the punches.'

'But I told you I don't want to marry.' I was running low on my stock of patience. 'Shiv, please don't rush me. I need time. I'm going through a rough time. The first one in my life. So I'm learning how to hold on and survive the way I want to. There's a lot of background I'll have to supply before telling you what it is. Some day I may be able to talk about it. All I can tell you now is that I have to decondition myself. Sahi family moulds its women into doormats. Those who are born as Sahis, as well as those who're inducted into the clan. You know the type of mats I mean? You must've seen, the jute ones. Colourful, with designs. Sahi doormats have "USE ME" on them.'

Shiv guffawed. 'I've seen one. Of all places while entering an art gallery. I had guests from abroad. The lady stood on it and said coquettishly to her husband, "Can we take one of these home for our bedroom?" I hope he took the hint if not the mat.'

After a prolonged laugh we were silent. He took the snifter from me, swallowd deeply and returned it. He didn't get up to pour another one. We shared, my sip to his two gulps.

He was quiet, contemplative for a while. Suddenly he got up and extended his hand towards me and said, 'Come, let's go for a drive. I don't know about you, I'm feeling claustrophobic.'

This time I sat, not on the back seat, but next to Shiv as he drove his Mercedes in a tender, caring way. He chatted, I hardly remember what he said. It was past eleven, Colaba was still bustling. It had not rained the whole day which had encouraged young people to come out and loiter on the roads. Marine Drive was relatively deserted, emptied of the day's humming traffic. Shiv speeded up on the familiar route my Fiat and I used to take, seemingly a long time ago. I hoped he was not going to drive by Sahi-Sadan, to tease me. I wasn't in a mood to enjoy that brand of humour. He had to slow up as we neared Chowpatty to allow the darting pedestrians to cross the road. Families had enjoyed their evening and were now anxious to get home with children sleeping on their shoulders. Young couples were dreamily walking from the gas-lit area of the food stalls, and unwarily stepping on to the main road. 'There you are,' Shiv said, I remember, 'love is blind. No exaggeration in that statement.'

140

On crossing the busy section of the beach Shiv parked the car. 'Let's walk on the sand. There's hardly anyone here.' Seeing me slip off my sandals he shed his loafers in the car before getting out and securely locking it. We walked on, holding hands like two children, to the edge of the Bay. The high tide was coming in relentlessly. 'During the height of the monsoon,' Shiv said wistfully, 'these waves kick up to giant heights against the tetrapods on the Marine Drive. Have you noticed?'

'Noticed?' I began to giggle, almost losing my balance in the sand. 'You'll think I'm real crackers,' I said when I could form words, 'but I have to tell you . . .' I described how I had forced Jeet and Kanta to come with me to stand under those giant waves, and how they had never stopped calling me monsoon-loony after that. In the dim light I could see that he was staring at me with disbelief. He must wonder, I thought, why he was getting involved with a girl who was not only wild, but mentally unstable.

Once again that evening he had a fit of laughter. He held out his arms and pulled me towards him saying in a choking voice, 'You are as mad as I am. I've stood under those waves so often. No one knows, not even Thomas.'

I could hardly believe him. 'Someone must. How can you keep it a secret?'

'I go at night. Drive myself. Great thrill to . . .'

'Oh, no!' I protested. 'This is unfair. I wish I was a man!'

We returned to Waverley in a jubilant mood. When he opened his front door with his key, I felt as if I had come there for the first time. The candle-lit dinner, my proposition, our conversation – the whole bit had taken place in some other segment of time. On entering his bedroom I turned around to him behind me. My hands reached out.

TWENTY

I felt something cold and wet on my neck. The reflex whip of my hand landed on Bhoot's snout. His snort made me sit up and apologise repeatedly. I was petting and cuddling him when I heard Dulari cackling, 'You were snoring, bitia, like your grandmother. You woke him up.'

That was one inheritance from Nani-ma I could've let go. I must have curled up in the chair and dozed off. Ludlum was lying on the floor. Bhoot was presumably waking me up to shift from the sun so that he too could get into the strip of shade near the wall. Nani-ma had already left the courtyard for the shady verandah. Apparently, I had hopped over a big slice of time.

'You're making fun of me, Dulari,' I had to defend myself. 'I'm too young to snore.'

That tickled her still more. 'Ask your Mamoo if you don't believe me. He also heard you and laughed.'

There was no use arguing her attestable statement. I gathered my shawl, picked up my unread novel, bid farewell to Bhoot, and said to Dulari, 'I'm going to sleep. No lunch for me. Please tell Mamoo I'll be ready to go to Sangam at four o'clock.'

'I'll give you a cup of coffee at three-thirty, all right?'

'That's very sweet of you, Dulari. Thank you. I'll need that to keep awake.' I was pleased to notice that I was winning in the field of beverage.

As it turned out, against my anticipation, I could not sleep in the bedroom. The chair in the courtyard had induced sleep that the bed couldn't. At the same time I had no desire to go back and ask for lunch. I wasn't hungry enough to

142

persuade myself to do that. I wished Bhoot had not taken my farewell seriously and followed me in to give me company. I had five hours to pass in isolation of my own seeking.

Wrapped up in my shawl from head to toe I lay down to hibernate. The cold bedcover extracted my body heat which was gradually replaced by my warm breath circulating inside the cover. Inside my stilled body-shell, my mind began to skip summoning memories at random, rolling the tenses of events till the time element didn't exist. Only the impact of happenings of the recent three months remained as intense experiences.

I shoved away the upsetting revelations which had robbed me of my child-like equilibrium. My mind selected the contrived loss of virginal innocence as my most precious experience. Precious and very private. Jeet and Kanta had desisted from probing knowing I would share the experience with them when I was ready to.

The experience of that night crystallised next morning into a hallowed memory when one by one my faculties surfaced. The first one to report on duty was my olfactory sense. The pervasive smell was unfamiliar, but evocative. I sniffed. Took deep breaths. It aroused me. It was later, when I could ask questions, that I was able to label it as Capucci's Punjab, Shiv's after-shave lotion.

I opened and shut my eyes. Hair spread across my cheek curtained my view. I remembered Shiv opening out my plait. My hair must be badly tangled, I concluded. No Saku Bai to gently comb it as she used to do after giving me a shampoo on Sundays. I imagined aching fingers and tired elbows on handling the mass with brush and comb myself. My leg began a pendulum swing on the bedsheet. I became aware of a dull ache between my thighs.

And instantly everything that had happened the previous night rushed into my brain, like the crowd at a suburban train station. Involuntarily, my hand pressed on the area of pain I had expected to experience, and didn't. Shiv had tenderly warned me, 'Now . . .' but I couldn't recall it happening at all.

I turned over on my side expecting to find Shiv on the

143

other half of the bed. The pillow was dented, the blanket and the drawsheet were turned back, the occupant was missing. The room was softly dark; I wondered why he got up so early on a Sunday. Being an unfamiliar setting, I didn't know if there was a clock somewhere which could tell me the time. I had no clue where my wrist watch could be.

As if summoned by my thoughts Shiv walked in like a genie, carrying a tray with two steaming mugs of coffee. 'I was going to wake you up,' Shiv said with a brightness I didn't feel yet.

'What time is it?' I asked lazily.

'About eleven,' he answered putting the tray down on the table.

'What?' I almost shrieked. 'Day or night?'

His laughter echoed in the room. He pulled the cord and opened the window drape slightly to let bright sunlight stream in. 'You haven't lost your Sunday totally,' he assured me. 'Come, let's have a cup of coffee together. How are you feeling?'

'Lazy,' I said getting up slowly inspired by the smell of coffee. I was halfway up when I saw the stains on the bedsheet. I sat up with lightning speed and covered my naked body with the drawsheet. 'Shiv, look . . .' I whispered.

He sprinted from his chair to the bed, 'What's happened?' On seeing the bloodstains he took me in his arms and held me tight. After a while he murmured, 'I'm sorry if I hurt you too much. I tried . . .'

'It's not that,' I blurted out. 'It's the stains. I want to wash the sheet.'

'Oh, that.' The relief in his voice was obvious. 'Don't worry. Thomas will take care of it. No one else will know about it.'

'No, no.' I pulled away to plead with him. 'I don't want him to see it either. Please, please let me wash the sheet.'

'He'll see the wet sheet and wonder which one of us did it. Since I've never done it before you'll stand guilty.' Seeing that my panic was still intact he said, 'I have a solution. Wait.' And he disappeared into the bathroom to return with a bottle of Hydrogen Peroxide and cotton wool. 'Now, you watch a miracle.' He waved his hands like a conjurer on Juhu beach. 'Have a last look at the badge you lost willingly. Never to be seen again.'

He set to work with soaked cotton wool, and magically the stains began to disappear. He kept on chattering like the magicians, the kind who suddenly sprout on the fairgrounds to entertain the children of the pilgrims. He was talking about the tribal custom in certain areas where a sheet is examined by the elders in the family, for the colour and the amount of bleeding, to predict how fertile the union would be. He went on and on relating other such customs imagining it was diverting me. I was more enchanted by the disappearing blood stains, releasing much more than just my anxiety.

'I hope Your Majesty is impressed by my magic?' Shiv asked with a bow.

'Indeed,' I said haughtily extending my hand towards him. 'Much obliged, I'm sure.'

He knelt to kiss the back of my hand saying, 'Your loyal subject, my Gung-o.' With a flourish he picked up the bottle and the soiled cotton wool. On his way to the bathroom he stopped in front of the full-length mirror. He mimicked Peter Sellers's South Indian accent to exclaim, 'Goodness gracious me! Heavens be praised. Lord above made me so handsome. Do you not agree, Gung-o?'

In the piece I had done on his interview I had mentioned his six-foot plus figure which is rare to find among Indians born in the regions south of the Vindhaya mountains. I presumed he was referring to that and urging me for an enthusiastic endorsement of his claim.

When I failed to second his statement, he struck the pose of a Greek statue and titled himself in a soft European accent. 'I am Golden Apollo. My reflection over there forces me to declare so.' My suspicion was confirmed, praise had gone to his head. Pointing to his midriff I said, 'Apollo will have to do a bit of a work-out. There's some sagging around there.'

'Neglected my squash this week.'

'Why?'

'Decided to chase a girl instead.' And after a bow he made a gallant exit.

I collapsed laughing in the rumpled bed.

TWENTY-ONE

It was just as well I had told Dulari to wake me up. She had literally to shake me, she said, before I responded with a 'hoonh'. I had no idea I was that tired.

I took sips of Dulari's sizzling coffee as I changed to get ready for the visit to Sangam. At some point of that mechanical activity I began to feel I was moving like a programmed robot. I should've found it upsetting since I was trying to control my life, but strangely enough, it had a soothing effect.

'I've brought the tonga from the stand,' Mamoo called out as he got down from the one-horse carriage I was excited about riding on, after more than a decade. 'Let's go. It's past four.'

I ran down the verandah steps. 'Have you taken a shawl?' Mamoo asked. 'It's going to be cold out there.' I held up the folded shawl on my arm. He had put on a thick woollen Nehru jacket; his dhussa shawl was propped on one shoulder.

'Good girl,' he approved.

'You refuse to think of me as an adult, Mamoo,' I said with a sham pout.

'You'll always be a little girl. You'll never grow up for me.' He tugged my plait. 'Last time I took you to Sangam you were wearing a frock. You were about nine or ten years old.' Carried away by his memory he took hold of my waist with both his hands to help me up the tonga step to sit on the back seat. I could almost hear Ma saying, 'Have you said thank you to Mamoo?' He was hopping to the other side to get up and sit beside me. It was exhilarating to see him as excited as I was.

147

'Take us to the Bund, bhaiya,' Mamoo requested the tongawalla who had leapt to his seat in the front. His whip stayed pointed to the heavens instead of prodding the horse into action. He twisted his neck around but, before he could ask, Mamoo answered the question in his eyes, 'I know, I know, it is far away from here. But we don't want to take the car you're looking at under the porch. Bitia here has come from Bombay to enjoy a ride in your tonga. She can't get this treat there.'

'Achha, achha,' he said proudly, promising on behalf of his horse to give me a ride I'd remember all my life.

It was truly a ride I was to remember all my life, but not for his reasons, or the fine performance he had presumed upon from his horse. At first I sat a bit stiffly holding firmly to the centre dividing board with my arm, bracing my feet against the rod down below. As we trotted along under the tree-canopied avenues of the cantonment I began to enjoy the scenes passing in slow-motion which whizzed by when riding in a car. I let my body go limp and sway back and forth, up and down, with the vehicle's motion as dictated by the tongawalla's whip, horse's gait, or the condition of the tarred road. Relaxed and swaying I began to rock between the past and the present. I chanted under my breath, 'Oh, minus fourteen from twenty-four, to be a happy ten as before.'

When passing through the bazaar area, I was amazed by the number of print-outs issuing from my memory section to match what I was looking at. Poor Mamoo was smiling indulgently but, I'm sure, he was bored stiff by my repeatedly calling out, 'Look, Mamoo, look. Look at that. I remember this . . . and that too . . .'

For him my most amusing recall was on reaching the Bund. This is a mud embankment along the Ganges when it enters the pilgrim township, Prayag. It protects the settlement along the bank against an overflow of the swollen river during the monsoon season. There is a road at the top and then it slopes down again to level with the flat bank of the holy river. This embankment is the central feature of the yearly religious fair that takes place for the whole month of

148

January. When we had come as infants on our first visit to Allahabad with Ma, Karan and I were brought here to be blessed by Nani-ma's Guru, an ascetic who comes down from his Himalayan seclusion for prayers and a holy dip at Sangam.

When we reached the age of reason Mamoo used to organise expeditions to this annual Magh mela for Karan and myself. He would rally our Kashmiri cousins to make a children's party. On reaching the base of the Bund, he would drill the servants assigned to guard us on the direction and manner of moving in the crowd. If there was an emergency our group's SOS was the cry of the koel. He explained it was safe to choose this bird as its mating calls are heard only in the summer. I don't remember any occasion at the fair when the Mayday koel call was heard by anyone in winter. Mamoo must have been a meticulous manager of frisky youngsters.

On Mamoo's shout of, 'Go', we would run up the daunting slope, dragging the protesting adult harnessed to each of us, and then run down swiftly on the other side enjoying the squeals and spills of our locked mates. Mamoo never scolded or restrained us. He understood our impatience to see parrots tell fortunes, bears dance, monkeys imitate humans, acrobats do awesome tricks high up on the ropes stretched between two poles embedded in the sand, snakes and mongoose do their fight unto death, see the cobras fan their hoods and sway to the piped music, and what scared me, but fascinated Karan, were the pythons slithering around the necks of charmers. We used to see all this with one hand held in a vice-like grip by a servant. The stretch and the pull used to hurt, but if we tried to yank it back, we were told in hushed, scary whispers that we would either be lost in the surging crowd, or be kidnapped by flesh traders who were forever prowling to grab weeping, lost children. There was no choice but to submit.

As far as I'm concerned – I haven't checked with Karan – I don't remember being part of the massive deluge of pilgrims I now see reported in press photos. For me at that time, only the side shows, and the endless row of shops with tempting things I wanted to buy, existed. According to Mamoo we stopped going since I was ten. I have to find out why. Was it our exposure to television? Allied with this could be the boredom of our Allahabad cousins who, most likely, had to accompany the visiting aunts, uncles and cousins from London, Canada, USA and so on to the fair. It was hard to believe that fourteen years had rolled off with no entry of a Magh expedition of Mamoo for the two visitors from Bombay.

'Mamoo,' I exclaimed, 'why have they chiselled down the Bund?' The mud bank looked ridiculously shorter than what I remembered.

Mamoo was counting out the money from his wallet to pay the tongawalla. My question made him explode into unrestrained laughter. The coins from his hand spilled on the sand. The tongawalla stared at me curiously before stooping to pick up the coins for Mamoo. At last, controlling his breath, Mamoo replied, 'No need to chisel it, we need its height. It's the difference in you. Between being ten and twenty-three, beti. May Ganga Maiya bless your growth.' And as he paid the fare he explained my confusion to the tongawalla.

I started climbing the mud bank slowly, trying not to feel mortified or sad. Standing on the edge of the road at the top of the Bund the receded river could be seen far away, like a glistening body sensuously stretched out on the flat bed of sand. As my eyes followed its length on the horizon it seemed to curl and uncurl sleepily.

'A month or so later you won't be able to see the river from here,' Mamoo said. 'You see nothing but people, and more people moving towards something they can't even see, but know the holy river would be there.'

It was a long bare stretch, with hardly anyone moving anywhere. There were no tempting shops where I invariably bought rag dolls with embroidered huge, staring black eyes and red pouting mouths. Black wool was stitched to the head and made into a plait with a tiny red ribbon at the end. They all looked the same. My crucial choice depended on the colour and style of sari wrapped around the rigid frame, indicative of my present partiality to style and fashion. After choosing the doll I had to buy a straw basket containing shining kitchen vessels, stove, stool *et al*. So did the other girls so that we could play house-house, or celebrate dolls' weddings, during the holidays. The boys must've bought footballs, cricket sets, tops, yo-yos – we girls didn't pay any attention to their shopping. That little girl, I thought wistfully, who showed a promise of being a wife and a mother, had disappeared into the one who was fighting to overcome her insecure world.

The enveloping silence recalled the sounds locked away inside me. The babble of the performers; the clapping of the spectators; the din of those yelling at the top of their voices to advertise their show; and the tantrums of the children asserting their right to stop and see every entertainment on the way to the river so very far away. It was a silence that dared me not to break it. Just for that I had to. 'Mamoo, you made a profound statement. In other words it's faith that keeps us going. When you become reflective I have to think over your words.'

'I'm a simple soul, beti. Uneducated. Limited. I say what I think. You know why they call this river maiya?'

'A river is a female gender, so they call it a mother who . . .' He didn't let me finish. I was off the track.

'No, no, beti. Like a mother, she feeds and what is important she's always there. Never disappoints. You note that. Maiya is a title you'll have one day, God willing.'

'Oh, Mamoo, now you're talking like all those elderly aunts.'

'I'm elderly,' he said. 'Come, let's start walking.'

And we began to walk towards Mother Ganges, a good half a mile away. Little do you know, Mamoo, I was thinking – that mothers do disappoint. You didn't have one so you have clung to an idealised version of motherhood. I hope, if and when I decide to have children, I do not disappoint them, causing an irreparable injury to the idealism they bring with them from paradise. Ma had given us her attention, love, and security, but she had also disappointed me, at least, by being submissive, almost servile, to the demands of Sahis at the cost of her self-respect. What was it that made her into their robot? 'Mamoo, tell me what Mother was like when she was growing up here?'

'What do you mean what was she like?' He squinted towards the setting sun to look at me sideways. 'She grew up to be as you found her. What's bothering you about her?'

For a moment I was tempted to tell him about her degeneration. Something clamped up inside me. It was my mother's private area. Besides, it would cause him pain and solve nothing for me. 'It was just a whim, Mamoo,' I began to fill the crack. 'What was she like at my age – that's what I really wanted to know?'

'Now, your age – that's twenty-three . . .' He began. I interjected to correct him as once before he had mentioned my age as twenty-three.

'I'm twenty-four, Mamoo.'

'One year is no difference.' And he went on to describe what I already knew about Ma as a doctor, hardworking and so on. Father and daughter working together was quite a novelty in those days, he was enjoying detailing on that. And he went on talking seemingly unaware of my wavering attention. But it was he who took me unawares when he stopped walking and once again squinted towards me to ask, 'This is not what you want to know. What exactly do you expect me to tell you?'

He was right. There was something I wanted to know specifically, but I had not yet given it identity with words. I stammered, halted, rephrasing somehow to convey finally that I wanted to know about her personality. Was she meek or assertive – positive or negative? Was she conditioned to be obedient, almost servile, to her elders?

It was Mamoo's turn to grope for words. 'You are . . . I mean, we're talking about Didda, aren't we?'

'Of course. My mother . . . your . . .'

'There was never this or that about her. She was always strong, still is. I know.' Mamoo sounded aggressive.

'She was? Always?'

'She's managed to get along with your Nani-ma, didn't she?'

'That was because she was Father's pet. That's why Nani-ma was hard on her. To discipline her, I guess.'

'Hoonh,' Mamoo uttered and kept quiet. I had to coax

152

him not to hold back from me. I had to learn from him. Who else was there who knew her as well as he did to make me understand what she was like and why she had so easily become . . .? Mamoo cleared his throat and said cautiously, 'Well, Nani-ma, as you know her, is different from what she was then. Didda had a difficult time with her, before Doctor Sahib passed away, and still more afterwards.'

'I should imagine, after Grandfather's death, Nani-ma would've got along better with Ma. Why didn't they?'

'Old habits are difficult to give up.' Mamoo made it sound like a newly minted saying.

'So marriage was an escape for her?' I knew that. I wanted to hear what he had to say.

He had nothing to say, rather preferred not to step into a private area. We walked on silently, each entertaining the thoughts reverberating from our conversation. It helped to shorten the long walk on the slipping sand.

Gradually the dry sand began to be wetter, becoming firmer to walk on. I shed my chappals, clapped them together to let the clinging sand fall off before putting them in the cloth bag slung from my shoulder. The wetness comforted the soles of my tired feet.

'Good idea,' Mamoo approved. 'I'll follow you.' He took off his chappals but refused to put them in my bag unless I'd let him carry it. So I shed my weight and felt as if I were ten and could skip, jump, swirl, hobble on one leg, or whatever I fancied, with Mamoo as my sole spectator. I chose to run, feeling the air I was disturbing rushing past my face. My plait appeared to have its own outlet of joy. It was tossing up high, and thumping down on my back, reminding me of Shiv.

I felt the rounded pebbles under my feet before I saw them. That was the end of my retrogression. I turned around. Mamoo was trudging up, smiling broadly at me. All around us was the expanse of land which the sun was illuminating with its slanting rays. It made the gentle waves on the surface of the river glitter like diamonds heaped on the blue velvet cloth of a jeweller. I stretched my arms out as far as I could to embrace the magic world all around me.

'The stones must be hurting your feet,' Mamoo called out as he came near. 'Shall I take out your chappals?'

'No Mamoo,' I seemed to be singing. My voice sounded unfamiliar to me. I sat down and felt the stones. 'See how slippery smooth they are, Mamoo. They can't hurt.'

'This is the shallow bed of the river in winter. The water flowing over them for years has rubbed the stones smooth,' Mamoo explained. I imagine he was talking to a schoolgirl who still had to learn applied geography.

This setting happened to be another enduring memory of my old visits. I remember collecting pebbles to take them to Bombay by sneaking them into my suitcase. It was only recently Ma told me laughingly that she knew about it all along. She had let me think it was my secret because it amused her to see me behave like a smuggler. After all the years I had spent in maturing they were still here hoping to tempt me. I stood up caressing a big one in my hand. As far as I could see the bank of a slim Ganges was littered with the smooth pebbles, big ones graduating to smaller ones nearer the glittering flow. I held out the stone to Mamoo and said, 'So much time has got locked in this.'

He said nothing. He looked at me sadly. I was perceiving myself as a tiny pebble among a trillion others scattered around us. The only way a pebble became significant was when picked up and kept as something special, something treasured and loved – like I used to. It was a pity I had no inclination to do that now. Fourteen years too late.

Stepping lightly on the section of smaller pebbles I lost balance and stumbled. As my knees folded, my right hand steadied me. Under my hand I saw a small stone with a colour deeper than the others around it. Old habit surfaced. My hand picked it up to examine it. It was an unusual one, unlike anything around it. 'Mamoo,' I called out, 'look at this pebble.'

He stepped over and took it from me. 'What a strange stone,' he exclaimed, 'I've never seen one like it.'

We examined it in turn. 'What would you call this colour?' he asked.

'Ma has a French chiffon sari of this colour. Sort of a blend of deep purple and black. Don't you think so?'

154

He didn't agree immediately. After some deliberation he said, 'This colour I've seen in the sky. Very early dawn. Remember the morning you came to the cattle-shed? It's at that time, or earlier – the first mix of the black of a dark night and the faint rays of the rising sun.'

It was an apt description, poetic. I tucked it away to use in my writing. The stone was a rectangle, with one angle rounded, a sort of off-centre diamond shape. A thin ridged line connected two opposite corners, as if a ruler had been used. On closer scrutiny I detected two tiny dips, identical ones, at the two ends of what would've been a flawless straight line. 'How did this line happen, Mamoo? It's like an electronic recording.'

Mamoo was fascinated. He bent down to look at other stones in the vicinity. 'There's no other stone like it here,' he announced. 'They're round and white like so many all over.' He paused, turning the stone to look at it from all sides. He handed it to me saying, 'Seems like a gift for you. Keep it.'

I took it, almost reverentially. I held it in the palm of my hand. 'It's a coded message, Mamoo. Some day I may be given the key to the code.'

I had meant to amuse him, but he took it seriously. 'It may be. Who knows?'

We tripped on watching out for another coded stone. There were hardly any coloured ones to be seen. It deepened the mystery of the one I was holding in my hand. 'Why don't you put it in this bag?' Mamoo suggested taking my satchel off his shoulder. 'In case you drop it,' he added unnecessarily.

We saw more and more people as we neared the ghat, some pilgrims, mostly sightseers like us. The water lapping on the stone steps was muddy. 'Is this Ganges water, Mamoo?' I had to verify.

'Yes, of course,' he sounded upset. The expression on his face was adding – what else could it be?

'Must be due to the incessant washing of pilgrims' sins.' I was happy to see him find my remark funny. I didn't mean to hurt his religious feelings.

Mamoo negotiated the fare with the touts who pounced on us before settling on the boatman who should take us to Sangam. Luckily, he was not a talkative man. The kind who take upon themselves to tell you the legend of the arrival of the holy river on the earth, and many other stories related to it. Or, perhaps, we looked the kind who knew our mythology. His oars shoved the water with a steady rhythm making the boat slither forward smoothly.

There were other boats around us. All we could see was the river meandering and disappearing from our view on the horizon. Flat, soft land and the clear, blue sky above. The sun was lowering itself, with its mathematical precision, towards the western edge of the earth. All of us on the boats could be the people living thousands of years ago paying homage to Ganga Maiya, and begging her to cleanse us of our sins. Where was the difference between then and now? Man had made a landing on the moon but he still needed gods and goddesses.

My educated concept of time in numerical factors disintegrated. There was no time before and after, only now and here. I felt myself dissolving like salt in water. I unfolded the shawl and flung it around my shoulders to contain myself. 'Feeling cold?' I heard Mamoo asking. I knew my head was nodding, my mouth was trying to smile. I spoke to make sure I could. 'Can I put my hand in the water, Mamoo?' Much like the little girl I once was.

Mamoo's laughter made me laugh too. He asked, 'You want to go back to the time when you had to ask your mother's permission for everything, don't you?' I nodded without thinking. 'Already tired at your age? There's a long way to go yet.'

There was no explanation handy to give him. I was relieved to hear the boatman's voice announcing that we were almost at Sangam. He pointed out the clear, blue stream of Jamuna swirling joyously from another direction, like a little girl hopping home from kindergarten school. Few more paddles and he had the boat exactly at the spot where the Jamuna and Ganga streams merged and became one. 'Devi Saraswati is down below, out of sight,' he added. He rested his oars to give us time for contemplation before making the return journey. So had some other boatmen. It looked like a picnic of boats.

The boat staggered as Mamoo got up to sit next to me. He cupped the Sangam water in his palm and sprinkled it on my head, reciting a Sanskrit shloka. 'May Ganga Maiya shower you with her choicest blessings.' He added his own blessing to the one, I imagine, he had invoked from the goddess of energy, Shakti.

'I need your blessings, Mamoo,' I said. 'Now more than ever.'

'That you have, always. Without asking,' he said in a soft tone, with misty eyes.

TWENTY-TWO

My twisting fingers in the river were creating patterns in their tiny wake as our boat pushed against the current in return to the ghat. I was thinking of the three rivers merging joyfully and becoming one for the rest of the journey to the sea, the usual destination of all rivers. It made me think of the three of us, Jeet, Kanta, and myself. Except that none of us was willing to be invisible. Also, we were not destined to stay together till the end of our lives. Ultimately, involvement with suitable males was our target. A naughty thought crossed my mind. Like Papa had often insinuated that we three friends must be lesbians from the time we became glued to each other in school, I wondered if these three rivers could've been locked in a lesbian relationship to have stayed together till the end.

'Mamoo, were Ganga, Jamuna, and Saraswati married?' I asked looking up from watching the wake patterns.

Mamoo hesitated, he wasn't very sure about all of them.

The boatman, on Mamoo's request, supplied the stories he had heard from his grandmother. What I could gather was that Ganga had married in her human form but left her husband when he broke a promise given to her at the time of their marriage. Jamuna was a beloved of Lord Krishna. So were many others, I said. Was she married to him? Perhaps, he wasn't sure. Interestingly, he observed that marriage is for humans, not to be applied to gods and goddesses. What both Mamoo and boatman were absolutely sure of was the maidenhood of Saraswati. Why wasn't she given a spouse? 'Goddess of Knowledge and Wisdom, I suppose, had to be unfettered,' Mamoo observed.

'The institution of marriage in those days also had many shades, Mamoo. Like now. What do you think? An intellectual like Saraswati is better off without the hooks of marriage. Also, a working woman, who has a promising career to carve out. Don't you think so?'

He didn't answer, just smiled. I had no choice but to return to contemplation with my hand making designs in the water. Suddenly, for no apparent reason, I asked, 'Mamoo, why didn't you get married?'

The question caught him off guard for a moment. Recovering his sense of humour he replied, 'Consider this, which sensible girl would've married a pint-sized idiot like me?'

'Nonsense, Mamoo.' I sat up, dried my hands on my kurta and launched a defence. 'How are you inferior to many other men girls agree to marry?'

'Their marriages are arranged by the elders. For different considerations. Match making can succeed for idiots also.'

'Nani-ma must have tried for you. You were not opposed to marriage, were you?'

He shook his head, a forced smile on his face.

'Why? Why didn't she? Obviously, you wanted to.'

'She wasn't bringing me up for the benefit of someone else,' he laughed and added, 'anyway, what is marriage? They call it a mousetrap. Those inside want to get out and those outside want to get in. A huge nonsense after a while.'

I asked, careful not to hurt his dormant feelings, 'Didn't Nana question any of her decisions?'

'He never accepted responsibility for me. He was kind and good to me. The rest was up to your Nani-ma.'

I had noticed that he always referred to Grandmother as 'your Nani-ma'. I had never heard him address his foster mother directly specifying his equation with her. I asked him about it now, a time when I could transgress respect of the elders in a search for truth. 'I wasn't told how I should call her. Just shows one can manage without formalities, doesn't it?'

'Hasn't it made you bitter, deeply inside you?'

'It did. For many years.'

159

'And then?'

We had arrived at the ghat. The sun had come down very low on the horizon in a diffused red glow, revealing a perfectly round face, to be looked at and admired. I spotted a group of women who had arrived for the sunset worship of Ganga Maiya. The mellowed rays of the sun were making their colourful saris glow against the darkening sky. I wanted to sit on the stone steps to watch their pooja.

'It'll get dark soon and suddenly. There are no lights on the way to the Bund. We should get going,' Mamoo urged.

Highly pleased with myself I searched in my bag that he was carrying to bring out a small flashlight with a powerful beam. 'I have this, Mamoo. Can we watch their pooja, please?'

The women started singing praises of the benign river whose blessings could take away all sorrows. Some of them were out of tune, some were muffling their words, one of them was bent on being louder than the others in order to be the first to reach the deity on call. Their faith transcended the tuneless hymn of praise and supplication. They had brought boats made from green leaves pinned with thorns to float their earthen lamps and flowers as offerings. As the sun dipped and disappeared they lighted the wicks and carefully placed their vulnerable green boats on the water. I watched the flickering lamps as they bobbed in the current which carried them downstream.

As we started walking back I repeated my question, 'How did you get rid of your bitterness Mamoo?'

'By turning the picture around,' he was quick to answer, showing his preparation while I was watching the sunset pooja. 'I thought of what my fate would've been if she hadn't brought me away from my stepmother.'

That must've scared him into total submission. I wondered if Nani-ma had used it as a whip. Quite possible, I decided. From the corner of my eye I observed him as he unfolded his shawl to wrap it around him. It was as if I were seeing him for the first time.

As we walked on in silence darkness fell like a curtain in a theatre. The flashlight projected a round patch which ran ahead of us. I was a little startled when Mamoo spoke. 'About that bitterness, I haven't given you a complete answer.' He took a couple of deep breaths before continuing, 'I want to tell you for a selfish reason. Can you keep a secret from your mother? This is only for you. I haven't told anyone.'

His serious tone scared me. 'Are you sure, Mamoo? I can keep it from Ma, or anyone else. You must know I won't tell since you decided to trust me. I hope you don't regret it. This . . . this place makes one talk . . .'

He said it was not an impulse but a need which was compelling him. He may not get another opportunity to find me alone. So I listened, prepared to be surprised. Yet, what he told me was beyond my imagination. A hundred-odd years ago I would've taken out my smelling salts.

He told me of falling in love with a widow, a Christian woman. She had two children who were now going to college. She was a nurse who was earning as much as she could in her private practice. Well enough to stay independent of her in-laws. In fact they had tried to live off her and save their income. I thought of asking how long this had been going on but I decided it didn't matter. After all, duration is no measure of depth. He went on to say that he was partly supporting her with his earnings from the repair jobs he did – radios, transistors, electronic equipment, and now televisions. He had taken some training to develop his natural flair to earn more money. Nani-ma had no idea how much he earned. He kept his savings in a post office account.

So this was the secret of the telephone calls which Dulari couldn't fathom. 'Why didn't you have the courage to tell Nani-ma that you wanted to marry her?'

'You've taken it for granted that she wanted to marry me.'

'Why, doesn't she?' I was intrigued about a secret liaison being preferred to marriage in conservative Allahabad. Cosmopolitan Bombay was different.

'Her experience with her first husband was a bad one. She doesn't want to be tied to any man with marriage vows.'

'Surely, she should by now know that you're not just any man?'

'Her Roman Catholic order wants to convert me if I want to marry her.'

'And you don't want to?'

'No, why should I? We can have a civil marriage but her priest is firm on my conversion.'

I restrained my mocking laughter. 'She prefers to confess every Sunday and do the assigned penance?'

'I suppose so.'

'Weird,' I couldn't help saying. 'How is it that Nani-ma's information bureau hasn't uncovered this?'

'Why only her? The whole Kashmiri clan has no clue. I'm over-discreet.' His voice was laced with pride. Good for him, I thought.

I remembered, 'You had a motive in telling me this. What can I do for you?'

'You may not have to do anything. I hope not. But just in case. If anything happens to me suddenly . . .'

I was going to protest out of sheer form when I told myself that this was the time to listen, not talk. He went on to tell me that in such an eventuality I should extend my hand and help her if she approached me.

My heart objected to a responsibility far beyond my age, but I said nothing to Mamoo. I told him to let me meet her, or give me her address so that . . .

He cut me short pointing out that I would be approached only as a last resort. It was enough for his ladyfriend to know who she could turn to if she needed to. Till then I could forget about it. I understood what he meant by being over-discreet. I was proud to be chosen by him to be a trustee-on-call. I felt extraordinarily proud of him, and from that moment gave up feeling sorry for him.

Soon we lost the lights and sounds of the ghat. It was so quiet that our heavy breathing seemed to magnify and intrude on our consciousness. We were two unidentifiable beings pursuing a round patch of light on the sand. Our isolation created dependence and closeness between us. I heard myself saying, 'I have a lot of bitterness locked inside me, Mamoo. I hope to settle that like you did. Perhaps it's unfair but I'm disappointed in Ma. Not as my mother, that

162

way she's been fine. She's what you'd expect her to be for Karan and me. I always thought of her as strong, made of unbendable steel. And I found her to be soft, bent by my father and his people. I can't tell you everything I've found out recently. But believe me, it's been very hard for me to accept the old order. It's toppled everything around me, like an earthquake does. It happened partly because of me, but mainly because Shafi Ahmed came back into Ma's life. That is what I have to tell Nani-ma tomorrow. That's why I've come here, on Ma's assignment. She's in Lahore right now, with Shafi Ahmed . . .'

'Stop, stop . . .' Mamoo cried out. He stood still, the trembling light on the sand conveyed his agitation. 'Don't say anything more. You might accuse and punish yourself later on. You told me you had to talk to your Nani-ma first. Keep it that way. For your own sake, wait till tomorrow.'

'But, Mamoo, you'll have a sleepless night wondering why and how it happened. And worrying about her.'

'It won't be the first night of its kind. I'll manage. But you mustn't feel you did something you shouldn't have.'

'All right, Mamoo. Let me just say this. I'm proud of what Ma is doing now. I'm worried for her. You know how it is in the game of bridge. Your partner is the declarer and you have to be the dummy. You watch, and worry over your partner's skill in playing the hand to fulfil the contract bid and held. Well, as the cards lie with the four players, Ma has to win by her endplay. She has choices there. I'm worried about what she'll choose to do.'

Mamoo started walking but the light patch was still shivering. His shawl had slipped and was frisking on the sand. I picked up the end and handed it to him. He absent-mindedly deposited it on his shoulder and said, 'About your bitterness and judgement of your mother I can't say anything. I don't know enough and also it's not needed. I see Didda once a year. To me she's still a strong, determined person. She doesn't wear her armour outside. Anyway, I have a right to tell you how I have managed a somewhat similar situation.' He was quiet for a minute before continuing in a softer tone, 'Think of the pebbles and stones we have seen lying all along the river-bed today. Now, we see them from a height, and up to a great distance. Our eyes can give us the idea of this stone world that the stones can't have. I'll explain that. If the stone you picked up claimed that it knows, understands the layout of the whole area – enough to pass judgement on the other stones, even those next to it, what would you think? Unrealistic, unjust, even foolish, right? That is what I realised I was doing when I was bitterly blaming your Nani-ma, and everyone else, for trampling on me. And I talked to myself for days and nights. And this is what I learnt from somewhere inside me. It has served me well. I've had no reason to revise my thinking, only improve on it. And it is this. I have to concern myself with myself only. Everything begins and ends here. Blame or praise myself, no one else divides either of those with me. What I make myself do is within my power. Wishing others would change for me is a waste of time. If change is possible it's with me. I can choose to do so, or not. I expect nothing from outside of myself. Does it make sense to you? Think over it. It has served me well.'

'It's very difficult, what you've chosen to live by, Mamoo. It's become smooth for you, like those pebbles. Like water, you've worked on your philosophy. It's beyond my reach, against my ingrained nature.'

'You can say that only if you've tried.'

Mamoo was Socratic in his discussion. He was surprising me with his intellect at every turn of our conversation. 'How long did it take you to complete your change of attitude?' The journalist in me asked this question.

'I don't know. Took a long, long time, and a lot of pain. But then you and I are different. Your mind is educated and disciplined. My thinking was slow. It's bound to be easier for you.'

'Nonsense, Mamoo. You're a sharp one. The difference between us is that you wanted security. I had too much of it. I became more and more vulnerable in direct proportion to my accumulated innocence. I should've been exposed to the reality around me. I may have then accepted Sahi standards by osmosis, like the other Sahis did. Instead I turned into an idealist. I'm reeling under the shock of falling from a height. You were a realist from the start. You steadied yourself before you could fall. Your way is not for me.'

We had arrived at the base of the Bund. We paused to catch our breath before starting on the uphill climb. 'In this infinite world nothing is too late. You can't use a calendar for it. You need to do it, so do it,' Mamoo said. I felt as if he were staring at me in the enveloping darkness to compel me.

'It's an uphill task, Mamoo,' I said lightly. 'Too much effort with no guarantee I'd succeed.'

He matched my cynicism. 'At least you'll have the fun of running downhill on the other side.'

'Well then,' I said forcing a laugh, 'let's begin this climb.'

On reaching the pilgrim's road on the top I took a last look at the dark side from where we had come. I looked on the other side where we had to go. Down the hill was the wide, tarred road blazing with street-lights at measured intervals. 'Do we have to return to the world of roads to make our choice of direction and destination?' I mumbled.

I could see Mamoo's twinkling eyes in the street-light bouncing off the sand. 'Well, we have walked a long distance for this, haven't we?'

'Makes me sad to go back.' I was almost tearful.

'You can always return to the other side. It will be the same, always. Next time even the Bund wouldn't let you down.'

That made me laugh, genuinely. 'Thank you, Mamoo. Thank you for bringing me here. Next time we won't let fourteen years go by.' I paused and added before starting down, 'Thank you also, Mamoo, for your trust. I'll do exactly as you want me to.' I suddenly hugged him impulsively. 'Thank you for your wisdom,' I said near his ear before running downhill as I must have done many years ago.

TWENTY-THREE

Our tonga turned into the gate of Atal-Retreat and, with the horse now slack, lumbered slowly along the driveway. Seeing the empty porch Mamoo was commenting that fortunately we had returned home before Nani-ma, when we heard the telephone ringing inside. 'This must be Shiv calling from Bombay,' I said, impatient to pick up the receiver before he should hang up. Mamoo gave me the front-door key to get going as he had to stay back to pay the tongawalla.

I managed to reach the phone while it was still ringing. It was not Shiv's voice. It was the telephone operator checking on the number before asking if I was the particular person, Gunga Sahi. 'Madam, call for you from Lahore. I'll just connect you. Hold on.' Her information made me happy but also anxious.

'It's Ma's call from Pakistan,' I called out to Mamoo as he came in. Just then the line went dead. We waited. The operator returned, the connection this time stayed alive. I heard Ma's two helloes. I hoped she heard mine too before the static filled our ears. We tried to shout to rise above it but the connection became soundless again. There was one more promise of a successful connection which failed also. I was still sitting there hopefully when it rang once more and on picking it up I had the second surprise of the evening, an unpleasant one.

It was Papa from Bombay. He didn't ask me how I was, or enquire after Nani-ma. 'Have you heard from your mother?' He came directly to the point.

I hesitated before saying a flat, 'No,' and not a word about the aborted calls from Lahore.

'Is she still in Lahore?' he asked.

'I suppose so. Is everything all right at home? Anything wrong? How is Karan?' My anxious questions unrolled without a pause.

'Why, what do you care about us here? You're like your mother. You've run off too.' I had unwittingly given him the pleasure of twisting my ear.

'That is unfair, Papa.'

'You didn't even tell me you were leaving for Allahabad. I thought you were with your lesbian bunch. I had to ring up there to find out you're camping with your grandmother. That's embarrassing. And you tell me I'm unfair? Henh?'

'Papa, you took a long time to miss me.' I countered with a laugh. 'Today is my . . . uh . . . fourth day here. I've been away from Bombay for five days.' I found I wasn't angry with him. He didn't touch me that deeply. 'Karan knew I was here. I'm due to come back now. I'm taking the train day after tomorrow.'

'I suppose I shouldn't ask why you've gone there? All well with your grandmother?'

'Oh, she's fine. Everything is all right with her.' I ignored his first question.

'I'll send a car to pick you up. What time and which train . . .?'

'Don't bother, Papa. I'm going back to my lesbian friends. It's quite convenient to take a taxi.' I amused myself by thinking of his reaction if he knew that Shiv would be meeting me at VT Station. Not that Shiv had said so, but I knew he would come.

There was a slight pause before he said, 'Do what you like. I've given up on you . . . and your mother.'

And he relieved me of his relationship by putting the receiver down.

About a week before I had left for Allahabad an equally unpleasant surprise call from him had come to my office, five days after Prime Minister Gandhi's assassination, the reason why I remember the day.

Ma had left for Delhi the day after the assassination as soon as she had briefed Rekha at the clinic, and spoken personally to her imminent delivery cases. This was the first occasion when I realised, and so did Ma I presume, how fortunate it was that Rekha Dhar, Ma's niece – my cousin – had decided to come to Bombay a year ago after her graduation from the Medical College in Lucknow to gain work experience with mother. Ma was very pleased about it as she had someone she could rely on completely in her private clinic. For me it was also a great relief but in a different way. I no longer entertained any guilt about not taking up medicine as Ma had wanted me to. One exposure to cadavers and I was done with even trying it out to please her. Now there was a family member to inherit her flourishing practice. For a while I had felt jealous of Rekha for the closeness which developed between her and Ma, but I found her too likeable to sustain the feeling.

Ma had heard the news of Mrs Gandhi's assassination at Bombay Hospital while she was bringing a child into the world. The Maternity Ward sister, an addict of BBC broadcasts, heard it when the world news at nine-thirty in the morning was interrupted to give the news as a flash. She had burst into the Labour Room with her transistor. While the hands of everyone in the white room attended to the mechanics of the birth they heard the repeats of the flash and then the confirmation of the report. One of the nurses said, as she held the new-born while the umbilical cord was cut, 'The PM is your cousin, isn't she Dr Sahi?' When I rushed to the hospital to be with her, Ma told me that she was so stunned by the news that she did need to be reminded of her relationship to Indu Didda.

The news of the assassination had stunned everyone motionless, like curled-up caterpillars who suddenly encounter bleakness of fear while crawling along energetically on multiple feet in their green world. For days there was only one topic of conversation, only one preoccupation everywhere. In the *Reflections* office we collected obituary material – photographs, articles, news items – while our attention was either on the television, or tuned to the radio broadcasts, our own and from abroad. In this setting I got the call from my father. He flung his question at me without any preliminaries, 'Who is Shafi Ahmed? You must know about him.'

I certainly did. Only recently I had found out at the dinner Ma had given for Dr and Mrs Davidson at Salaam, a new restaurant Karan's friend Ravi Nath had introduced to Bombay. I happened to catch an unfamiliar expression on Ma's face when Dr Davidson mentioned that it had been a problem but he was able to get their visa for Pakistan just before leaving. That they were now planning to stop in Lahore and Karachi on their way back home to England. Was it possible, without much trouble, to contact Shafi Ahmed from here to let him know of their visit? Ma's voice was constricted when she said it could be tried but it was difficult to cut through red tape. With my natural curiosity aroused, in the next five minutes I ferreted out from Rekha the significance of Dr Shafi Ahmed in my mother's past. But I denied the information to my father: 'I've never met him, Papa,' which was true. Through the years I had acquired a voltage stabiliser to deal with the variable currents from him. It effortlessly plugged in whenever I talked to him. 'Why are you asking? What's come up, Papa?'

'There's a courier letter from Dr Davidson. He sent it from Lahore. It mentions Dr Shafi Ahmed . . .'

I couldn't help interrupting, 'The letter is to you, Papa?' That seemed unlikely.

'No, to your mother.'

'You opened it?' My question carried an accusation based on social rules and norms.

'Naturally. She's not here. What if it had an urgent message for her?' His defence was impeccable. But I knew it was curiosity which compelled him to tear the letter open.

'What does it say about Shafi Ahmed?' I asked.

'As I presumed it's an urgent message. He's got cancer, terminal. Dr Davidson has written a brief note. He felt she might want to know that. That's all.'

That's all . . . that's all . . . that's all . . . – my mind kept repeating. I couldn't talk to him any more. I heard the click of his receiver as he dropped it on its cradle.

When I could depend on my speech I rang up Rekha to

give her the news. I told her I had decided to meet Ma at the airport. I wanted somehow to prepare her before she read the letter on reaching home.

Miraculously the flight from Delhi arrived on time. Through the smudged plate glass of the arrival lounge I saw her walking up in a white sari with fatigued shoulders, and a sorrowful face. She looked as colourless as her sari. With a start I realised she was not wearing the only make-up she used, light lipstick. I remembered just in time that the nation was in mourning for twelve days. I quickly wiped off my lipstick with a tissue I fished out of my bag.

On catching sight of me leaning on the visitors' railing she stopped walking and stood staring at me. Other passengers passed her from both sides. I waved out. She slowly gathered momentum and on coming within hearing asked in a faint voice, 'How is it you've come to receive me? You hate airports. How is Karan? Everyone else? – Some bad news?'

I had to say as cheerfully as I could, 'Being a journalist I was curious to hear about Delhi, and . . . and the Gandhi family.'

She tried to make my effort worthwhile by talking about anything and everything that came to her head on the drive home. Most of what she had to tell me was familiar as I had been watching television. Her personal account of Mrs Gandhi's family I heard with full concentration. My mind was wrestling with the problem of when and how to tell her what I had to. I couldn't decide till the only choice left was to break the news when she would lie down to rest in her bedroom.

Saku Bai opened the door; she tried to say something. I thought it was her speech of condolence. I steered Ma quickly past her. As we entered the living-room Papa was sitting in the chair where he read his newpapers while drinking his morning tea. 'Papa,' I exclaimed before I could censor my reaction. 'How is it you're here and not at the bridge table at Willingdon?' I could now guess what Saku Bai was trying to say to warn Ma.

'I stayed back to give Bimla the important letter personally,' he said taking out the letter from his pocket without waiting any more.

'What letter? What's the important news in it? Why didn't you tell me at the airport, Gungoo?'

Pre-empting Papa I disclosed the news to Ma at break-neck speed. A horrible way to do it but I didn't trust Papa's motivation in depriving himself, and Aunt Chanda, of their usual outing.

The moment Ma finished reading Dr Davidson's brief note Papa asked, 'Who is this Shafi Ahmed?'

'A friend. I worked as his assistant in the Allahabad Civil Hospital.' Her voice was firm, much to my surprise.

'Wasn't he more than just a friend and a boss?'

Ma looked up; her hands folded the letter as she said in a crisp tone, 'Yes, he was. I wanted to marry him but my parents didn't allow me to.'

'Why haven't you told me about him all these years?'

'I didn't think it was necessary. It didn't concern my relationship with you.'

'Your virginity was my concern . . .'

Ma got up suddenly; turning her back on him she started walking towards the door. I followed her. We heard Papa ask, 'What do you plan doing about this letter? You'd better let me know. Now it is my concern, is that clear?'

'I'll inform you when the time comes,' Ma said slowly and clearly without stopping her walk.

TWENTY-FOUR

As I followed Ma I prayed that she should reach her bed-room without collapsing. When she lay down and I for-ced myself to look at her face, I found she was still combat-worthy after the ugly encounter which had left me feeling limp, and fearful.

Ma lay quietly, simmering down perhaps. I sat by her side, with no desire to talk. I felt mad with myself for being slow-witted. When Father had said that the virginity of his wife was his concern – as if it were his birthright – I wish I had retorted, 'Papa, your daughter is not a virgin. What are you going to do about it?' The expression on his face would've been a compensation for me, if not for Mother.

I don't know how long Mother and I stayed in that state of shock, but I was glad to see Rekha knock softly and walk in with her medical valise. Seeing the still form on the bed she came to a stealthy halt and asked in mime if Ma was sleeping.

'Ma, Rekha is here,' I announced. Ma turned over and asked, 'How is everything at the clinic, Rekha? Any problem in my absence?'

'All the imminent preggies are holding on for your return. No one seems to trust me, Didda,' Rekha reported as she opened her valise and took out a disposable needle.

'What's that for?' Ma asked.

'For you. Diazepan. We have to extract Delhi fatigue and tension. The cases in waiting may start landing up tonight. Who knows, these strong-will types may suddenly let go when they ring up and hear your voice at this end.'

Rekha had no idea of the skirmish in the living-room or

172

she would've doubled the dose of Diazepan in the injection. Ma didn't resist Rekha's thoughtful gesture. Her eyes were on her moving hands without really seeing. She said in a flat voice, 'Rekha, they'll have to trust you. You are a very promising doctor. I wouldn't have taken you under me if you weren't.'

'In their eyes I'm fresh. Inexperienced. You can't quarrel with that.'

'No, I suppose not. You hold on to those who want to stay with you. Those who want to shift you pass them on to Dr Sharma. I'll speak to him to be on call as a senior doctor should you run into trouble. That should . . .' Ma's face winced as Rekha injected the medicine.

'You're here now,' Rekha said. 'You do that next time . . .'

'I'm afraid the "next time" is here,' Ma said sadly. She told her about Dr Davidson's letter and her decision to go to Pakistan as soon as she could arrange it.

I wasn't surprised. I knew inside me that she would do that. Rekha disposed of the injection, left her valise open and bent down to hug Ma. 'Everything will be all right, don't fret,' Ma said. I wondered if she was referring to herself, or the clinic and her waiting patients. It was at such passages that Ma and Rekha's close relationship irked me. I got up and moved over to lie down on the chaise-longue.

I could hear their shop-talk from where I lay. I saw the injection taking effect slowly. The mask Ma had kept intact for years started cracking and peeling off. I suppose as she discussed the details of arrangements with Rekha she was absorbing the happiness of meeting Shafi Ahmed. The worry of his illness was receding to the back of her mind. For her he was coming alive, a reality again. As her eyes began to dip into sleep, I saw glimpses of the way she looked in the pictures of her young and carefree days in the albums I had pored over in Atal-Retreat.

I had seen her look like this once before. I recalled how youthful and lively she had been at the dinner she had given for the Davidsons. The restaurant belonged to Karan's friend, Ravi Nath. As he had done the interior entirely on

173

his own, Ma had asked Ravi to take us around before seating us.

Ravi's father was a compulsive buyer of antiques, anything and everything that caught his fancy on his regular Sunday-morning expeditions to the Thieves' Market. He brought back carved rosewood furniture, blue china, cut glass, Tanjore paintings, an old typewriter, sewing machine – it could be anything from a beautiful to a nonsensical item. Ravi's mother dreaded his return from the Market. She had a preference for the new and the modern in everything. Very rarely did she find something in his purchases that she liked enough to use. Many items she gave away as gifts for birthdays, marriages and anniversaries. Ravi's father just liked to buy and bring home something. He didn't care if it was used or stored, or given away. When the storage space in the apartment was exhausted the overflow was kept in the garage, which had to disgorge their two cars. And yet the acquisitive hunger was not satiated.

The Sunday excursions began to cause serious marital cracks. This was when Ravi came up with the solution of using the miscellaneous items as décor for a restaurant. He called it Salaam because his father was greeted by the Thieves' Market shopkeepers with warm and tempting salaams every Sunday.

When Ravi took us around he gave an enthusiastic bio-data of all the items in the décor which aroused our curiosity. The Davidsons were fascinated by the items used which had no affinity to each other apart from their age and bygone value. An old double bass was suspended, seemingly precariously, from the roof. The pedalled stand of a Singer sewing machine was converted into a cosy table for two. The old typewriter had become a lamp to keep company with the carved furniture used for an elite dining corner. The table he had reserved for us was a delightful conversion of an old four-poster bed. The canopy and curtains were intact but the bed boards were sliced from both sides to fit in six chairs on the two sides of the centre piece, saved to serve as a dining table.

There was a Country Club corner with Raj pieces of fur-

174

niture and pictures. The Davidsons burst into laughter on seeing the hanging frames of huntsmen gravely posing on their horses. Port was served to us here. We raised our glasses to the serious riders and their still more handsome horses.

Mother was ahead of us when Ravi led to the right of the L-shaped area. Ma squealed with delight, clapping her hands like a little girl as she exclaimed, 'Look what's here.' It was a gleaming, highly polished convertible blue vintage Ford car. Ravi had made it functional by placing stainless steel trays on its seats to serve as a salad bar from one side and a tempting chaat station from the other.

Beyond this buffet he had parked a victoria, its brass polished to mirror efficiency. There was imitation hay on the floor but no pretence of a horse. One could sit on its seats and eat all the courses without fear of being trotted off the scene. Ma and the Davidsons couldn't praise Ravi enough for his innovative ability. He shyly said that it all germinated from the desperate need to recover space and peace in his home.

Salaam made the evening for us. Both Karan and I had come resigned to an evening of utter boredom. After the tour we sat down at the four-poster table, Mother and the Davidsons on one side – Rekha, Karan and I on the other with an extra chair shoved in for Papa, whom I fully expected not to turn up at all. Afraid to fall into a belt of boredom, Karan and I made ourselves interested in critically appraising Ma's ebullient mood which persisted after a slight fall when Dr Davidson had asked her if it was possible to contact Shafi Ahmed in Lahore. Karan said softly to me, 'I think old Davidson must've had a crush on Ma in the good old days. What do you say?'

On finding a chance I asked Rekha if she agreed with Karan's speculation. It was then that she told us it was Dr Shafi Ahmed – just mentioned in their conversation – and not Dr Davidson who was the man in her life. The next day we dug the whole story out of her. When we asked her to authenticate it she revealed it was known to the whole clan in Allahabad. We could find out for ourselves when we went there next time.

Both Karan and I were intrigued by this revelation. It gave an interesting dimension to Ma. It also heightened our enjoyment of the evening. But the quality of the evening underwent a change after the late arrival of Papa. Ma's vivacity vanished and so did her transient rejuvenation. The Davidsons became circumspect in their conversation. Papa was at his sarcastic best. I became apprehensive about the impression he was making on the Davidsons, who must, naturally, be comparing him to Shafi Ahmed. I felt sorry for Mother also because I knew she had handed out another loan to Papa for his and Aunt Chanda's bridge debts. For the first time I had heard her requesting him to return early from the club to be on time at the dinner. The food selected and served by Ravi was superb. It shifted the tension we all felt, according to our perceptions, to the back seat.

I felt a feather-touch on my arm; my eyes flew open. It was Mother bending over me. I had dozed off. 'You must be exhausted, poor darling,' she said stroking my face.

'Has Rekha left?'

'A little while ago. She said she'll get in touch with you.' I was wondering why Mother had to wake me up to tell me that. She sat down and put her arm across to hold me close and said, 'Don't be so upset and frightened. You'll be all right.'

'I'm all right, Ma,' I lied. 'You're not going away for ever. Don't worry about Karan and me.'

'No, I won't. I'm more worried about what's ahead of me in Lahore,' she said slowly. 'I had to wake you up to help me. Can you ring up Anil Dhar in Delhi? Tell him about the Davidsons' news, and that I want to go to Lahore. Ask him if he can get me a visa for Pakistan. I feel hesistant to talk to him about Shafi. You tell him.'

'He's sure to get you the visa, Ma. He's in the core of bureaucratic power in Delhi. How long are you going to be away? He'll want to know,' I asked in a practical manner. I wanted to camouflage the child inside me which had started to fret.

'As long as Shafi wants me to stay with him,' Ma replied.

'What if he wants you to stay with him till . . .' and I stopped appalled by my lack of sensitivity.

'. . . till he dies?' Ma finished for me and left me gaping at her. 'He's not a selfish man. I wish he had been selfish enough to make me marry him.'

I kept quiet. I knew what it must've cost her to say that to me. I decided to be selfish. 'Why are you in a hurry to go, Ma? Please wait a few days,' and hastily added, 'Not because I hope you'd change your mind. I expect you have to snatch the time left . . . to . . . to fill so many blank years.' When she said nothing I added slowly, holding back the tears that threatened to flow, 'Gives me a chance to adjust to your going.'

'I'm not going tomorrow, my pet,' she said soothingly, laughing softly. 'I plan to attend the thirteenth-day observance of Indu Didda's . . .' and she faltered over naming the event. 'I wouldn't want to return here after Delhi. I want to go to Lahore from there. Gives Anil time to arrange the visa for me.'

'Ma, I'm feeling uneasy. I don't know why,' I said and at the least expected moment the tears broke through. I said between sobs I didn't know why I was crying when I was so happy for her, and proud that she had the guts to decide on going to Lahore. Next moment I knew I was crying because of the crudeness of my father, and because I had twenty-three of his chromosomes in each life cell of my body. This was plain self-pity which I would have to suppress later.

Ma squeezed herself on to the chaise-longue beside me and held me tight and said in a whisper, 'All this has been too much for my baby. Don't ever think that my decision to go to Lahore is impulsive. One day, in retrospect, you'll be able to assess it differently. Give my selfish action the right weightage then.'

Mamoo, followed by Bhoot, was back looking fresh and rested after a bath. 'Arre, you're still sitting here? Why don't you bathe and get ready before your grandmother returns? She's got interested in a family gossip otherwise she doesn't take this long on her visits. I don't think the Lahore call will come again. If it does I'm here. I'll call you.'

I slipped away without telling Mamoo that I'd given up on the Lahore call a long time ago. It was just as well he hadn't overheard me when I'd talked to Papa. I would've found it difficult to tell him about him and Aunt Chanda and why my feelings had changed towards them. And more so relate to him how Papa had behaved when Ma had announced her decision to go to Lahore.

None of us, Ma, Rekha, or I, anticipated what was to happen although Karan was warning us in his own vague style. He wanted to remain neutral – neither with Ma, nor with Papa. I had advised him that in clear-cut battle lines one had to jump to one side or the other. I think Mother was upset about his observer's position although she said nothing to pressurise him in any way.

I had moved back to Sahi-Sadan to be with Ma for the seven days before she was to leave for Delhi and then for Lahore. As luck would have it, all her choosy patients delivered, or chose to have induced deliveries when they heard she was leaving on the eleventh of November. Rekha was perceptively relieved of her main worry over Ma leaving.

Ma had returned home after two induced deliveries on the evening of the eighth of November, and was telling me about them when Papa sent Saku Bai to ask Ma to come to the living-room. 'This is strange,' Ma said. 'Surely he knows his way to my rooms.'

'Looks like,' I suggested laughingly, 'he would've if he needed to borrow money from you.'

It was fortunate that I decided to ignore my office fatigue and followed her to the living-room like a shadow. The reason for the summons became clear the minute we entered. Papa had made his father and mother descend from their lofty perch and fortify his planned confrontation. Ma touched the feet of the elders before sitting down. Papa frowned at me and indicated that I should leave.

'I'm here for Ma,' I said and sat down next to her. Ma whispeed she'd be all right, I could leave. I clutched her hand and said nothing.

'Let her be,' I heard Lalaji say. My existence was overlooked after that. I noticed a door to my left move ever so slowly. This was Karan's old trick of widening the hinged side of a door to peek through.

'I hear you're leaving for Lahore from Delhi,' Lalaji began.

Ma nodded. Lalaji was fully informed but he spelt out everything as if it were necessary to make Ma put her seal on the wax.

Having accomplished that, he held forth on the propriety of her action as a married woman and a mother of a grown-up son and a marriageable daughter. When Mother didn't respond Papa asked angrily why she had to go to this man, a Muslim at that. Why now when she had abandoned him long ago? The choice of the word abandoned startled both Ma and me. I could see her backbone stiffen. I knew they'd never be able to bend her now. Ma spoke up, 'Shafi will understand why.'

'What kind of an answer is this?' Papa was furious. 'That means you've been carrying on with him without my knowledge. Is that so?'

'If I had, his cancer wouldn't have reached this stage,' Ma answered in a sharp tone.

'How will it benefit you to go now?' Lalaji asked.

Ma stared at him with disbelief. She didn't answer. The room grew nervous in the silence that followed.

'How long do you plan to stay there?' Lalaji approached from another angle.

Ma shook her head. 'I don't know. It'll depend on how Shafi is.'

'Well . . . well,' Papa began. I remember distinctly feeling as if he were just waiting for this point of the confrontation he had sought. 'If you don't return in four days we don't expect you to come back here at all.'

'What about us?' I cried out. 'Don't Karan and I count at all?'

'Ask your mother,' Papa said at his best biting pitch. I regretted my stupid remark.

We were all surprised to hear Grandmother, when she was expected to be a mere witness, say in a firm voice, 'How can four days be enough to go so far and return?'

179

'All right then,' Papa said gallantly, 'I'll make it a week.'

'Ten days at most,' Lalaji exercised his right of the last word.

And that is why Papa had anxiously rung me up to find out if I had heard from Mother. His anxiety was based on self-interest. I had learnt from Karan about Papa declaring to Lalaji, after Ma left, that if she didn't return after the generous allowance of a ten-day visit, he would be within his rights to do as he wished. Asked to clarify he said he intended to marry Aunt Chanda. Both of them were tired of keeping up a phoney façade in their life. 'He wants an uncomplicated life only on one level of Sahi-Sadan,' Karan wound up his report roguishly.

After witnessing the living-room episode through the peep-hole, Karan had swung off the fence and dropped on Ma's side. It was a tremendous relief for Ma to hear from me that both of us would never accuse her of 'abandoning' us. And I assured her that we were both old enough to take care of ourselves. While I said all this my hands were stretching up to her to pick me up in her arms and hold me. It was at that vulnerable moment in my life, when she requested me to go to Allahabad to explain everything to Nani-ma, and deliver her special message.

'Why don't you send Karan, Ma? He has the gift of the gab and the charm of the devil's disciple. He'll . . .'

'Your Nani-ma will not be impressed by words or charm,' Ma said.

Rekha, busy at the writing table making notes on the instructions she had received, chuckled and said, 'That's true. She's tough in every facet.'

I resented her grim estimation of my grandmother, and her great-aunt. 'I don't know why you say that,' I said. 'Karan and I have always found her soft and loving.' There was a tinge of a challenge in my voice.

'Quite conceivable for one month in the year,' Rekha insisted.

'Karan is good at sparring in the boxing ring, Ma. He'll do a better job than I could.' I ignored Rekha's unsolicited opinion of Nani-ma.

'The assignment needs skill in rational arguments. You argue like a lawyer. I have a good reason for choosing you.' Ma made it sound like a compliment, a privilege to be trusted with her assignment.

She briefed me again and again, till I knew my assignment like the multiplication tables I had learnt by rote long ago. Even at the airport, when Rekha and I had gone to see her off, she had something to add to the litany.

'Ma,' I had to laugh off her anxious tutoring, 'don't waste your time, leave everything just so and go,' I said lightly, but I was cringing inside.

I was also in a rage because except for Aunt Sita no other Sahi family member had come to see her before she left. Despite my dissuasion Ma decided on going to the sixth floor to pay her respects before leaving. She didn't want to be accused of discourtesy to her mother and father-in-law.

Lalaji was not back from the office at his habitual set time. Grandmother graciously came out to the baithak and silently put her hand on Ma's bent head. There was no blessing to give to her daughter-in-law on such an unusual departure. We could hear Aunt Shanta yelling obscenities in her barred room.

I asked Rekha to go down with Ma. I went to Lalaji's terrace garden and asked his valet to pluck some hibiscus blossoms for me. On the way home from the office I had dropped in at the Taj and bought an exquisite orchid for Ma. Since it was packed in a transparent plastic container I knew she could carry it with her. Its stem being in saline water in a tiny test tube I expected it to last for at least a week of her visit. When Karan showed up at the airport I gave the orchid to him to give Ma.

Tears welled up in Ma's eyes when Karan gave her the orchid with trembling hands. But my hibiscus wrapped in cellophane overwhelmed her. 'These are not from a florist shop, Ma,' I said with happiness surging inside me. 'I got them from Lalaji's penthouse garden. After all the shrub belongs more to us than to him.'

'We appropriated it long ago, didn't we?' She looked happy too. As she hugged me she said near my ear, 'The sunshine fairies always return to their flowery bedrooms . . . at dusk.' She kissed me on the forehead. I murmured, 'Ma, the fairy should run off before the flower closes up.'

'She has,' Ma said as she turned to Karan and Rekha to hug and kiss them.

She picked up her overnight bag and turned away. She hurried off without looking back, and disappeared out of our sight into the security check area.

When I came out after my bath Nani-ma had still not arrived. Mamoo was exercising Bhoot with a ball in the courtyard. I was happy to hear that the Lahore call had not come through since I had no news to give Ma.

My thoughts shifted to Ma in Lahore. I wished I could know how her meeting with Shafi had worked out. Both of them had aged. Was it possible for the old spark of their passion to revive? What if they found they had to strain to reach out to each other for old times' sake? What would they do if they felt they had nothing to give or take from one another? Would they dare to be honest? Or would they fake their reactions so as not to embarrass her for coming to him? If so, how would Ma cope with that shattering experience? I wondered if she had thought of all this before returning to her past. Feeling uncomfortable, I transferred myself back to Allahabad from Lahore to concentrate on what was ahead of me.

My befuddled brain had cleared up. My thoughts, impressions and experiences of the last few months were tidily arranged. I had exonerated myself by determining the causes behind the cracks which led to the fall of the centre beam of Sahi-Sadan. All that I had done was to sound the walls of the containing edifice and set myself free. And I liked to think that its side effect had been to put Mother in touch with her own inner strength.

TWENTY-FIVE

For the first time in Atal-Retreat I slept soundly that night. So soundly that I woke up effortlessly at five-thirty in the morning, with a refreshed body, and an alert mind.

My first thought was that this was my penultimate day in Allahabad. A day's train journey and I would be back in Bombay, to Shiv waiting for me. While lolling in the warm bed I sketched a variety of scenarios of our meeting. I had to throw them all into the waste-paper basket, and accept the reality of my joy at the sight of Shiv ending up with a ridiculous – 'Hello, how are you?' – in the presence of the milling passengers on the railway platform.

I was shifting the locale of my day-dreaming to Waverley when reality interfered. I had been aware of the curtains on the east window gradually acquiring visibility till I could see the flowery print on them. Just as I shut my eyes to continue with my dreaming there was a burst of sunlight on the curtains. The sun had arrived punctually. I realised I had to get out of bed to be ready to meet Nani-ma. I decided to add a bath to my morning's ablutions to make a start on an even score with her.

Nani-ma was bathed and waiting for me to join her on the divan on the verandah. When I did my namaskar she opened her arms to embrace me. I hugged her tightly, nestling my face in her bony shoulder.

Despite her well-scrubbed appearance, and a fresh change of clothes after her morning bath, her skin still smelt of a blend of cow's milk, ghee, and wood-smoke from the kitchen stove. Karan had complained about it when he was four years old. Fortunately he had said it in his newly acquired nursery class English. I remember Ma promptly taking us to her room and giving us a lecture on the importance of controlling one's tongue. Karan had listened to her patiently and then said, 'I not want hug Nani-ma.' I had no problem. I always liked her special homespun fragrance, it was comforting.

'This is a new perfume on you. I haven't smelt it before,' Nani-ma remarked.

'It's Youth Dew of Estee Lauder, Nani-ma. A friend gave it to me recently.' I almost said Shiv. She would've latched on to that and not been as easily placated as Mamoo at the station. I thanked the guardian angel on my shoulder.

'Nani-ma, I'm ready to talk to you,' I opened the session. 'Where's Mamoo? Ma wanted me to ask him to sit with you.'

Mother had warned me that Nani-ma pinned her intentional lapses to something that was not said, or that she hadn't heard, or that it hadn't been explained properly. This made Mamoo an asset as a witness. Anyway, I was keen to have him hear and know Ma's message.

'He must be somewhere doing something,' Nani-ma said. 'First you eat your breakfast before we talk,' she dictated to me.

'I can talk as I eat, Nani-ma.'

'No, one thing at a time. Eat first,' Nani-ma ruled.

'What about you, Nani-ma?'

'I've had mine. No hurry. Plenty of time to talk.'

She called out to Dulari and ordered a sumptuous meal for me. Papaya to begin with, followed by a spicy omelette and hot parathas, wound up with a large glass of milk flavoured with Nescafé. I realised I was hungry. When Dulari coaxed me with her third, soft paratha I was tempted into over-eating. 'Dulari,' I said, 'no one in this world can make an omelette and parathas as delicious as you do.'

'Chh, bitia,' she purred, 'you're making fun of me.'

'I mean it, Dulari,' I defended my statement. 'Truly. I'll swear on . . . on . . . on . . .' I faltered.

'On me, bitia,' Dulari said laughing heartily.

'No,' I protested. 'I can't swear to you, on you. I know

what I wanted to say. I swear on my namesake, Ganga Maiya. Isn't that impressive?'

She shyly covered her face with her sari. 'You are too clever, bitia. How can anyone win from you?' she said and scampered off to the kitchen.

I hoped it was prophetic, a good omen for what I was expected to do. And I also hoped that Ma's call from Lahore would come when I had finished the task.

As soon as I had drained my glass of milk Nani-ma sent for Mamoo. He was standing near the divan when I returned after washing my hands. 'Namaskar, Mamoo,' I greeted in a lilting, high key. 'Ma wanted me to talk, to both of you. Can you spare fifteen minutes and sit with us?' He said nothing, just gave me a hug in return, and sat at the edge of the divan behind Nani-ma. I sat down cross-legged, facing both of them.

I plunged straight in. According to Saku Bai, if one has to have a cold-water bath one shouldn't sit staring at the bucket. Dip the mug and pour the water on the body. One may jump up but after that warmth creeps under the skin all over the body. It's better than a hot bath which cools one as the water drains off.

So I said, 'First of all I want to tell you that Ma is not in Bombay, or Delhi . . .'

'Then where can she be?' Nani-ma interjected.

'She's gone to Lahore after attending Mrs Gandhi's Kriya ceremony.'

'Lahore? You mean, Pakistan? Why?' Nani-ma was so surprised that her voice rose a pitch higher with every question.

'She's gone to see Dr Shafi Ahmed,' I said. Nani-ma had interrupted my opening statement, forcing me to shock her more than I had planned to. I said quickly before she imagined it was their delayed rendezvous, 'Shafi Ahmed is not at all well. He has terminal cancer.'

She sat quietly for a while with her hand on her mouth before asking, 'How did she come to know about it? She promised her father they wouldn't keep in touch with each other.' Her voice was so soft, I had to lean forward to hear her.

185

'Dr Davidson wrote to her. He found out when he met Dr Shafi Ahmed there. In Bombay he had asked Ma if she knew why Shafi had not replied to his letters. She had said they hadn't been in touch at all. I think she did keep the promise she'd given to Nana.'

'Then why has she broken it now?'

'It was unfair to take that promise from her, Nani-ma.'

'If that promise was not there to restrain her she might have got tempted to go years ago,' she said contemptuously.

'In my opinion she should've gone after Nana died. Promise or no promise.'

'It seems she hasn't brought you up as well as she was. You don't break promises, especially given to those who are dead,' she said angrily. 'Bimla was always selfish. Spoilt by her father. Never thought of anyone but herself. As it's said, you can try but you can never straighten a dog's tail.' I began to feel I couldn't be related to this person who had so expertly, so mercilessly attacked her daughter's jugular even after so many years.

'Why, what difference does it make to the dead?' Her righteous, holy pose was irritating me. 'What made you so sure you were right in opposing her marrying Shafi Ahmed?'

'What do you mean by that?' Her voice was rising. 'It was for her own sake, for her own good.'

'If that was so you should've stopped her from marrying my father. Circumstances made her choose the frying pan. Didn't you see that?' I tried to restrain my voice from rising to match hers. I gripped my throat. I hadn't foreseen the direction our talk had taken. Easy, easy, I was repeating to myself.

'Do you think she told me what she was going to do?' Nani-ma's eyes were piercing into mine. 'If you want to know, this was the marriage of her choice. Even then I had told her she was making a mistake. That one day she would come running back to Allahabad.'

I felt like retorting that Ma had stuck on to the degrading bargain she had made rather than come back to her. But I was not going to let her have the satisfaction of knowing that Ma had suffered as she had predicted, or maybe hoped for.

186

I still had to tackle the real purpose of my visit. All through this opening passage of arms Mamoo was looking down, his head drooping lower and lower every time I looked at him over Nani-ma's shoulder. I could guess that he was embarrassed by my exchanging blow for blow with Grandmother without any restraint. That I had let myself down by ignoring to give respect due to an elder. I did some deep breathing and counted to ten a few times.

'Anyway, Nani-ma, I suppose you were right. Ma should've listened to you, like she expects me to take her guidance. Young people make mistakes and suffer. Probably, I'll do the same thing.' I couldn't do better than this balmy speech. I wanted a lull before opening my second front.

'When is Bimla coming back from Lahore?' Nani-ma asked.

'We don't know. It depends on what she finds there.' I didn't feel like taking the cue right then.

'What do you mean by "what she finds there"?' I should've known she would accept only precise answers.

From the corner of my eye I could see Dulari lurking behind a corner to hear the conversation. There was no use in pulling my punches because of her and losing ground to my adversary. In any case there was hardly anything going on in the family that Dulari didn't know. Fleetingly I realised I had never bothered to find out what her opinions were, or where her sympathies lay – with Nani-ma or my mother.

'Well, Ma didn't spell it out,' I began slowly. 'I imagine it would depend on how ill Dr Shafi is.' Ma had no chance to define her intentions, if she had any. No one at Sahi-Sadan had asked her, not even Lalaji during the confrontation with her.

'Bimla hasn't gone to treat him, she's not a cancer doctor,' Nani-ma said belligerently. 'She has her own patients in Bombay. Why couldn't she decide how long she's going for? Didn't Dr Davidson say in his letter at what stage the illness is?'

'Seems it's pretty bad, Nani-ma.' I had anticipated this

question. 'Dr Davidson also wrote that Shafi didn't marry. He has no immediate family member to take care of him. He's at his brother's home, not in a hospital.'

'Why didn't he marry?'

'Your guess will be as good as mine.' I patted myself for keeping my tone and manner respectful. Mamoo's head had come up to the normal level.

'Hoonh.' With this Nani-ma indicated that she had registered what I had said but was reserving her opinion.

I kept quiet and absolutely still to signal that she had the privilege to ask questions.

'What did your father say about all this? And his family? They couldn't have liked her going off to Pakistan to meet . . .' She left her sentence unfinished.

'You're right. They didn't.' I paused and then continued when she didn't comment, 'Their reaction was as bad as yours. Naturally.' Don't hustle the elders. You get nowhere that way, I had advised myself.

My strategy extinguished Nani-ma's rise of temper and restored her to her usual form. She asked a series of questions about who said what, and how was it said when Ma's decision to go was disclosed. What answers and explanations she had given then? How had she tackled the family's opposition?

I gave her as candid an account as could be ingested by her. Her reaction, comments and questions began to worry me because they were more incisive than Papa's or Lalaji's. Every answer I gave her she punctuated it with her 'hoonh', paused, and then hurled her next one fixing me with her penetrating eyes. I began to feel uneasy at this stage about tackling her. Mamoo's presence was keeping me from keeling over.

I was becoming almost mechanical in my answers since I had anticipated them all, but her next question made a greater demand on my alertness. 'How did you and Karan react? What do you think of her selfish action?' She softened her voice to convey her concern. 'After all her action is going to affect both of you, more you than Karan, because your marriage has yet to be arranged. You both are going to suffer more than anyone else.'

188

Foolishly, I had not anticipated this most obvious question from her. I thought for a while before saying, 'Both Karan and I saw her off at the airport. We are grown-up, Nani-ma, over twenty-one. We understand why she had to go to Shafi Ahmed. After all that she's done for us she now deserves to do what she wants to. We'll be all right.'

'Hoonh,' was her response with a derisive chuckle added to it.

On looking back, I think her chuckle released the adrenalin building up under my imposed restraint. I managed to monitor the outflow. I said in a tone dipped in honey, 'She sent me specially to explain all this to you so that . . .'

'Why didn't she come herself before leaving? Why load this on you? She could've thought of coming here on her return.'

She took the wind out of my sails. I held on firmly to the rudder. 'Ma had to be in Delhi for the Kriya ceremony for Mrs Gandhi. It was logical to fly out from there. As for coming to Allahabad on her return,' I lied without wavering, 'I offered to come here to tell you myself. I wanted to do that.'

'If you didn't mind her leaving why have you been so unhappy? You look like a wet hankie crushed in the hand.' I had to laugh at her novel simile. It did describe me very aptly. All I needed was a bit of ironing. She looked relaxed and happy about my appreciation of her turn of phrase. She went on to ask, 'Why didn't you talk about Bimla the next morning after your arrival?'

'I was pretty wrinkled when I came, as you said, Nani-ma. I first needed to put a steam-iron on my own problems. Many things happened that bothered me. I'm bothered about Ma too. Not her going, but her return . . .'

Just then the telephone rang. I looked at the watch, it was half past ten. I had expected Ma's call at eleven. Mamoo had gone to the hall to pick up the phone. Nani-ma asked me, 'What are your heavy problems? What's gone wrong?'

Mamoo came back to announce that the call was for me from a friend in Bombay. 'I'll tell you later, Nani-ma,' I said unfolding my legs to get up. I thanked Mamoo, smiling to convey my appreciation of his holding back the name of the caller from Bombay.

I scrupulously avoided taking Shiv's name, as well as cut off the warmth in my responses to him. Nani-ma knew enough English to grasp more than just the words. I had to explain my situation when Shiv asked me why I was so uptight. 'It's like my office – full attendance at the desks. Get me?'

He did and asked me how the mission was going. 'Rough weather. Pretty cold. I'm beginning to feel very chilly. I need a wishbone.'

I was grateful he didn't sympathise or give pointless advice. Most of all for not prolonging our inane conversation. Also for releasing me ungrudgingly to go back to my task. He ended by saying that he was impatiently waiting for my return, that he was missing me too much, and that he would be at the Victoria Terminus to receive me. And that I should be sure there was no drop in the mercury as far as his love was concerned.

'You can say that again and again to me and expect a full return,' I said avoiding the use of the word love which even Dulari would've understood.

Nani-ma was waiting impatiently to ask, 'Why are you so bothered about Bimla's return?'

I figured this was a good opening for coming to grips with Nani-ma. The mere clanging of swords between us should be over. Also I was keen to deliver Ma's message so that I would have the answer ready for her before she should ring up.

'It's just that I don't want Ma to come to Sahi-Sadan on her return. She doesn't want to either.'

Both Nani-ma and Mamoo were shocked. I could imagine in her corner Dulari's mouth had hung open. I gave them a few seconds to absorb and then went on, 'You see, the reason why I waited to talk to you was that if Ma returned before a week was over she could return to Bombay. Since she hasn't she has to think of another option.'

'Why? Who gave her this kind of ultimatum?' I had to admit Grandmother was lightning quick. Admirable, even if it threw one over.

'Papa at first. It was made a week by Lalaji.'

'So Lalaji has taken an interest in this?'

'You know how it is, Nani-ma. Nothing of consequence can happen in Sahi-Sadan without his knowledge, and silent or sought-out approval.'

'I should think so. He's the head of the family.' After this she kept quiet for an unusually long time. She didn't ask the question I expected her to. So I made a dive on my own.

'Nani-ma, Ma wants to come here to live with you. It would be easy to start a fresh practice here. Maybe work in the hospital too. Whatever it is she'll find out for herself.'

'Is she going to divorce your father?'

'It may come to that.'

'And all this for a visit? Wasn't it foolish to stake her twenty-five years of marriage for a gamble of this type? It's not even a gamble. She's like a child. Breaking everything around her, smashing her home. Your and Karan's home and life. How can she expect her husband and her in-laws to be as indulgent as her father was? She should know that when one spits at others some of it falls on oneself too.'

'It does look like that, but in her case there are other humiliations involved. At last she had the guts to do what she should've done years ago. In fact she's wasted twenty-five years, frittered them away.'

'Making a home for her husband and her children is her prime duty. Not risking it all for the sake of visiting a dying man she didn't see all these years. What can he mean to her now? Senseless.' Nani-ma made her pronouncement without answering the important question I had posed.

'He's a man who was everything to her once,' I said without straining my thoughts as they flowed. 'She was made to give him up. She didn't forget him. Or abandon him. If she wanted to see him now before he ... before he passes on why is she being served with ultimatums? How is that justifiable? This is no way to treat her, not at this time of her life. Leaves her with no dignity.'

'I don't understand all these things you say. All I know is that a woman has to stay posted to her home.'

'Like a cow tied to her peg,' I retorted.

191

'A cow is worshipped for the good it does for a family's health and wealth.'

'That's it, Nani-ma,' I pounced on my advantage. 'She should be worshipped not whipped. You've said it your way what I've been trying to say all along.'

'Then why don't we agree?' she parried.

'We're using different words, that's all,' I said weakly, laying down my arms.

I was nowhere near getting the answer Ma wanted about her welcome to Atal-Retreat. I had thought it was odd that she was giving so much emphasis to Nani-ma's consent. She was an equal inheritor to this home. When I said so to her Mother had replied cryptically, 'You'll understand in Allahabad.'

This time I phrased my question in unambiguous words and served them out straight. 'So, Nani-ma, Ma wants to know if she can come here to live in Atal-Retreat. She's going to ring me up from Lahore. She tried last night but the connection didn't work. I expect her call any moment now.'

'What about you and Karan?' she asked promptly, showing she had done some progressive thinking in anticipation of my question.

'Karan and I will stay on in Bombay. He's prepared for his role in the Sahi business. I've got my work . . .'

'What about your marriage? Isn't it Bimla's duty to see that a scandal due to her leaving her husband doesn't spoil the chances of arranging your marriage into a desirable family?'

'You know times have changed, Nani-ma. I've asserted my right to choose the man I want to marry. That's why I haven't been married off like my cousins, daughters of Uncle Dinesh.'

'Soon you'll be too old for marriage. Twenty-five now . . .'

'Twenty-four to be exact . . .'

Once again I heard, 'What difference does a year make?' This time it had a razor-sharp edge to it. 'Like mother, like daughter,' Nani-ma ended on a triumphant note.

'True, very true.' I had to laugh. 'I may never marry – that may be a variation on the old theme.'

192

'How can she then leave you and come here?'

'I'm beyond the chaperone age. I'm a working girl, Nani-ma. She doesn't have to latch on to me.' It seems to me that somewhere there was a catch in her concern for me.

'Can't she stay in Bombay on her own? She'll have her practice and all of you will be together too.'

'Cost of apartments have sky-rocketed in Bombay. It won't be easy to afford one near her area of her work. Anyway, she wants to leave the big city. It will have too many associations to deal with. It's better for her to return here.'

'I don't think she should come here.' Nani-ma jolted me more with her tone than her words. I saw Mamoo get up and leave just when I needed his presence the most. There was no apparent reason for his departure. The telephone was silent, no servant or visitor had needed his attention. I almost stopped him from leaving but I instinctively felt he wouldn't do it for a frivolous reason.

'Why, Nani-ma? Why shouldn't she come back to her roots?' I had to ask.

'Because she left me when I wanted her to stay with me and give me the support I needed. She has no roots here.'

'She got married. She had to go where her husband lived. Isn't that how it is?' The face of the bride in the train, the picture-pendant on her brow, passed through my agitated mind.

'She used marriage as an excuse to leave me. You think I didn't understand that?'

'But she's been coming here every December to meet you – carted us here from our pram days. Forced us to come here when we protested about spending every winter holiday here.'

'Oh, I didn't realise you and Karan didn't like to come here. You had to say so only once for me to stop her from forcing you to visit me.'

She hung and quartered me on the explanation I had given in the heat of the argument to reinforce Mother's case. 'Well, it just shows how much she cared for you to do that. That's the important point I was making. Never mind us. Coming here did us a lot of good too.'

'She did it for her guilty conscience.' She pronounced it like a judge.

'Am I understanding correctly that you don't want her to come here?' With Mamoo not there my adrenalin had begun to gush through.

'It's not my wanting. I don't think it's fair on her part to do what she likes, and expect me to take her dictation. Just because I'm a widow I'm not a monkey dancing to the beat of the small drum, afraid of the stick in the hand of the Monkey Man. I've lived on my own here. I can continue to do that till I die.'

She had overlooked Mamoo who lived for her. He was the monkey on a string in her hand, if the metaphor had to be applied correctly.

I weighed my next move before saying, 'Nani-ma, Ma has a right to come here. She's a joint owner of Atal-Retreat. Have you considered that?'

'Yes, I know. She'll have to go to the court to evict me from here.'

I couldn't breathe for a few seconds before saying in a muffled tone, 'You know very well Ma will never do that.' I was barely able to hold my anger. 'It's for you to be the court, the prosecutor, the defender, the jury and the judge.'

'My decision is not something I'm making now that you can snap your fingers and ask me to change just like that. For years I've expected this to happen. I've been prepared for it.'

My throat felt dry and my palms were sweaty. Nothing had gone as I had anticipated. I had considered myself very clever as I had prepared and rehearsed for all the mutations I could encounter with Grandmother. I had not allowed for my inexperience, or given serious weight to Mother's conflict with her. I had always claimed that I found Grandmother agreeable and caring.

I needed a drink of water. As I was leaving for the kitchen I asked, 'Nani-ma, can I get a glass of water for you?'

'No, I don't need it!' she replied. I detected a smear of rejoicing in her voice.

At the corner turn to the kitchen Dulari detached herself

from the wall she was stuck to like a lizard. She speeded ahead of me to the kitchen. As I reached for the fridge she silently raised her palm asking me to wait. She pressed oranges on the glass squeezer, collected the juice in a tumbler and gave it to me when it was full. I sipped it slowly standing there instead of bringing it back with me to the verandah. I did a quick re-run of the arguments and stiffened my spine for the next session.

As I walked back I had a long-shot view of Nani-ma sitting in a spotless white, starched sari on the white sheet of the divan. Her shahtoosh shawl defied the cold wind. Her chin was resting on her folded knees. She was calm, in perfect control of her milieu. A symbol of purity and power. From my visual memory I extracted a similar sight of Lalaji on the morning of the breakfast interview he had given me. The two were kindred soils in the management of their domains.

This time I didn't climb on the divan to sit cross-legged. I sat at an angle from her. I found I could speak in an even, calm voice. 'Consider this, Nani-ma. Ma has been paying the taxes, maintenance and what-not on this establishment for years. Doesn't it give her a moral right to . . .' This was the last weapon in my armoury which she was obviously also prepared for. She cut me off.

'No, it doesn't. I wanted to sell this house and move to a small bungalow I had found in Katra next to Dharwallas there. I haven't known peace and happiness here myself – it's full of memories I don't want to be reminded of. I wanted to make a new beginning in a small place more suitable for my lonely state. She didn't let me sell it. So she had to pay for holding on to it.'

This was truly unsettling as I had no clue of this. I took a wild gamble; I had nothing to lose now. 'Ma sent you money regularly for your expenses and for the house too, didn't she?' I was happy to see her shaken up for a change. Her knees dropped, she sat up stiffly with her chin in the air and said, 'It was her decision, no more. I never asked her for any money. If she has said that then she's lying outright. My household expenses come from shares invested for me by

Dharwallas, and from the rent of the shops I bought years ago on their advice. Then there is my dairy which gives me more than I need. The money she sent I've always used on the expenses of your December visits. Whatever was left I've kept in a separate bank account. You'll get that, and my share of this house when I die. It's meant for you.'

I recognised her masterly thrust. Divide and Rule, an old Imperial trick. Plus a sweet revenge from a daughter through a daughter. I pulled up my plait from under my shawl and brought it over my right shoulder to the front. I made my movements very slow, watching Nani-ma's nervous observation of my act.

After a vibrant pause I said, 'I'm not going to actually cut my hair to qualify for disinheritance by you. Only because there is someone else who loves it, adores it. From this moment I'm keeping it for him, not you. I want you to know that. You can consider that I've bobbed my hair, like Mother's. I don't want to be bound to the half of your Atal-Retreat. Mamoo deserves it for his ascetic living and serving you as a male protector.'

I got up to make an exit on this excellent line but Nani-ma had not finished with me. 'Who is this man who loves your hair?'

Her curiosity made me reckless. It also gave me better exit lines, 'Not only loves my long hair, but loves me too. He is forty-five years old. Married and divorced. Has two teen-aged children. He is from the deep south, Kerala. Dark in complexion. His name is Shiv Menon.'

It was not to be my exit. Nani-ma said smugly, 'So, this is the problem which has been bothering you. No wonder you were so unhappy.'

'No, he's not my problem. He's keen to marry me.'

'Who is stopping you?'

'No one. When I go back to Bombay I think I'll have enough courage to decide to live with him.'

'What do you mean, "live with him"?'

'I don't want to marry and be tied down to a peg, like a sacred cow. I want to be free, unburdened. No vows around the holy fire to plague me. I'd stay with him as long as I want to. Remain a mistress of my own destiny.' My mind owed this inspiration to the bride on the train.

I walked away with quick steps, pulling up my dragging shawl back on to my shoulder.

TWENTY-SIX

It was not long before I was back in the arena, but for a different purpose. Nani-ma was still sitting on the divan in the same position I had left her.

After my grand exit I had rushed to my room, rather Ma's bedroom. Mamoo was there. I went straight into his open arms and let my tension melt into sobs which I tried to muffle on his shoulder. I didn't want Nani-ma to have the pleasure of hearing them.

I tried to suppress the outburst to ask Mamoo's opinion of my confrontation on the verandah. I needed his honest estimation to get the right perspective on my toppled mission. I was still clinging to him and trying to smother my hiccups when we heard the telephone ring. 'I think this is Didda's call,' Mamoo said softly. 'I'll take it and ask the operator to hold it till you come. Wash your face and drink a little water.'

Mamoo was right. It was Ma's call. A clear and strong connection this time. She said she had kept on trying last night for a long time before giving up. This time Shafi's brother had brought her to the Home Minister's office to get through to me.

'How is Dr Shafi Ahmed?' I asked formally in case the call was being monitored.

'Not as bad as I had feared,' she replied; her voice was buoyant. 'He had given up. His family couldn't persuade him to go to New York for treatment. It can't be cured but his life can be prolonged with the latest treatments. I want him to take that chance. Very much. Can you understand that, Gungoo?'

'Yes, I can, I can, Ma,' I replied almost at the top pitch of my voice.

'Hey, Gungoo,' Ma said with a laugh, 'this connection is a good one. I can hear you very well.'

'Can you hear me clearly?' I turned my volume to low. 'Ma, I'm so happy for you – I just lost my head.'

'Can you guess what I want to do?' she asked almost conspiratorily.

'I know what I would do, Ma. I'd take him to Sloane Kettering in New York without losing time for the latest cancer treatment.'

It was Ma whose voice rose to a high pitch, 'Yes, Gungoo, yes. That's exactly what I want to do.' She continued in her normal voice, 'Now, listen, I don't want to misuse the privilege of this call, and abuse Shafi's friendship with the minister. I'm going to be brief. All right? How was your talk with your grandmother?'

'Bad. I've failed, Ma, in all my approaches. I couldn't make a single dent.'

'I expected that.'

I had to have a brief pause to take the impact of what I'd heard. 'Then why did you send me here? On this abortive mission?'

'It wasn't abortive. Not at all,' she contradicted instantly. 'I wanted you to understand why I decided to . . . to leave Sahi-Sadan for this . . . this very brief living with . . . with Shafi.'

I heard her silence, for a long time, before I could whisper, 'Yes, Ma?' to urge her to continue.

'I wish I could look at you. This . . . this instrument in my hand . . . this is not the way to talk about . . .'

'Try, Ma,' I said, and choked the break in my voice to add, 'It's important to me.'

'Some day. Soon, maybe,' she started hesitantly. 'I do understand that the past few months have been hard on you. You've had too many disillusions one after another. I know you've been . . . been groping . . . trying to find a meaning . . Gungoo, I wish I could've . . . Anyway my purpose in sending you to Allahabad was . . . I wanted you to come to

know your Nani-ma as my mother . . .' After a pause she
continued, 'Gungoo, don't worry about losing my case.
never expected you to win it for me. Besides, as it happens
I have no intention of returning to Bombay, or to
Allahabad.'

'Good, very good, Ma. You do that.' And I felt wetness
on my cheeks. I took Mamoo's handkerchief when he held
it out to me.

I let Ma talk. I had nothing to ask her. I paid careful
attention to the instructions she had to give me. I was wondering what I should tell Karan when she said, as if she had
read my mind, 'I'm going to ring up Karan after talking to
you. I'll keep in touch with you both. I should ring you up
at Kanta's place, right? Give me her number.'

'I'll return to Sahi-Sadan at first. Ma, I want to witness
the crumbling of its walls and hear them crash around me,'
I said with no joy in my voice.

I waited for a while, then panicked in case the connection
was dead, 'Hello, hello, Ma, are you . . .'

'Yes, hello, I'm here.' She kept quiet again, I could hear
her breathing. 'Who am I to tell you not to feel so bitter?'
she said slowly. 'I think it will suit both of us to do exactly
as we want to. I don't want to bind you to anything I may
think is good for you. You're lucky to have learnt your
values early. I wasted a lot of years. Anyway, I'm fortunate
to have another chance to make a choice. Just don't forget,
or let Karan forget, that I love you both. Too much.'

After another trip to the wash-basin, a touch of lipstick,
and patting down of my hair I stalked out to the verandah
and faced Nani-ma once more.

'That was Ma's call from Lahore, as you must've heard,
Nani-ma.' I paused to let her, as usual, preempt me with her
question. But she didn't this time. She had fixed her eyes on
me questioningly to hear from me what she had already
understood, from my clear and loud answers on the phone
when I had deliberately spoken in Hindi only.

'Ma is not coming back to Bombay, or to Allahabad,' and
added after a second, 'not just yet anyway.' I wanted to keep
Mother's right to her father's home on a shelf she could

reach whenever she wanted to. 'Right now she's interested in Dr Shafi Ahmed's treatment in New York to prolong his life as much as possible. To her it's worth giving up everything to stay with him till the end, whenever it comes.' I was proud to have been able to articulate what I had choked on earlier. 'She'll make her decisions as she goes along. That's about it, Nani-ma. You don't have to worry about her returning to Atal-Retreat.'

I waited for Nani-ma's counterblow. When it didn't come I stole a glance at her. She was sitting absolutely still, enveloped in her shahtoosh shawl.

As I turned to go back to my room I almost stumbled on Bhoot. He had stationed himself close behind me to stay out of sight of Nani-ma. I bent down to hug him and invite him to Ma's room to give me company while I packed.

On my way I had a glimpse of Dulari standing on the kitchen door-sill. On catching my eye she smiled – a smile I haven't been able to fathom yet.

ALLISON & BUSBY FICTION

Phillip Callow
The Magnolia
The Painter's Confessions

Catherine Heath
Lady of the Burning Deck
Behaving Badly

Chester Himes
Cast the First Stone
Collected Stories
The End of a Primitive
Pink Toes
Run Man Run

R. C. Hutchinson
Johanna at Daybreak

Dan Jacobson
The Evidence of Love

Francis King
The Widow

Colin MacInnes
Absolute Beginners
City of Spades
Mr Love and Justice

*The Colin MacInnes
Omnibus*

Henry Miller
Quiet Days in Clldry

Adrian Mitchell
The Bodyguard

Bill Naughton
Alfie

Dolores Pala
In Search of Mihailo

Boris Pasternak
Zhenia's Childhood

Ishmael Reed
Reckless Eyeballing
The Terrible Threes
The Terrible Twos

Françoise Sagan
Engagements of the Heart
Evasion
Incidental Music
Those Without Shadows
The Unmade Bed

Budd Schulberg
The Disenchanted
Love, Action, Laughter
    and Other Sad Tales
On the Waterfront
What Makes Sammy Run?

Debbie Taylor
The Children Who Sleep
    by the River

B. Traven
Government
Trozas

Etienne van Heerden
Ancestral Voices